Peru

Remember me, and see what
happens in the next book.

Robbie Wolf

The
INHERITANCE
LETTER

BY

RALPH G. DITCHBURN

Enjoy Ralph G Ditchburn

Book One of the
Robbie's Adventures Series

To wonderful Chris
Enjoy Ralph

Produced by:

FriesenPress
Suite 300 – 852 Fort Street
Victoria, BC, Canada V8W 1H8

www.friesenpress.com

Distributed to the trade by The Ingram Book Company

Table of Contents

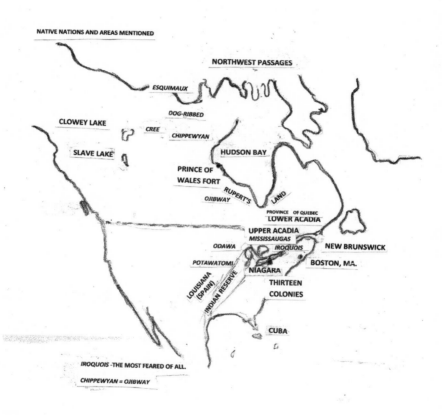

NATIVE NATIONS AND AREAS MENTIONED

NORTHWEST PASSAGES

ESQUIMAUX

DOG-RIBBED

CLOWEY LAKE

CREE

CHIPPEWYAN

SLAVE LAKE

HUDSON BAY

PRINCE OF
WALES FORT

RUPERT'S

LAND

OJIBWAY

PROVINCE OF QUEBEC

LOWER ACADIA

UPPER ACADIA

MISSISSAUGAS

NEW BRUNSWICK

ODAWA

IROQUOIS

POTAWATOMI

BOSTON, MA.

LOUISIANA
(SPAIN)

INDIAN RESERVE

NIAGARA

THIRTEEN
COLONIES

CUBA

IROQUOIS -THE MOST FEARED OF ALL.

CHIPPEWYAN = OJIBWAY

To my grandma 'Bubba', who constantly encouraged me to read by example and gave me my first copy of *War of the Worlds*.

And to Dorothy, who allows me to indulge in fantasy.

THE CATCH

Dark blue water flowed with a ferocious intensity inches from her feet as the snow began to turn some of the far river bank white. The snow and sleet had fallen all afternoon, making everything cold and wet and hard to see. She gritted her teeth, smashing her fists together and wailed, "Wait a bit more, Kiwidinok."

Her name was borrowed from the Chippewa language, meaning Of the Wind. Her patience was wearing thin, and she said aloud with determination, "You need this."

She knew that fishing would stop in the barren lands for it was late January and even this river would freeze over.

Key, as she was often called in nickname, had lost her pregnancy weight and had her slim and trim figure of youth. Not too difficult to do when food is scarce. Small framed, with soft shoulders standing just over five feet, at twenty-five and a half she was beautiful. A not too prominent front brow and small features including her narrow straight nose gave her a delicate soft look, unusual for Indian features. The small features she got from her father Keezheekoni. His name was also taken from the Chippewa language, meaning Burning Fire and he was a Dog-Ribbed tribal chieftain. Key, his daughter carried strong blood lines. But Key was now worn down and suffering.

Just as she was about to give up, two very large brown speckled fish, simultaneously swam up and were caught in her net. Not believing her luck, she pulled hard on the line. Her small yet hardened hands wrapped in pieces of deerskin rags gave good grip. The fish netting was made from a twisted rope of twine made from the inner bark of birch. The Dog-Ribbed tribe had successfully used this method for years. She pulled again leaning back with all her strength. There would be no denial of fresh fish for dinner tonight.

Looking up through the thick falling snow she could see no sky. "Thank you, Sky Father," she said anyway. Key wrapped her heels and ankles with her few pieces of deerskin binding. She immediately stood, grabbing her few belongings, a deerskin drinking flask filled with water, her small fishing net wrapped around two trout and a knife shaped from a five inch piece of iron hoop. She placed the parcels under her arm and then jammed her hands into her warm furry coat. The warmth of the thick rabbit fur coat was comforting. Made from many small pieces of fur the coat did make Key feel very sensual. The way she had tied it just so.

Key was trying to decide what fish bones she would use to finish decorating her freshly-sewn warm covering. The rabbit provided her food, clothing and bindings for nets and snowshoes, snares and sewing for her clothing. Painstaking work these chores. It involves a good deal of time to draw the small tiny sinews of rabbit ligaments together to create bindings. Tomorrow she would finish her moccasins, cute and furry, white and puffy with brown tinges at the end of the hairs. Little rabbit fur offerings that would keep her feet warm after today. Somewhat durable she thought and adorable. She smiled faintly at that thought. Just like the plain but beautiful ornaments that were to adorn her furry coat.

On her journey Key followed the river bank and in her haste her half-bare foot found no grip and she went down fast. Gasping for air in the chilly cold she winced in pain as she fell hard onto her belly knocking the wind from her. Her warm coat slid up to her shoulders exposing her chest and belly to the wet snow. The snow rose quickly by her bare sides as she sank deeper. Her back exposed to the elements became snow white. She slid a few good feet farther downhill. Snow caked all around her bareness like a clinging blanket of leeches. Key rolled slightly and felt sleep wanting to consume her. She lay still fighting for her breath in the freezing air. It was as if she was holding her breath but there was no air inside. The cold numbed her. Key's thoughts slowed. Pulling her last bit of might together she took in the air she so desperately needed and tried to move. The heavy wet snow bent a pine tree branch over, covering her further and prevented her from rising. Tears flowed as Key wrestled with desires of giving up against the need to survive. A howl could be heard in the distance.

For her husband she would endure. He had to be told. Little by little Key inched her right arm out of the deep offensive whiteness. With all her effort she managed to rise and poke through the snow as it lay all about her. Holding on to the bent branch she pulled herself to her knees. As best she could Key pulled her rabbit coat down and about her. Shivering and shaking she looked where she had fallen and saw a large cleared area of snow.

The snow was coming down hard and fast now. So thick she thought that there would be no need to cover her tracks; usually a branch from a pine she would drag behind her or she would create detours to throw off any trackers. The temperature was dropping fast. She could feel the cold in her bones. Key re-wrapped her feet in the strips of deerskin rags and stumbled back to her camp in search of her deerskin walled lean-to and warm bedding.

Key's only risk was when she was hunting or fishing. For that was when she must leave her temporary homemade sanctuary. She did not want to come across the Athapuscow tribe just west of her from which she had escaped. Any other tribes were also a threat. She'd gone through enough torments. Things no woman and mother should ever have to endure. But still she stood. She wanted to just go home but it was so far. In the spring she would embark on her journey home, she guessed. *I have a story that needs to be told* she kept reminding herself as a reason to continue.

Key thought back at what had just happened. Despair and humiliation were mixed with feelings of relief at her escape. Little hope was really felt anymore. Happiness would never return. A tear froze immediately on her reddened cheek.

In a pocket of lower land our isolated young princess had previously found a small redoubt. By fighting through a thicket of Hawthorne trees to a curiously small opening in a wall of rock she had gazed upon a low cliff. Through the small fracture in the wall of rock, she could see a drop down area. When she descended the four feet to a ledge made out of rock she found her winter hideaway. This ledge overlooked this little paradise. Another twelve feet she paced down the side hill until she reached ground level. The sun would shine above tall trees and drop onto this thirty foot square playground. From all around this area it was invisible. Trees, rock walls and the natural contour of the land made this oasis undetectable. When the sun shone it was warm. At sixteen feet she was protected from the cold winds, except for those really bad nights when the wind would howl. And the tall trees blocked a lot of snow from descending. She had built a habitat to hold herself over the winter out of branches and the one remaining piece of deerskin she used for a wind wall.

Key headed for her warm lean-to momentarily happy, with her catch under her arm. She looked back with dark and tired eyes on her path and turned her face toward the afternoon white-flecked sky and reflected on her recent past.

"My husband I am so sorry," she apologized to the clumps of white in the air in front of her. She had failed miserably and probably would never return to tell her story. She did not know her life story was far from finished.

ACADIAN RANGER

Overlooking the Niagara escarpment, two Upper Acadian militia members stood facing each other. Corporal Thomas Johnson was an identical twin. His brother Private Jeffrey Johnson had the same thin build with thick, curly, dark-brown hair and was laughing at something his brother said. Arms in ready position with bayonets attached, a total of five militiamen stood at the ready.

They peered at the man who had just arrived.

"No advancing past here. Not today anyways," Corporal Johnson stated flatly, his young face determined. He was the man in charge.

The new arrival looked around and realized that in his haste to find travel to southern Virginia he was not being careful enough.

"Well, what of it? Who are you? We don't want any foreigners around here!" The group noticed he was unarmed but spread out and started waving rifle butts at him. One held back and had his rifle aimed right at him.

The young man threw up his arms. "Let me explain. My name is Robbie Wolfe. I came with reinforcements for the 49th Regiment. i I was an Acadian Rangerii hired as a scout to bring fourteen recruits down to Fort Niagara. They were to establish that this area was still safely under British command and to report back if there were any French invading forces close by. As things are secure they released me of my duties and paid me."

"I heard you Canadian Rangers were paid well," said another of the group.

"Twice what everyone else makes, I heard," another commented.

5

"And foreigner?" Robbie sneered. "I'll have you know I was born about five hundred miles north of here. Isn't that good enough?" He brushed an imaginary fleck of dust off his sleeve.

Robbie was dressed in black derby, dark business jacket, no waistcoat as was common in the day, a tan shirt, and brown woolen trousers. Polished black boots rounded out his gentlemanly attire. His clothes did mask his capabilities as a scuffler.

Robbie gave a gawky lift of his head and glared at the man pointing the rifle. "Put that gun down. I don't want you accidentally shooting me and then saying you're sorry."

The man with the musket dropped his barrel down and the mood changed swiftly.

"Okay, we cannot be too careful round here. On the first of last month the Brits just marched into Boston and took over. October 1768 will be written down as not a good month for a lot of people."

"So what happened in Boston?" Robbie inquired. Any information south of where he was became important.

The Corporal glanced across at another in the group and pointed, "He was there. That's Vernon Mills. Go ahead Vern, tell him."

In his best south Boston accent, "Hold your shauts on! Was my brother John really, see. So I says to him not to go south. He went anyways. So he gets himself mixed up with the colonists there and almost got arrested. Word was, British ships came in. The soldiers came marching out and took over. Just like that. Everybody is up in arms over it. There are a lot of people supporting the colonists there. This business ain't finished." Vern was interrupted by everyone voicing their opinion all at once. Robbie could not help notice the freckles all over the man.

Overheard among the men, "Back in August, a crowd gathered in Bauston under a large elm tree at the corner of Essex and Orange Street to protest the hated Stamp Act.[iii] Patriots who later called themselves the Sons of Liberty had hung Andrew Oliver, the colonist chaus'en by King George III to impose the Stamp Act. There on the branches of the tree hung a British cavalry jackboot. Grinning from inside the boot was a devil-like doll holding a scroll marked 'Stamp Act.' It was declared the first public show of defiance against the Crown and has since spawned a big resistance. The British didn't like that.

"British troops in response landed in Boston this October and just took over. All this ever since the Brits introduced the Stamp Act three years ago."

"What's that?" Robbie inquired. *Better to have stayed home*, he thought.

"In March, the Brits started the first direct tax on us colonists taxing documents, newspapers and even playing cards. Totally unfair. And, we have no say on what the funds are used for."

"Certainly spent on the European campaigns," Patrick Henry[iv] put in.

"They were fretting over poor hanged Andrew Oliver," Vern continued. "What makes everything worse is the Quartering Act. Two days later the British required all colonists to provide temporary housing to any British soldier. So we get martial law, taxed and we are required to house them."

"We have to pay extra for our tea, gentlemen," Patrick Henry put in.

"And the rest of them got everybody nervous," the Corporal said.

"Who is the rest of them?" Robbie asked.

"Loyalists hold most of the institutions around here," Corporal Johnson said.

"They're loyal to the British," his twin butted in.

Corporal Thomas Johnson waited and then continued, "A group of French were rumored to be heading north. We keep losing ground in European court too. For every time a treaty is signed, the French gain some North American land back. Acadians do not know who is on whose side, used to be the British against the French. Now that most of the French are tamed we have people who have strived from hard work here or who were born here who do not want British rule. Their laws are faulty, they do not work here when you are ..."

"... trying to tame an uncivilized hostile world." Jeffry finished the Corporal's line again.

I guess twins do that, Robbie thought. *How hard it is to follow a conversation when they finish each other's sentences like that.* Robbie was left wondering what triplets did.

"Oh, and not to be putting this down as a real bad thing but there are militias forming up everywhere. Every group of settlers a few shy of a community got their own militia taking shots at each other. Don't think the British got a clue what they are doing either. They strut around and then downgrade us. We took just as many casualties against the French."

Corporal Thomas Johnson looked at his brother and then looked across the beaten down ground to Robbie. "Here comes the Lieutenant. Go report to him. Have a good day," and then turning to the group of five militiamen pleaded, "Come on everyone, get back to your duties now." The Corporal looked in earnest and paused in hopes the men would listen to him. He saw them for what they were: Under-trained men who grasped warfare the hard way; in kinship with poor living conditions, violent weather and severe hardships.

They all nodded to each other and turned as one and retook their positions of lookout hoping no one attempted to go south, for they were not sure of what to do to block the road. How much resistance should they put up with? How much force should they expend? Should they shoot to kill?

MOSS TO BURN

Her hair was long, fine and black. Her petite frame, wrists, hands and feet added to her femininity. A small waist contrasted with the nice curves of her hips. Her radiant tan colored skin, sculpted facial features added to her status as heir to the Dog-Ribbed tribe. She was a young woman of fifteen; at an age when she should have been given to an elder as a wife two years earlier. Only her father being a chief held back her suitors.

Then one day she met a young farmer boy the same age. He was Acadian born and of British descent. He fell for her while she visited at the fort off of Hudson Bay. She was young, slender and beautiful and a princess of her tribe. Her large eyes constantly looked as if she was surprised. Key's smooth complexion and long slender legs added to her allure. He was a tall strapping young lad full of eagerness, with broad shoulders, a thin build but muscular with a handsome outdoorsman ruggedness to him. He exuded confidence and independence. Robbie sported dark hair and the deepest blue eyes she had ever seen. With her father's blessing, they joined their lives together before her tribe. Their love for each other brought a son very soon.

Key's dreams were crushed when she and her family were ambushed. Her entire family was brutally slaughtered. Only she escaped. Her husband was on a twelve moon journey and would probably be late coming back. Key looked around desperately for moss to burn.

LOVE, LAND AND MONEY

The Lieutenant was a young dashingly good-looking specimen of a man. His face was shiny and clean. He smelled of a fragrance that made Robbie wince. It was impossible not to notice that he was immaculately dressed. His accoutrements were polished and shone like diamonds. Robbie's jacket showed signs of being recently brushed but still carried a lot of dust from the road. And the Lieutenant was in quite a jovial mood.

"Well, what is it? What are you doing here? Hurry up! I have a honeymoon trip to prepare for." The Lieutenant stared into Robbie's eyes.

Robbie felt uplifted by seeing such a jovial and spirited soul this deep into the new country. *No need to hide anything from him. A man of his word I trust.*

An officer and a gentleman and probably very rich. What more could one aspire to?

"I have left my family in the northern lands to see if we can settle in South Carolina. They say a man named Mr. Mason will give fifty acres to settle there. I heard they are going to become independent. Start a province called Tennessee. I need to know if he will accept my native wife. If all this happens I will fight for him. I will help start an independent democracy. If he accepts my native wife and family then I will bring them here."

"It is that simple, yes? Love, land and money is it? Very well. You cannot stay here. I suggest waiting a few days in the woods till things settle down before heading south. The rumor is a group of rebels have come up from the south to stir up trouble. They don't like being taxed for their paper. I can't believe it. All paper has to have a British tax stamp on its packaging or it shan't to be used. There is only one thing I use paper for."

"I cannot believe it. I can't relieve myself without being taxed."

"Definitely cannot get worse than that!"

THE ESCAPE

The rolling and dense forest in this small cove of an area abounded with deer, moose and bear. Black bears were stealing the last of her berries. She needed to awaken to prepare for the harsh winter that was coming. There was so much to do.

Her child's voice awoke her. She sat up, clutching her breasts and in her bewilderment called and looked for her daughter. She was nowhere to be found. She sobbed, remembering the horror. For when she was a new prisoner of the Athapascow tribe she lost something more precious than her pride. After a few weeks of rapings and beatings she was given to a man who liked her and was willing to take her in as a third wife. Key, in her usual stoic way, never complained. She just kept things to herself. She could never be happy living with people who slaughtered her family.

After less than three weeks, Key was finally allowed to wander away from her tent. Waiting for the appropriate moment she slipped out the side of the village of the nomadic settlement. It was not far to go to the same place where she was so surprised and captured.

"Please, take my coat ..."

REDCOAT

Robbie was full of excitement when he and a few troops had first arrived near Fort Niagara. It was a long trip aboard a supply ship. Getting so much closer to his destination he was fidgeting. Jubilant might have been his word of the day after meeting the Lieutenant. The thought of having his journey reach fruition this fast was reviving. Soon he would be home with his family, packing them up for a return trip.

Imagine, the Lieutenant asking me to enlist. Me, a Redcoat. Fancy that, Robbie cringed at the thought as he looked away. Just as they started getting comfortable and started to relax and let their guard down, Robbie's thoughts were interrupted by the crack of musket fire. A scream and a shout of hurrah was heard.

Turning back to see the Lieutenant, remembering he didn't even get his name, Robbie watched him spin and fall. Hit in his lower abdomen. It looked bad. He knew he was a goner. Just a slow and painful death would be expected. Only a shot of rum would help now.

"Robbie, come here please," the Lieutenant whispered.

Robbie looked over at this group of men who were dressed in wool overcoats with their waist coats sporting watch and chains glittering out of their watch pockets. Their tri-hats and derbies were turning all around making them look comical. Everyone was real jittery and fully armed. Out of the corner of his eye Robbie noticed a figure in the shadows. It was that Private. That twin who was with the rest of the militia who so suddenly disappeared. Private Johnson was on the other side of the building going off behind it to disappear into the woods. Outnumbered, they took flight. Robbie took a step and knelt down on one knee close to the British officer. Wondering what he was going to do he pulled out a small flask of rum and placed the beverage within hands grasp. Robbie left his ammunition and supplies in a crook of a tree before revealing himself to the militiamen. He was now unarmed with an empty musket and in a strange land where there was brutality everywhere. He sent up a small prayer for his life.

"Please take my coat. In the pocket, I beseech thee," the Lieutenant exclaimed.

Robbie raised his head and put a watchful eye to the gloom. He must observe the actions of the rebels to see what they would do next. He gave the officer a rag from his pocket to press against the wound. It bled worse now, a deep red. It was getting darker and bitingly cold. The rebels seemed to have disappeared in the darkening hour as well, content with the single kill.

The Lieutenant sat up holding out his jacket, gasping for breath through his pain. "Please take my coat. Inside the pocket on the inside, you'll find gold. Take it. I won't need it anymore."

Robbie shuffled with embarrassment. He did not expect to receive gold at a time like this. Robbie could see the man was losing a lot of blood. He looked inside the jacket and sure enough there was gold in there. A fair-sized pouch and also a finely wrought drawing of a most desirable woman. She was wearing a fashionable French designer gown that sported a frilly front that revealed more bosom than thought possible. It took Robbie all he could to take his eyes off the picture and hand it to the Lieutenant.

The Lieutenant stared at the picture, his eyes full of tears. He winced as he dragged in a painful breath. Tears flowed down his cheeks.

"I've been married over six months. I'm scheduled to return now to meet her at the Prince of Wales Fort off the west coast of Hudson Bay. She has arrived six months behind me at the wrong port. We have not even consummated our marriage. I married minutes before sailing off to here, Fort Niagara."

He cried out in despair, "Give this boring hell hole back to the French. I don't care. Oh, it hurts."

"What is your name?"

"Whiltshire, First Lieutenant Ian Whiltshire. Please I ask of you — one unselfish deed. For the love of Christ. The pain."

The Lieutenant bent over double for a second and then sat up a bit before continuing. "In the same pocket you shall find wrapped in double paper a letter written and signed by me. It authorizes the release of my recent inheritance to be bequeathed to her. I had this letter done in case something happened to me. I have failed her. I promised not to get hurt. Through duty I did not fulfill our marriage vows. She's still a virgin. Take her this letter. Let her live not in poverty. Do this one thing for me. Swear to me."

Robbie grabbed the coat and used his own coat to cover the once happy and friendly man he had just met. Knowing now why the Lieutenant was so happy with a beautiful bride waiting for him. A large inheritance to have been received, a Lieutenancy that guaranteed a retirement income that would provide adequate means. Coupled with his sums of money to be gotten they would have lived comfortably for the rest of their lives. A Captaincy or Major ranking would provide a much nicer retirement package but those ideas would all be cancelled now.

I don't know, perhaps after Tennessee. I have so much planned. My family waits. They could starve if left too long without me. Something could happen, Robbie mused.

Robbie turned to see the man had thrown off the coat. His eyes remained open in a pained expression. His breath was no more.

The air was so damp and cold and with no moon it was becoming quite dark. The wind swirled up the autumn leaves and the temperature felt like it had suddenly dropped significantly in the last few minutes. Shivering, Robbie wrapped the officer's wool redcoat over his thin clothing and huddled in the woods close by.

Where are those militia guys? They could sure help out, Robbie thought. *Maybe those rebels can get me down south. Bejeezers, maybe they are from the Carolinas. I better call them out.* Robbie picked out the gold pouch from the pocket and hid it deep in the lining of the dead man's redcoat. He gathered up his powder horn and ammo pouch. He crouched. He did not want to look like a threat to anyone. He would hold on to the inheritance letter and the drawing of the dead Lieutenant's wife. For some reason Robbie could not let the picture go, and because of it he could not let the inheritance letter go either. He ripped open the other side of the lieutenant's jacket seam with his fingers and slid the papers and the picture inside the lining. He pulled out a pocket watch that he had gotten from his father and rubbed it nervously. The timepiece didn't work. Maybe he would come across a watchmaker one day and get it fixed. *A keepsake for my son,* he thought and put the watch back in his pocket.

Robbie took a deep breath and hollered, "Hello, searching for rebels?" He stood up. "Hello, don't shoot." The darkness made everything unreal. There was nothing to see except shapes of tree branches moving in the darkness. Shadows of pinchers ready to grab and pull you into the trees and hold you. It was too quiet and very eerie.

Just then a tremendous weight fell on his shoulders. A giant of a man came rushing at him from behind. The man wrapped his arms around the redcoat on Robbie's shoulders completely straightjacketing him. His heart pounded. Robbie could tell the man was a blacksmith by his smell and the size of his arms and chest, which did not allow for Robbie to breathe, let alone move.

Robbie was pinned, trapped and surrounded. A group of about fifteen rebels encircled him. "It's that Lieutenant. I thought you shot him, Carl." Robbie heard one of them call out.

"No," Robbie screamed "No." The air was being compressed out of him.

Just then Robbie thought of his wife. Only the feelings he felt rocked him so badly, that it shook him like a shiver. *Oh why did I ever come down here?*

Robbie's saving grace was that the officer's coat was only over his shoulders and he was able to squirm out of the big man holding onto him and stood up in haste. Holding up his hands in front of him, he bellowed, "Wait, I ..." Robbie was unprepared what to say. Stammering he called out, "I'm an Acadian Ranger. Or I was. Do you know a man named Mason? I say, do you know a man named Mason? No?"

One of the men facing him said something he couldn't hear. He strained to listen. Just then an agitated young lad of about fifteen years of age but with broad shoulders came up. He swung across with his rifle butt hitting Robbie across his upper back. Robbie jumped up with the blow and then dropped to his knees. Not to be gotten the best of,

Robbie rolled up with a right elbow to the lad's groin, screaming, "You big ... PIG!"

Robbie pushed the big offal away from him and stood up again. Only this time four muskets were aimed right at him. The big lug was bending over holding his privates squealing like a baby for his mommy.

Robbie, thinking fast said, "Have you heard of a Mr. Mason? I'm heading a long way south and trying to make a place for myself there. I don't want any trouble."

Wearing a redcoat did not garner much chance of negotiation or success at survival amongst these southern activists.

"Let's teach this Brit a lesson," a voice yelled out. Just then a fist came into Robbie's blind side hitting him in the back of the head knocking him face down to the ground. And then Robbie saw a shovel. Robbie remembered a pain in his leg, being pulled up, falling down again. Later, he awakened briefly as someone shouted, "Chain him up. We'll tar and feather him in the morning."

And another voice, more authoritative said, "Put him in that tool shed overnight and we will heat some tar in the morning." Robbie was beaten, bruised and doomed.

THE TRAIL

The following day was warm, melting a lot of the snow. Where Kiwidinok, or Key had fished the day before a foreigner approached. He stopped and noticed how the deep snow had melted. He noted how the runoff of melted snow filled up beside the stream. Caught staring by one of his comrades, he looked away.

One of the other braves said, "That is just a flat rock below the stream's surface. The water was collected in a depression where the snow melted down a slope."

"No," the first young Indian stated. "It is more."

Blocking anyone from advancing he picked up a rock and placed it at the top of the path interrupting the path of the melting water. Immediately, the flow of water stopped its downward direction and instead started to overflow the ridge. Slowly, the area in question exposed a two inch deep depression and a smear of mud on the ground. It was if an animal had slid a few feet and just stopped, an all too common sight. However, at the end of the slide in the mud and marked clearly a frozen footprint was visible – a most recent footprint with five toes.

After a pause for reflection, the first warrior turned to his friends who were trying to embarrass him. After having feelings deeply hurt, he rebounded with great joy and jumped and howled back at his aggressors pushing his closest adversary to the ground, hoping to be further successful and gather followers from the young tribal group.

"I will show the way. I found the footprint." The brave who was right would lead. He in turn would attract other followers. All members of the tribe tried to be the strongest, bravest and most of all right for then they would have the best women and many followers for themselves. For that is the way. A man may be a follower or lead a few men or many but still be under the tribal council rule.

"I am the greater scout. Do not move while I look for more prints." He had a high-pitched voice full of venom.

"No, I will lead. I am closer to the hill. The footprints have to go here," said one of the others as he pointed toward the distant terrain.

"I will lead. I found the trail." His authority was being challenged. Angry and full of rage he pulled a knife from his belt, a ragged piece of shale stone carved into a point.

"Quiet! I will lead," said the senior warrior who was coming up from the rear. "You argue like children. Go eat with the women. While I the great Matonabbee[1], best of the Northern Indian warriors take over."

It was no understatement for the man was well over six feet and built big. This man knew a few native tongues and learned English while growing up at the Hudson Bay fort after his parents died. He was the representative and self-appointed leader of the Chippewyan people. He made a loop motion with his finger and the young scouts went scurrying.

"I will take this direct path. You all shall circle around here." Pointing his arm out it was clear he was to have the advantageous and shorter route while the rest of the men would have to circle around and take quite a bit longer to continue the hunt. Eventually, another print was discovered in the melting snow. And then another. Their excitement grew with each find.

---

1   See Author Notes

REBEL ROASTING

In the morning, the rebels must have slept in. But then they came. They yanked him out into the bright January sun. Blinded by the shining rays, Robbie squinted. They only had a small cast iron pot but it was full of tar and bubbling over. A small splash hit a man on the back of his hand and he jumped away from the pot tiptoeing and shaking his hand.

Robbie turned at a shriek and watched as another of the men brought over a live rooster to be plucked. The red comb looked like blood mixed within white feathers. The fire was stoked up with a long stick poking and poking into the reddened chunks of log and branch. The cast iron pot was put further into the flame. They dragged him, one grabbing his shirt on each shoulder. Kneeling him by the fire they wrapped the redcoat over his shoulders. Ambers sparked from the fire and Robbie felt heat pricks touch his face and started to cough from the rancid smoke. Robbie did not shiver in the cold. Death crossed his mind and he put up a cold face. Closing his eyes he removed himself from the group and also imagined himself a hero. He would stand up and kill these bullies. Knock them all down with just a few clean sweeps and daggers to the throat. He could feel what it would be like to be a hero – everyone congratulating him for subduing the foe. A slight brush against him brought him back from his reverie.

Somehow, the picture of the Lieutenant's wife had fallen from his jacket and onto the ground. One of the rebels picked it up, looked at it and jammed it back into the open lining where it would stay.

"Pretty one, mister. Sorry you're had." The rebel thought for a moment. "Proves you're a Brit. Look at her, you got a Brit woman for sure."

Robbie's mouth was so swollen he could not talk. Every syllable this man uttered made the veins in his head pound. The Blur. Robbie could not focus and was unable to stay fully conscious. His right leg was swollen, probably broken and cut at the calf.

"I should never have come here. This is not what I expected. Why me?" Robbie blurted out. He looked around with an embarrassed grin to see if anyone had heard. He fell back unconscious.

After a time lapse that Robbie was unsure about, he woke to a ring of shots. A barrage of smoothbore muskets had exploded. The smoke of the blast hung in the air like a giant cloudburst. Only a disciplined regiment in line could have fired those shots. The rebels fell in numbers. Few would escape – hiding only prolonged their death. The only saving grace was the fact that the accuracy of a smoothbore at fifty paces although registered as one hundred percent accurate had a misfire ratio of three in ten. Combine that with thirty percent of the shots being wild due to design. Loading too small a shot in a wide non-grooved barrel produced a ricochet effect. Still, it was better than the blunderbusses most of the militia used. The troops had used up most of their standard issue thirty-seven rounds of shot before the killing was done. Certain unmentionables would never reach the history books. A man's life was many times just that, a Man's Life, lost to war, famine or hope.

Robbie looked up as a big, fat and burly Sergeant walked over to him.

"Oh, so what do we have here? Can't talk? A few teeth knocked out, swollen face, sore head, hmm." The Sergeant deceitful, jealous and coveting as always surveyed the surroundings surmising the situation. Seeing the markings on the epaulettes of the officer's coat he immediately straightened and kept his eyes on the gold buttons sewn to the coat.

"Wait. What's this? A rich lieutenant or what's left of one. Can you respond? They did a good number on you I'd say." The air was really getting chilly. The Sarge could see his breath and spit tobacco juice onto Robbie's face to see if Robbie was awake. The yellowish brown bile slid from Robbie's cheek to his jaw.

"Corporal Freeman, Private Murphy. Pick this man up and takes what's left of him back to the hospital wagon." Just then, the Sarge pulls out his bayonet and picking up the redcoat he sliced off every gold button.

"Won't need these any time soon, eh?" Turning, the non-commissioned Sergeant bellowed all over a smallish cowering private.

"Private Strutsenburger! Take this damn coat and cover him with it. Hurry on now. A slim short man in his thirties limped over and grabbed the coat and turned away. As he was leaving, the Sergeant kicked him in the ass, pushing him a few feet forward to hurry him on. The three men with orders converged on Robbie hoisting him up onto a mule wagon.

Just then the Sergeant nodded to Thomas Johnson who just happened to walk by, "Thanks, Militiaman. Never would have found them without a word from you."

Thomas glanced at Robbie, seeing the beaten man before rushing off. Robbie acknowledged being saved with a head nod.

"Sergeant Devil, sir," the dark bearded British corporal said. "Corporal Maxwell Freeman, sir. Permission to carry on, sir." The last was a slow exaggerated pull on the word sir, more like saw-err. As if he was being cheeky with the Sergeant.

The Sergeant walked over to Robbie who appeared barely alive. Fiddling the gold buttons in his big, fat clammy hand in a quiet tone he said: "Do not worry, son. It'll be warm where you're going. The officers' hospital changes their bandages regular they does. And cleans the wounds and keeps 'em wet. Not that that'll do you much good. I just as soon leave you here to die." The Sergeant twitched his eyes in thought.

"But I will do my duty I will," the Sarge lamented, then belted out, "Strutsenburger, get back in line. You can move out now, Corporal Freeman."

The Corporal smiled at his buddy Private Jimmy Murphy and put his foot out, tripping little Sam Strutsenburger flat onto his face. Sam got up without looking, accepting his punishment as if it was a habit and got into line. There were men to bury, beers to drink and stories to be told.

LITTLE ONE

The rich foliage in Key's little paradise was abundant in herbs and plum trees. The red Tamarac bushes and tall grass were still four feet high and not flattened by the early snow. It was only August of 1770 but this far north winter consumed nine months of the year. There was plenty of small game. Squirrels and rabbits were in surplus. There was only one porcupine she had found but plenty of partridge. Life was serene in her hidden lean-to.

Key awoke from her dream and lunged upright. She screamed in her native tongue: "Ayashi!" Little One. For that was the name of her daughter. She had dreamed of hugging her baby. She was alive just a little while ago and for so little time. She was two moons maybe three at the most when she died. Key was sweating from the dream and then started shivering in the cold of the morning. It was important not to perspire. The sweat would freeze under her clothing and make it almost impossible to warm herself. As she was weeping over her loss of her daughter the bushes moved.

I'm found! she thought. Her heart skipped a beat. Her eyes darted back and forth. If she did not move maybe whoever was there would not see her. Just then, a large caribou buck with a fourteen point rack came out of the brush. Somehow it had found its way into her clearing. Key did not waste time. She arose in a split second and stumbled for her one and only staff. She had sharpened it to a very fine point. It would stick into a tree. It would not break. A fine piece of ironwood, it was slender enough for her to wield while carrying with it formidable strength. She blocked the caribou's path to the ramp. The beast kicked its hooves, pointed its giant antlers at her and challenged her. She started shivering all over. Shaking, beads of sweat formed on her brow, her heels dug into the ground. *I will do this. I must!* Hunting was man's work in the family but she had no doubts of what to do.

"Come on!" she bellowed. A stinky odor came off of the beast. Clouds of hot vapor came from its nostrils, a mixture of fear and a wild anger was clear in its eyes. Charging, the beast came running at her, feinting at the last moment and instead of trying to shoulder her out of the way, hit her with its rear quarters, sending her flying. The smelly odor of a dirty animal and hundreds of small hairs enveloped her. Stumbling up the path the caribou started to get away. Key had only one chance. Scrambling to her feet she raised her staff with both arms leveled and released. The throw had true aim, hitting the beast just behind the front shoulder. Key jumped in the air. The animal squealed in pain. The well intentioned missile bounced off its target with little effect. Little Key did not have near enough strength to kill the mighty beast and she watched it disappear before her. A disappointing end to the morning's excitement.

She walked back to her lean-to and lay back in her bedding of ragged deerskins and rabbit pelts. There was much to do today. One of her snares kept getting knocked over and she would have to deal with that. More meat needed to be hung, dried and pounded. The leftover fish would need to be smoked, and there were still berries and herbs to pick and roots to try and dig out. It was so daunting. Her helpless situation was further underlined by the morning's event. In spring, she would travel back to her native tribe, the Dog-Ribbed Tribe. She needed to know what direction to follow. The river paths were winding and confusing. She would endure till winter's end. If only she had some deer meat. She daydreamed about fresh deer meat and how good it tasted.

THE HOSPITAL

Robbie awoke to soft lamp light shining down on him. He knew he was in one of the barrack buildings made for new recruits that had been turned into a hospital. They would not need the extra soldier accommodation now that Captain Thomas Sowers[2] was re-engineering old Fort Niagara into a new fortification capable of defending itself with just forty men. Either the French or southern colonists might easily take the fort with such a small planned contingent.

"There you are. And what have you been dreaming about? Probably rum, women and fighting," a young cute brunette said.

Robbie gazed up. She had turned her body around to face the doorway. Leaning out gave her body away. Robbie could not help but notice and admire. Nice plump curves on a well developed body.

"Sergeant, your man is awake now." She looked down the hallway and did not appear to see anyone. As she turned back Robbie could see the girl was very well-endowed under her nurse's smock. The extra weight he believed to be some baby fat.

"How old are you? Robbie inquired.

"I might be eighteen. But in any case I am not far from that age. Why? Have I not looked after you so far? Look at your leg. It was awful when you came in. We cleaned and dried your wound every day. We learned from the Jew, Lieutenant Noah Chapman to stop keeping the wound damp. Changed the old bandages two times every day till the

---

2   Thomas Sowers was a British engineer for Fort Niagara. His job was to prepare the Fort for a defensible position of just forty men. Fortunately, the fort never reduced their register below ninety-nine personnel.

puss stopped oozing out. Lucky no one wanted to bleed you. You had lost a lot of blood."

"Ah the gentle medieval art of bleeding," Robbie responded. "Thanks. I would like to keep all of mine. Oh and keep the bonesaw away. Half the surgeons cannot even spell bonsaw."

"It says here on the inside of your coat that your name is Ian ... or is it Robert?"

"Whatever you like, my dear."

"When you were talking in your sleep you sure mentioned Key a lot and said you were Robbie, no last name. And you sure thought something of a Mr. Mason."

Robbie had a head that ached. He could see beauty in her eyes. Big brown eyes that were forever looking for acceptance. The poor girl looked scared out of her wits. Something was troubling her and she could not hide it.

"What is wrong uh ...your name?

"Laura Le... I mean Laura Strutsenburger." She stated it with so much pride and defiance.

"How long have I been out?

"Well, you came in at the end of January. I do not know which day it is. I heard someone say it is March 9th. But I'm not sure anyone really knows for sure around here.

"What year?"

"Seventeen sixty-nine of course. Now aren't you being funny! You had better rest awhile." She leaned over and her ample bosom brushed Robbie's chin. She grabbed the blanket she was after and spread the army grey woolen blanket about him tucking him in good and snug, before turning down the lamp,

"We will see you in the morning, Lieutenant. I will speak to the Sergeant, goodnight."

"Laura?" Robbie called out. "You are so pretty. I just wanted you to know that. And thank you. I'm not a Lieutenant, so you know."

She glanced over at him and he noticed her giving him a once over, just a glance askance from top down. His dark blue eyes stayed focused on her. She looked away, blushing as a tear fell to her cheek. She did not dab it.

"What is wrong, Mrs. Strutsenburger?" Robbie asked quietly.

Finally she broke, "I am in trouble," she said.

"Can I help, be of some assistance, surely I can repay your kindness?"

'My real name is Laura Leblanc. I live not far from here. We are one of the mixed families. My father was French and three of his brothers. That explains my last name. My mother and her parents were English. We lived on the farm next to the English settlement not far from here. The soldiers under British command came one night. Private Strutsenburger was there. He is a short and mean man who never spoke, but he has such a haunting vicious look to his eyes. I knew I was in trouble. My older sister was taken into the neighbor's barn the year before. With her murder we all have been warned about it."

"This does not sound good. I am so sorry."

"Ha, that is nothing. So I have to go around and pretend I am married to that bugger. So as I don't get left for the whole pack of them."

Robbie gently reached out and took her hand in his.

"I might as well tell all. The Sergeant may be here any moment. He is very rough." She spit the last words out with a shake of her head and tucked a stray wisp of hair behind her ear. Her beautiful brunette locks were all but hidden under her bonnet. Her hospital uniform underneath her hospital coat hid full curves that were voluptuous and tempting. Her story created a cross between feeling sorry for her to an intriguing intercept of passion. Whatever it was, Robbie just knew he wanted to help her.

"I am sorry, Lieutenant, for I have sinned. I have to live every day knowing the men who killed my family have me imprisoned here and I have to allow that Sergeant to touch me."

"Why?"

"Because Sergeant Devil made up some trash that Private Strutsenburger got caught stealing the Captain's rum. The first time it cost him half his rum rations every day. The quartermaster Noah Chapman knew this so he always gave Sam just a nip over his half ration. Noah would look over his wire rimmed glasses and give a bit of a wink. Really it was more of an eyebrow raise. But the kind point was always made."

"But why?" Robbie prodded.

"Hold on, I'm trying to tell you. I hear the Sergeant. I won't tell him you are awake till morning. It is probably March 8th... seventeen sixty-nine.

Robbie whispering back: "Thank you for your trust. You really have nursed me back to health."

"It is my job." She smiled as she extinguished the lamp and closed the door.

Robbie could hear her arguing with a gruff loud male voice just in the hallway. *That must be the Sergeant,* Robbie concluded. Just then a smack was heard and then clothes being torn.

'No,' Robbie heard her muffled scream.

Then the Sergeant said, "My dear, you must play along. Your husband still owes me a debt. And I comes to collect."

"He does not owe you by now, you filthy bastard," Laura shouted.

"Now dear, who's do you think is responsible for paying the interest? I'll take that now ma'am."

"You just keep coming up with new stories and scams. Why me?"

"Because my dear, your husband ain't really your husband, which means you ain't nothing. And I will cut the skin off your ass so you will never sit down again unless I get my way. Life is cruel for some and I might lessen the debt considering I am feeling sorry for you and all."

Robbie was sedated earlier with a few swigs of whiskey. He was not sure of all he heard but he had heard enough. He threw off his blanket and swung his feet to the floor. Standing on legs that had not walked for a month was impossible. The muscles once strong and defined from years of hard country work had no strength left in them. Robbie fell and fell and fell into oblivion. The last thing he remembered thinking was of her sweet smile and how young she was.

Blood poured out onto the floor from Robbie's wound. His skull was cracked from bouncing off a rock on the hospital room's earth floor, leaving him senseless.

DREAMS

K ey lay in her bed of furs and crossed branches and rolled over, dreaming. Sweat broke out on her body. She dreamed ...

The camp was a group of seventeen Dog-Ribbed Indians. They were all old friends of the two senior members with the exception of Key and her two-month old baby Ayashe and her son Kuckunni, meaning Little Wolf, aged eight years and two months. The two aged members were dressed in ceremonial deerskin pullovers. They were the two selected to be brought out to their favorite place to be left to die. The tradition of the Dog-Ribbed tribe and most north Indians was to abandon their old and sick, left usually with a small amount of supplies. When the food ran out they would starve or freeze to death. Usually, when weakened, the wolves would take you. Key knew Robbie had a sinister view of it all. But, tradition would not be changed.

Turning in her dream she saw her father. An elder of the tribe, he was respected for his experience and knowledge. Just then he disappeared behind some bushes. She pulled the branches apart ever so slowly and gently. Key looked through the bushes and saw her father's face close up, full of blood, staring at her and him screaming a frightful shrill. She awoke in a fright. Damp with sweat she awoke with the realization that her father was already dead. He was the first to disappear in the ambush that night.

Right then I knew we were in trouble. No sound except father going to relieve himself and not returning. We were attacked right after that, she shook her head in sorrow. *I was taken captive. Everyone else was brutally massacred. The Athapascow warriors came in the night and killed.* During her dream, she could hear vividly the screams of death of her family and the excited yelps of the Athapascow Cree as they slaughtered all around them.

Key lay awake in horror. The truth had been dreamed and she now realized it to be reality. The news was again sinking in. If only she had been awake that fateful night. She might have been able to scare off the band of attackers. They would not attack if they thought they were at a disadvantage. *If only I could have snuck everyone away.*

Key's mind turned to think about her husband. He could never accept the "Indian way." He asked her, "How ruthless can be the inhumane treatment of Indians against each other? Now I understand. I accept fate because that is the way of life here. I have seen it all my life. But through this pain I know how you feel now; when it becomes personal and lives get shattered. I am sorry I failed you.

"But, as you say," she remembered Robbie saying, "the people failed themselves by not uniting and forming some sort of central governing body to make advancements and rules for the protection of its people. A small upgrade in the standard of living from possible chance of surviving to anything better would have helped." *I can remember him repeating this over many times.*

Key lay back down. She was still tired. She knew she had to finish preserving food and then finish her new moccasins. They were made from the rest of her deerskin leggings and rabbit fur. But, she needed more rest. She feared she could not survive all winter. She slept again, hoping no dreams would come.

RUN LIKE THE WIND

During the time Key's family was being attacked, a boy of eight lay hiding in the bushes. This boy was Key's son. You could not say he escaped. More like not found *yet*, might be more like it. The warriors would be thorough in their sweep of the land for survivors and prizes. This woke him up to reality and terror at a very young age.

Slowly creeping backwards he slid under the leaves and brush. Being so small helped. *Make me big now*, he wished. *They killed my mother, I'm sure. That answers how grandpapa disappeared.* He loved being picked up by his grandpa. He rubbed the little wood doll that Chief Keezheekoni had made for everyone in his tribe, including Kuckunni or Little Wolf.

Crawling back without a sound Little Wolf shook with fear. But he was making a go of it. After fifty feet he stopped to rest. At seventy-five feet Little Wolf turned and ran like a scared jack rabbit.

The Athapascow invaders were too content over the many new deer-skin outfits the Dog-Ribbed patrons wore to continue to check around. New deerskin coats could take up to twelve deer just to make one coat. Making a coat involved a lot of scraping, drying and painful work. Prepared every summer for the severe winter season they welcomed the extra coats.

Lil Wolf knew he could run fast like the wind just like his father. Many times he could remember being in father's arms laughing while his father ran deep into the woods. Even though the trips would be scary, Robbie never dropped him and the worry was held in check by Dad's continued confidence. Lil Wolf would run all the way home.

SIMPLY A CASE OF
MISTAKEN IDENTITY

Robbie came to the next morning thinking about his wife at home and how he had failed her and his young children. As he lay there, he realized a bandage was around his head. The events of the night before flooded back in his memory.

Just then, a flicker of ash fell onto his mouth. He blew it away as he raised his head and sure enough, as if the devil had brought him, stood the loud-mouthed British Sergeant.

"I knew you were awake. Nurse, get in here. Get this man sitting up." Nurse Strutsenburger walked in. She had a bruise on her left arm and sported a doozy of a black eye. She kept her head down as she approached Robbie. She looked like she hadn't slept. Her eyes were red and bloodshot from crying. She grabbed some extra pillows and hugged Robbie with one arm around his chest and their heads met cheek to cheek as she slid the other arm gently under his back and pulled him forward. With a quick motion she jammed the new pillows under Robbie's back – the smell of her perfume was intoxicating.

"I'm okay," she whispered.

"All right, Lieutenant. I needs to be asking you some questions." The Sergeant pulled out a gold button and started to twirl it in his fingers.

"Nervous twitch there, Sergeant? Maybe you should do something for your nerves," Robbie said.

"Oh I am quite fine, I am. Yes, as long as me and the officers have an understanding. You don't upstage me. Don't make me look bad in front of the men or other officers and we gets along fine. Just letting you know the rules around here. So, being as I look after this area so as you knows.

And if you be needing anything, Sergeant Devil at your service." The Sergeant looked about and stared straight into Robbie's eyes. His cigar breath was mixed with stale beer and garlic even in the early morning. The right side of his face was scarred as was his right upper lip. As if skin was burnt off there. The skin was a pinkish color and from the cheek he had white flakes of skin falling off of him. But it was his eyes that stood out, maniacal eyes. Eyes that would help 'a picture be worth a thousand words.' Eyes that would make that statement ring true. Menacing, threatening, get even if you crossed him, radical, would always want to get the upper hand against you were just some of the impressions that could be made from this obviously mad and conniving man. The Sarge stood biting at his lip allowing drool to drip at the side of his mouth.

"The girl, Nurse Struts-her-ass-off, she has a nice – pair of – legs, don't you think? But you probably weren't looking at her. That is good too. But don't think you'll ever get your hands on her. She's married. And to a good man. He pays his debts he does. Not a better soldier."

"What do you want, Sergeant?" Robbie asked.

The Sergeant looked at the nurse and then back directly into Robbie's eyes. "The nurse, she says you said you ain't a Lieutenant."

"Of course I am not a Lieutenant. I'm a Canadian Ranger. I just helped bring down some new recruits to the fort. I showed them the way so to speak."

"What? You're not an officer?"

Robbie sat up, grabbed his undershirt and pulled it on.

The Sergeant stood up and squinted making his face real wrinkly and moved to within an inch of Robbie's face. "This is an Officers' Hospital. We do not take civilians, enlisted men or non-commissioned officers here. You dirty scum ... Mrs, Struts you hear that? Your pretty boy soldier is not what we thought he was. Come on. Off to the Surgeon's office at the pig farm. That's where you should have gone. Get up."

Robbie gingerly tested his legs. "This is a case of mistaken identity. When can I leave?"

"Impersonating an officer you have been," the Sergeant concluded. "Come on, we're going to make a visit to the Captain. He'll want to have a word with you. Let's see what he wants to do with you."

Robbie's heart sank. Just as he was feeling better, now this. He wondered about it all and then suddenly remembered—the coat. The Lieutenant's redcoat. The Sarge left the room to call in a pair of guards for escort.

Robbie pulled up his trousers and did up his belt. He turned to Nurse Laura, who was looking away.

"You shouldn't let him talk to you that way or do that to you," Robbie pointed to her bruised arm.

"There is nothing I can do. I need protection, food and shelter. I have no family now, nowhere to go." She helped Rob walk a bit and helped him out the door.

"I'm ashamed. I really don't know what I shall do."

The Sergeant had two soldiers grab Robbie by the arms and helped get him down the front porch and out onto the landing.

Robbie's legs were still weak. Before his injury, Robbie was in such good shape that he suffered less than most people who lay in bed for a month. But his balance was off.

"Bring him along Max, I mean Corporal Freeman." Corporal Maxwell Freeman was recently promoted to Corporal by the Sergeant's recommendation. Just an extra slip of paper for the Captain to sign. Captain Knobbs never noticed or would probably not care if he did. A sort of thank you gift from Sergeant Devil to his helper for certain favors. It seems the Corporal was quite adept at getting rid of the settlers' husbands when their wives complained or keeping quiet the native girls that the Sergeant scars and rapes. Even the whores were bruised and crying when leaving. Corporal Maxwell would always be able to find a spot in the open courtyard in the middle of the night to deposit the sobbing victims. Their wounds would heal. The native women at the fort were not very particular about who they slept with. Pain and suffering seemed inbred in them. Their welfare was regarded with little value all of their lives.

The Sergeant bellowed, "Private Murphy, give a hand here. Get our Canadian Ranger down to headquarters."

Captain Neil Rae Knobbs was a straight thinking kind of man. He had made his rank by being careful. When it came to any problem or situation, he would take the course of least confrontation, the least trouble with a fast decision. Get the people away from him and on to the next problem. Then the same thing on the next conflict brought to his attention. Not always did this work out.

Full at attention and saluting Sergeant Devil held there for a reply. The captain waved his right hand in a flap away as to show he was not bothered by formalities. A new confrontation was about to be sprung on him on this sunny spring day.

"Well, what is it, Sergeant? I don't have all day."

"We have here an officer impersonator. You see, this derelict of a person we thought was a Lieutenant was only acting like he was an officer. Led us on so to believe."

The Sarge continued, "Well he ain't. Just a bloody Ranger. Born here, he is. Imagine. Not even British!

Robbie winced, *not my fault I still have a British accent thanks to my parents.*

The headquarters' room was small. An old oak desk, a chair on each side at the front and back. These chairs would creak and moan every time you shifted your weight on them. The Sergeant sat his wide derriere on one of the chairs in front of him. Holding his left knee he lifted his right cheek as if in terrible pain. When he did so, the chair vibrated as he passed wind. Everyone turned to look at the Captain.

The Captain looked at his men with a smirk. Then he roared with laughter. The men guffawed. More whips of real gas were tooted, causing more laughter. Hard to hang a man after that.

As the laughter subsided, Robbie spoke up. "The jig is up, gentlemen. I never would have even been here if it was not for the Sergeant and his patrol. They saved me from death. Getting tarred and feathered would maim and blind me if one was to survive such an ordeal. I tell you what. You gentlemen are short on recruits. I already have on-duty experience and feel a lot better. I mean it was my job to get fourteen raw redcoats down from Prince of Wales Fort. I like soldiering. I have not had a home for awhile and looks like my plans are about to change. It felt like home being a part of a regiment. I'll enlist. I'll enlist and take an immediate Captain's position based on what I can do for you and have done for you. My qualifications, what more can I say?"

Private Murphy interrupted, "Well, the boys have heard of him. Does carry a bit of conversation about him."

"Well, why not?" the Sergeant said.

The Captain grabbed one of a pile of papers on his desk. "Here, if you can read this you don't have time. That is your agreement. A three-year term to fight for his Royal Majesty, that or a hanging for impersonating an officer. Sign here, *Private* Robbie and get out. I mean all of you. Turning to the only other ornament in the room, Captain Knobbs stared into the small mirror hanging on the post and mumbled to himself, "I need time to think and relax."

No sooner than the ink was starting to dry the Sergeant growled at Robbie, "You're mine now. Special duties for new recruits. I just so happens to be in charge of all new recruits. And the stipend for signing you up now gets used up in the payment for some of your gear including your boots, redcoat, undershirt, derby, musket and bayonet, belt, ammunition, and ammunition pouch, horn and powder. All supplied by his Majesty's service. As soon as the wool redcoat goes on the lice start getting onto you. Hard not to. They will be just be meeting cousins in your night sack. It is all in what you get used to. A tot of rum will be issued every day and a pint of beer. A roll of tobacco per week rounds it out if you're a smoker. Sometimes there is peppermint or lemons."

As soon as they had all marched out of the Captain's office, the Sergeant growled, "Private Robbie, you're under arrest. You're to undergo an interrogation.

"Put him in the brig, Corporal Freeman. Private Murphy give a hand and make sure he is tied up good. We'll be paying him a visit shortly."

FIRST TRIP

L il Wolf thought about this recent trip. He was out on a trek with mom to the favored grounds of the two elders who were to be left to die. Burial grounds, or more like wolf fodder grounds. The barren lands had bands of the starving canines. Clowey Lake was to the north. Slave Lake or Athapuscow Lake was west. Home was east eighty miles to Prince of Wales Fort then north half as much again, very important things to worry about when it was your very first trip from home.

"Oh give me a piece of dried deer meat," he wished aloud. *I don't have anything, not even a knife. I think I know how to make a fire. Now what am I going to do?* His thoughts were in panic. "I am almost eight," he said to the sky.

The young Indian boy who looked like his father, a white man, could not think clearly. Slowly he started to feel more and more disheartened. The threat of wolves did not overtake his tiredness. He lay propped up beside a tree. He could hear no more screaming or crying. Only the cold wind. Weeping to himself he fell into a deep sleep.

BRANDED

Robbie awoke tied up. He was sure he had lost another back tooth. One of his ribs was surely broken or misplaced. His whole spine felt twisted. His lower lip was quite swollen. Someone was coming. Robbie could hear shuffling close by. The room stank. Dank and dark, the old soldiers' sleeping quarters were in disrepair. Some of the wood beams were missing and used for firewood. The coldness from outside blew in with the wind. It actually felt good; the cold numbing his wounds. The Sergeant came around the corner and took a look.

"You're mine now, Private." Sergeant Devil walked up to Robbie. As always, the smell of cigar smoke and rum was strong on his breath.

"It really was a case of mistaken identity. No one asked if I was a Lieutenant. I couldn't talk for a month. I had no concept ..."

Aghast, Robbie watched as Corporal Freeman came walking in. Robbie recognized him as one of the assailants who participated in his beating from last night. Maxwell held a branding iron. There was no special branding face. Just the letter 'S'.

The Sergeant went on, "Make me look like a fool you did. I bring you in thinking you're a Lieutenant and you screwed me over. Corporal Freeman, give me that branding iron." The Sergeant licked his lips.

Robbie squirmed. Sweat was starting to form on his brow. Weakened by his plight and still restrained by well-tied knots to both wrists he had no chance. His legs were free and he thrust up, hitting the Sarge on the outside of his leg as he went to block. The hot iron came in fast. A sizzle pinned Robbie to the log wall. Scorching pain hit Robbie in his upper right chest. The Sarge was pacing back and forth panting like a dog, spit drooling from his mouth. Sergeant Percival Devil had the villainous eyes of a mad man. Forever envious of everything and every one, he also wanted to control everything and know everybody's business. His eyeballs would shake, no waiver back and forth as he looked at you. As if he was so full of hatred he could not stare at one spot. He rubbed at his scarred cheek. "Not going to kill you. We need you to work. Let this be a lesson not to make me embarrassed again."

Robbie raised his head from looking at the blistering wound. Fuming, he could handle no more torture. The agony was just keeping him from passing out, his humility no more.

Why did I ever think this was right? Robbie thought. *Oh Key.*

Robbie's cry of anguish tailed off as he saw the Sergeant raise his arm and pull loose one of his restraints.

"I have decided to let you go. There will be a penalty of half your rum rations for as long as you're under my command. Go clean up and report to Noah Chapman. He's the Quartermaster Lieutenant. He's in the office in the supplies building, the tallest building that has one window, in front of all the tents."

Robbie rubbed his raw wrists. He was not sure the army life was what he wanted anymore. At least the punishment was over and he could transfer to Prince of Wales Fort, which would get him forty miles from his wife if she and her family were still camped where he had last left them. He didn't know she would travel on a death walk with her family being gone since January 1768.

Walking over to the supply depot Robbie watched a few workers who were rebuilding part of the rampart. A rampart consisted of the fort's defensive walls, which assisted the defenders of the fort from land attack. These walls and landscape led to the only fort opening; a gate house with three walls to provide a three-sided defense against an attack against the entrance. It had taken British troops nineteen days to take Fort Niagara by land. The French surrendered after learning their supply ship was intercepted by the British navy. Now the British had cleared a lot of native American threats by alliance and drove most of the French from America. Now there were more important issues.

The southern colonists had a large following of independent thinkers who wanted justice by way of eliminating concessions of the new American immigrants and an end of the British duty tax. The British would stop world shipping and any Americans would be pressed into naval service for the Crown. Robbie had desperately wanted to join this new group. Bring his family down south. Receive fifty acres and a new start in warmer country. Robbie was well schooled by his mother before the pox got his family. He studied and understood some great points in literature written at the time on politics and freedom. But, it was time to return home and live at the Prince of Wales Fort with his family, as a British soldier.

Robbie lamented, *if I ever come across those bandits who called themselves southern rebels I will get even.* In afterthought, there might have been quite a few escapes. Robbie put aside his back and forth train of thought and entered the domain of Lieutenant Noah Chapman.

"And what do we have here? They send me a sick man. You look terrible! Guard! Get me a man who can work. Return this deathly looking thing."

"I can work," Robbie blurted out.

Noah paused and took a curious eye to Robbie. "There is a hand cart outside. You should be able to put six bundles of flour on the cart. You should start with five and see how it goes. Pile the potato flour bags here. Hurry on."

"Not to appear stupid but could you tell me where I get the bags? I have been down for a few days, I believe." Robbie said in an understatement.

"Oh, of course. The supply ship came in last week. See Lieutenant Gordon Drummond.ᵛ You'll be able to tell him by his energetic nature. I do believe he is the first Canadian-born officer of the British Army."

Off Robbie went, thinking it would be wonderful to be an officer with power, wealth and people who would admire him. His first duty was lugging bags of potato flour. Might have been one thousand potato flour-filled cloth sacks. The west had not brought the influence of wheat yet to Upper Acadia. That would not be for fifty years or more.

Ships were sailing up and down the St. Lawrence by the numbers. They brought new immigrants and supplies. Robbie went up the ramp to the tall ship and waited in line.

A BOY NAMED LIL WOLF

Key had been thinking of her son. She did not remember seeing him killed. Kuckunni looked just like his father, a white second generation British colonist. She remembered Kuckunni or Lil Wolf always running away and laughing. She had trouble catching Lil Wolf because he was so fast.

Her father had gone missing first. Obviously, he was bushwhacked. The whole group of family members was massacred and she was kidnapped. *My Sky Father*. She shuddered with embarrassment on her first time being raped. How she had fought and then for the sake of not getting hurt went along with it. Faking happiness she moaned. This made the first warrior laugh and made her flush red and get flustered. When the act was repeatedly administered by others she knew to lie still and accept that this was the Indian way of the north. When motherly, she brushed some hair out of a young warrior's face but the lad laughed and embarrassed her further. Share and share alike was what it seemed like. Take or be taken. This made survival have a better chance for the poor desperate creatures living in the desolate north. It was their way.

CAUGHT

The day was colder and he awoke shivering. The reality of his situation came rushing back like a gushing river heading straight for him. Sitting up, his awakening thoughts ended on a violent shiver. He got his bearings, stood up and immediately lit out. He had to cover ten thirty-mile days and winter was coming. Snowshoes would be needed soon. No food for ten days except some dried berries and a few roots. Onward Lil Wolf endured. The rivers were many. Most waterways were not crossable without a canoe. They would not freeze over for at least two or three moons. Many of the detours resulted from the woods ending in too thick a brush to continue. Frustration was worse given the immediacy of the situation. Finally, having covered no more than five miles, Lil Wolf eased to a slow run wondering if he could go on. The area was heavily forested with poplar and pine, and straggly branches he did not know. The ground was damp and slippery. He could only see thirty yards ahead at best. There was no clearing.

Which way do I go? he asked. As he passed by a big tree on his right, a knee came out and stopped him on his chest. A leg came out bent at the knee and stopped him right in his tracks. The warrior who stepped out was obviously not worried about getting hurt by the way he herded Lil Wolf to a stop with his knee. Lil Wolf had no chance to escape. His breath was gone and all he could do was drop to his knees, fall onto his back and pant. Staring up at his aggressor he was frightened to silence. Death was sure to follow. Lil Wolf wondered if the pain of death would be slow and torturous or torturous and fast.

ALTERNATE MOTIVE

Robbie had moved so many bags of potato flour his back was feeling stiff and pained. Being so tired he drifted into memories. Thinking of his wife he smiled. She was the prettiest in any group, and he was proud of it. Unlike many Indian women, who tended toward larger fat bodies, bulky and bloated, she was petite and strong with long slender muscles like her father.

Robbie was finally feeling his strength coming back in his legs and feeling a little more confident. But even though he was feeling better he could not straighten his back after so much lifting all day. *After a night's rest I'll be okay.* First chance he could get he would transfer to Prince of Wales Fort and from there take leave and check up on his family. A change of plans is all. The southern colonist idea just was not clicking in. *A few years as a soldier and I'll have a bit of a nest egg. Just a few more months and this journey will be at an end. What can stop me now?*

And along came Sergeant Devil. Like the Devil himself sometimes Percival had tusks of hair stick out of his head that took the form of horns like the Devil. Sarge had a whole head of curly brown locks. The big lug did have some ruggedly-handsome good looks. His size was just so intimidating. The size of his forearms, hands, forehead and back were astounding. He carried his extra hundred pounds of weight around handily. This time, Sergeant Percival Devil was in good manners and addressed Robbie cordially,

"How do you like the army now, Private?" The Sergeant held out his big fist and opened up his palm to offer a handshake. Robbie took his hand. Robbie felt some warts on the Sarge's palm and then his hand was consumed by the sausage fingers. No squeezing, just a firm grip. Robbie straightened and they backed away from each other.

"How did you get a name like Devil? You change it?" Robbie changed the line of conversation with his query.

"I kind of like it. Don't you?" the Sarge replied in a deep voice.

"The Devil is a good name, you Devil you," Robbie teased poking an index finger into the Sarge's rather large belly. Robbie sometimes liked to instigate for no other reason than disliking the man.

The Sarge stood erect pushing Robbie's hand away with a push of his stomach.

"Well now I never got baptized properly, I didn't. You see I was to be baptized Horace Wartnabbee. The priest was on a trip. It was a late hour. The stupid drunken janitor placates himself and everyone by putting himself in charge at the church temporarily. Me parents were members there. Me parents were in a rush you see. Well the drunken old fart forgot to write my name down and put down where he thought was below the name space of the Baptismal form 'The Big Precious Devil.' Because I was big even as a baby you see. Anyhow, the janitor's added note was made legal. Because the bugger made it official with a stamp on it.

"My parents would not take me to church with a name like that. School was hell. But I am here and made it to Sergeant. And do not forget it. I changed my name to Percival from Precious. Percival Devil. Nice eh? Got a ring to it, it does."

Robbie soaked all that in and was quietly amused. The guy was off to a rough start right away from childhood. *No wonder he is so off base*, Robbie chuckled to himself. Horace Wartnabbee would not be appropriate. *He has lots of warts. Just look at his hands.* Robbie started wiping his hands on his pants.

After a moment Robbie realized the Sarge was opening up to him. Robbie thought, *Seems like the Sergeant is being a little easier on me. Maybe things will turn around and we can get along now.*

Sergeant Percival Devil was showing extreme politeness in his manners and voice. "So did you say you were married? A good looking fellow like you surely has a wife, no?"

Robbie nodded. "Kiwidinok is her name. A very beautiful Indian princess. I met her outside Prince of Wales Fort. It was love at first sight. We were both fifteen almost sixteen."

It was not uncommon for girls as young as twelve and they came to blood to be mated with the senior tribesmen. She was fortunate to have travelled to the fort considering the alternative.

"I left her with her family just west of the Fort. When I left, I remember that day distinctly, January 14th, 1768. And my son was seven years and three moons old. He would be now …"

"It's March 69, uh, you figure it out," the Sarge said, befuddled. "That's a tough one. Ya got it?"

Robbie nodded. "My son would be eight years five months old right now. I was to go get them as soon as I finished my scouting job and had arranged land in New Tennessee. Seems they like to give away land for free. But all that's changed now. I've been gone too long. I will go home to see my wife and son. I will accept the next transfer to the north. Some of these ships sail right out to Cape Breton. From there, a supply ship will take another month to get to Prince of Wales Fort."

Robbie thought, *While there I will drop off the inheritance letter.*

"From there I am going home as a British soldier." About the opposite of what he started out to do but a lot simpler. "The south can go to hell." Twisting away before the Sarge could read his thoughts and blinking away tears of being homesick he jumped when Sergeant Percival Devil slash Horace Wartnabbee, slash many warts I see on the big bugger asked, "What did you say your wife's name is? Kini ... din ..." Sergeant Devil pinched his lips together and kept trying different syllables.

Percival Devil's question commanded an answer. The type of intimidating interrogator that could get any answer from you just by a direct accusing question.

The Sarge appeared to be trying to remember. "Kabbey? Canobie? Kiwi Haha? Kiwidin..,"

"Pronounce it Ki-widi-nok, with the accent on nok," Robbie proudly announced as if everyone had heard of her. Many had. "She is her father's daughter. He is a wise elder of the Dog-Ribbed Indians who have been at the Prince of Wales Fort many times. His name is Keezheekoni. He made these little wood carvings that we kept with us. They were not worshipping idols, just toys for us to give to the children to play with or just keep for good luck. We all had one.

"We were all afraid of the Iroquois that sometimes accompanied the French. The savagery of scalping we could never get used to." Robbie could not help himself from rambling and thought of his son because he had given his Koni doll to him. He realized he was homesick.

New Tennessee was a land full of rich soil and pastureland. Now he was looking at months to transfer to the frozen, barren lands of the northern part of the continent. Robbie had already discussed the transfer with Captain Knobbs and was pleased when he approved his request to transfer to the Prince of Wales Fort on Hudson Bay.

Robbie knew it was a suicide mission to go most places the British sent new recruits these days. The South Seas, Cuba and India all held their peril of disease while in France, Portugal or Spain you were liable to get killed by close enemy fire. Even Britain itself wasn't safe. Although the Scots and the Irish were allowed to enlist and finally wear their kilts or colors with regimental pride, they fought each other constantly. England, Scotland, Wales and Ireland all retaliating or instigating trouble. *Lucky there are any of the buggers left in the homeland,* he mused.

Going to northern North America was also suicide. Freezing temperatures or famine would get you. And there were constantly muggers killing each other there too. Staying here the Iroquois, sickness or soldiering would get you anyway so it really did not matter. Robbie was brought back from his reverie when the Sergeant interrupted.

"I've heard of your wife. A dog Indian," the Sarge smiled.

"Dog-Ribbed! Dog Flank is the actual translation," came Robbie's retort.

Sergeant Percival continued, "The Athapuscow war party came in and massacred a group of Dog-Ribbed Indians and captured a beautiful woman named Kiwidin ... what you said. She was killed escaping." Right then and there Sargeant Percival Devil's heart sank to his lower belly. An airy achoo sound came from Percival's lips as he expelled his air. This matching up of information meant the Sergeant had no need to put on an air of liking Robbie. He had no wife to steal. All new recruits since Private Sam Strutsenburger endured the same treatment. First, half their rum rations would be penalized. Then an excuse to have the recruit fall into debt of some sort and be threatened with a flogging. Have death hanging over their heads. Get another soldier's wife to do his bidding. Pay the interest till the debt was paid. Hopefully never.

"Your wife is dead, Private. And by the looks of you I bet you will never get another. You're done. Bloody bastard is a waste of my time." The Sarge started walking away.

"You can't be serious. You lie." Robbie stared in disbelief. He jumped forward to catch up to the burly Sergeant.

"I will bring the Indian who told me when I can find him. Call me a liar again and I will have your tongue, I will. I'll rip it out!" screamed Percival. Spittle sprayed over Robbie.

Robbie thought of all that was happening in his life. This news could not be true, could it? The past few months had really turned his situation around. Robbie, who seldom drank for need or want, needed a beer. They departed with their own agendas on their minds.

SLAVERY

The air was warm around the fire. The smell of fresh fish cooking made his mouth water. Only moving his eyes he spied a stick of delicious looking dried venison about a foot long. The dried meat was within his grasp. Where was his captor?

"Na hacha!" spoke the Indian.

Lil Wolf, recognized the voice as the man who stopped him. He must have passed out. He must tell him his story. Consoled that he was not dead Lil Wolf sat up and grabbed the dry piece of deer meat. He would pay dearly for such a bold move.

The Indian screamed a high pitched yell at him and went eye to eye one inch away. Lil Wolf pulled down his brow touching his eyebrows together. The Indian grabbed Lil Wolf by the hair and smashed him to the ground and kicked him in the back. Another stomp on his ass and off he walked turning once to see if Little Wolf moved. He did not move. Not till much later when he would feel very sore. He lay face down in the dirt.

ROBBIE'S WATCH

At the end of his shift, Robbie went to the food shelter to get his dinner and his daily ration of beer. Nothing like beer. However, the beer here was fermented from spruce wood. Kicked a wallop from the first sip. Only trouble was most of the time it tasted diluted. And no one had cheesecloth or proper straining equipment. Run it through a dirty woollen shirt with lots of holes in it and one would get a ton of sawdust with each beer. Some pieces were bordering on splinters. Putting back six quick big mugs of room temperature fifteen percent or more alcoholic beverage would result in someone walking you home. Robbie was on his sixth, generously donated by Noah.

He was sitting on a pine wood bench for the soldiers to sit on to eat. Each bench matched the length of the twenty foot tables. Wood pegs were the fasteners. Broad Axe was the saw. Short chip strokes to square up the timbers. Joints to fit it all together. Life was a lot of hard work just to make tables. There was always a shortage of furniture.

Looking up, Robbie stared across the road. Out of the Headquarters building came the Sergeant. Sergeant Percival had pulled out a pocket watch. Robbie, with a few drinks in him got up, knocking over the last of his beer.

He staggered across the road and proclaimed, "Sergeant, is that my watch? I plumb forgot about it. May I look at it? Where did you find it?" As Robbie swatted at the air, an elbow in his stomach knocked the wind out of him and down he went into the mud.

The Sarge sneered, "This is not yours. A likes of you would never have something so nice. Belongs to an officer it did."

"You stole it out of my pocket when I was unconscious. It doesn't even work." Robbie clutched his stomach.

"As I said, you stole it off that officer that was shot back then," the Sergeant threw back in defense.

"No, sir. I have had that watch for a long time. My father ..."

Cutting Robbie off Sergeant Devil put it straight, "I am keeping it in safekeeping for evidence. You had to of stole such an expensive watch. I will see what punishment there will be for having it. In the meantime, I will keep it for some of the interest you owe on your debt."

"What debt?" Robbie took a step forward.

Corporal Freeman and his companion Private Murphy stepped forward quickly to block Robbie from the Sergeant.

Over their shoulders Sergeant Devil sprayed as he belched out, "That outburst is going to cost you your other half of your rum ration."

Robbie took a few steps forward and leaned into the two soldiers blocking him and gritted his teeth. He placed evil eyes onto the Sergeant. Percival chuckled at first watching Robbie fume then started to fume himself.

Neither one of them spoke. They stood there glowering at each other.

SON'S DILEMMA

In a deep dream Lil Wolf could see his mother. Although his features would mistake him as white like his father, he still had a slight brow and the dark straight hair that hung long over his shoulders inherited from his mother. He would have his father's tall, thin athletic build and his wide shoulders and rugged good looks. He was already over three feet and he would turn nine soon.

He remembered things of his father either by memory or the constant stories Mother had told. He wasn't sure which. An image of his father came into his mind with questions. Would his father come back to save him? Would he have to go and find his father? Tell him what happened? Lil Wolf continued to dream and heal.

A WITNESS

The tension broke between the Sergeant and Robbie. Robbie knew he had to back down; there was not much he could do. A full garrison of troops would have cut him down if he had tackled the Sergeant and caused a scene. As he was defeated again he saw what appeared to be an older Indian approaching, wearing two feathers in his hair, beads about his neck and a deerskin ensemble that was quite popular for the day.

The Devil of a Sergeant, Percival Devil regained his composure and broke through two soldiers and screamed, "Here you go Robbie. There's your proof. This here is the Injun who told me of your wife's demise. Go ahead tell him, Injun."

Even in his drunken state, Robbie cringed at the Sergeant's disrespectful language. *He has no respect for the true hosts of this land. As a matter of fact, he doesn't respect anyone.*

Robbie thought how good it would be to lay a beating one on one with the Sergeant. They stood off to the side so fewer of the men could hear the sad tale. The strange Athapuscow native stood with a grin on his face. Robbie wanted to wipe that smile off his face. Oh what restraint he grasped at. Tears were forming in his eyes. His vision blurred. The beer was turning in his stomach and his head began to throb.

The Indian talked on and on. "Key would not stay with a tribe that massacred her family, including her son and daughter."

"I have no daughter," Robbie shook his head. Was it possible he had a daughter? What if Key was pregnant when he left her in January of 1768?

"There is a possibility. Only makes things worse. Go on," Robbie said.

"She escaped into the deep wilderness and has not been heard of since. She could not possibly survive the barren wilderness for all this time. The people killed were all her family and elders."

"What was she doing there? Did she say what she was doing there?" Robbie started to realize the possibility of the horrible truth now.

"She was on a death walk to leave two elders with a few provisions to die. I heard one was called We Cha-ha. I do not know the other name. They went just south of Clowey Lake where we found them. That was the old ones' favored hunting grounds." The name brought no recollection to Robbie.

Robbie was now totally aghast. The last few months of torment had done its job. Robbie, head down with a forlorn expression, drooped his shoulders and slunk away to his bunk. He had to be alone. Sleep off this news and booze. Tomorrow he would figure it out. As Robbie staggered away, the Sarge and his cronies chuckled loud enough to be heard.

The next morning was no better with the exception that the work detail kept him busy. He was out in the yard lifting sand buckets up to barricade a thirty foot small area of the wall that had collapsed. The air was warm in the sun and the smell of lilacs tickled his nose and brought a smile. White lilacs were his mom's favorite. The land was full of the colorful blooms. As he worked, a seductive full-figured native girl passed by. Robbie watched the nice sway of her full hips as she walked. She turned back and gave him an eye and a head nod in acknowledgement of his admiration. Obviously she was going to keep someone warm tonight. She was quite attractive really and cute with a well rounded derriere – a nice cushion to curl up to. *Native girls are so pretty when they are young.* Robbie thought of his native wife. He realized he had been away from his wife for too long and was not there to support her when she needed him. He threw his shovel across the sand pit in frustration. He had not been home for a long time. Add that on to the list of problems. *Now I need to find someone else. Not yet I hope.*

Sergeant Percival was in his office waiting for Corporal Freeman to finish writing up the punishment form for Robbie.

"I'm sure I can bribe the Captain into signing the punishment form. Threatening a non-commissioned officer. It's worth ten lashes I would say. I will order the drummer boys to lay down a fast beat to their drums and have Robbie's back beaten till his skin is red with blood. Give him a taste of what will happen if he continues to mock me. I'll keep the order in my back pocket till we finish tomorrow's patrols. Heard he was good out there in this huge forested wilderness. We certainly can use another hand. Bring him along tomorrow on the patrol, Corporal."

"Yes sir, Sergeant." Corporal Freeman said.

He glanced at the Corporal who took no notice as he blew dry the last of the ink. "That makes all of it." The Sergeant put down his quill and folded the charges.

"Throw it in with the rest of the papers." He knew the Captain never read any of them unless they came off a new ship.

"Don't bother me. I am thinking," Captain Knobbs said as he always did. One of his subordinates would gaze over the files to make sure there were no infringements against the natives that would block or hamper the trade for their rich fur laden products. His subordinate faked the signatures and did not dare ask the Captain any questions about any forms in fear of conflict.

Meanwhile, Robbie watched every step the curvaceous native girl made till she was out of sight. Oh he was homesick. That smiling Athapuscow Indian mentioned that Key was kept alive for her beauty. They would not kill what they craved.

After a time she was given to one of the older men as a third wife. She would have to carve, cook, sew, carry and give her time to the man. Treated more like a slave than a wife.

Robbie felt sick as he remembered how the old Indian had stepped toward him and moved his hips back and forth suggestively, screeching like an owl, arms out and feathers flying. Robbie fumed. He wanted revenge. She would have to do anything and everything she was told to do or risk a beating or worse. In despair, Robbie recounted his losses — his energy gone.

Robbie thought of his time with his wife's tribe. The men did the majority of the hunting and fishing. The women made the fish nets and did the carving, drying, pounding, powdering and the cooking of the meat. The men ate first and the women might have some if there were leftovers. We live, we suffer, and we perish. Such is the way of life. Robbie wondered how much Key might have suffered from starvation, beatings and abuse. And anguish over a lost family and no husband for support.

Robbie wept. And wept some more. *I should never have left them for so long. Add this to the many mistakes in my life. A person can't make as many as me.*

Robbie walked off to get a mug of beer. Nothing mattered anymore. The soldiering, Tennessee, being a rebel colonist. *Our daughter. Oh my dear wife, I am so sorry. Life is hard in North America. Life is not good anymore.* Robbie was shattered.

SIGNS OF ATROPHY AND
SELF ISOLATION

Lil Wolf had lived and after a few weeks he had down all the rules. He was to gather as much firewood as he could forage all day. Not stand and tend the fire by the warmth. Just follow, walk, pick up, carry back and pile. He also did not eat till even the women and children ate. If there was anything left he could have and horde as much as he could grab. Lil Wolf did not eat every day.

When travelling he had to carry a heavy rock. If he sat for a break the rock would remain with him. This rock had birch strips that wrapped around the rock and tied to his leg. There was no escape. And where to? When he had time by himself he re-visited his recent experiences. Killed were his mother, baby sister, grandfather, great fathers of tribe members who were the old wise men. All perished.

After a few beatings, all Lil Wolf would do was sit and stare off in the distance when taking a short break from working. No one talked to him. No one heard him speak. The group of Northern Dene had a few children a little older than Lil Wolf. When they kicked him for fun or poked him Lil Wolf would curl up and shake, scared of all physical confrontation. Even scared of his own shadow. He could not help himself. From fun and love of a family to drama involving death and an end of everything he knew and then to be cast to slavery and starvation and horrible unloving treatment.

Lil Wolf remembered, *I was to be my father's son. I look exactly like him. I will be tall, lean, big and strong.* But, he despaired, *I will die young in slavery. Because I look white my punishment is extra harsh.*

He managed to stand on his injured ankle. He had sprained it after tripping while carrying too much wood a few days ago. If he could have stayed off his feet for two or three days the ankle would heal. Instead, his ankle would heal in five or six months as he was not able to rest it. "Pain for six months I am sure, maybe forever. Great! What is there to care about now?" he said out loud. Lil Wolf dreamed of a bear coming out of the woods and killing him to end his despair.

ANGUISHING MEMORIES

Key thought of how the women had attacked her and killed her three-month-old daughter Ayashe. She had carried the baby one moon short of the usual time and Ayashe was very tiny and quiet too. She never cried beyond the normal even when wet or hungry. As if even as a baby she knew her fate. A quiet resolve of her life to be extinguished early – surely not. The brutality was common among the tribes. It was not uncommon for the women to help during war years by killing enemy wives and children. They were expected to do it. They expected to do it. To savagely kill young and old enemy survivors left at camp. Some were made into slaves or used to replace a family member. But there were very few. Most would be attacked with venom.

Key could not consolidate her feelings and stood looking up to the sky. Stretching her neck, as a wolf howls to the moon she howled out, asking why she was picked for this fate. Slow in movement and glassy-eyed, she had thoughts of further doom and anguish. Further indignities. Key wept for her daughter. Lonely and insulted beyond what any woman should have to endure she collapsed to her knees. *Stand up and get through this for Robbie.*

"Oh, Robbbieeeee ..." she pined.

CUBA

By August 1769, Robbie realized that he had left his wife one year and seven months ago. He also realized that her family had been massacred thirteen months ago. *I will not go to cover the bones of her family. Of my children. By the time I get there, no evidence will be left. The bones would have been scattered by wolves.*

His transfer had been one month in the waiting to be signed by Captain Knobbs. He never rushed anything. Now there was a wait for the proper ship that was going all the way to the eastern coast.

Speaking aloud, "I don't know what to do. Maybe I should ask to go to Cuba. What does it matter if I do not return? And how am I ever to start another family. Key! The tortures she must have endured," Robbie felt so much hurt.

OFF TO SEE MOSES AT THE
PRINCE OF WALES FORT

S top, please." Lil Wolf was curled up in a ball. A boy of about six was
throwing rocks at him. After about five minutes the boy got bored
and walked away. Lil Wolf, bleeding on the front of his calf from the
rock that cuffed him, looked around in embarrassment. Shaking with
fear and crying over his realized loss of his family and the recent plight
sent a lightning bolt of sorrow through his heart. *I will not speak again to
anybody at all.*

His immediate slave master Conneequese, the Indian who captured
him called out, "Time to pack." The horde was moving to Moses' fort.

Despite the short time he was with these people he was learning a
few words of the Chipewyan tongue. He would not let them know.

The group headed off in unison. Lil Wolf overheard that they were
heading to the Prince of Wales Fort on the west coast of Hudson Bay
to trade their furs for guns, ammunition, iron and knives. Scissors and
pepper and iron pots and awls for the ice. The Governor of the fort
was a Métis named Moses Norton. Half French and half Cree. He was
believed to be a fair man when it came to bartering.

There was also word of a crazy white man who wanted guides to
the Copper River, which was north of Clowey Lake and where it was
rumored that an abundance of copper was cached. They had a long
trek ahead. Lil Wolf had no need to go to the fort area again. His only
desire was to show everyone he did not care. He would never speak to
them again.

"WHERE EXACTLY IS SHE?"

That same day in the late evening Robbie was rocked. The bucket of spruce beer was about empty. "Oh, got to go relieve myself gentlemen." Robbie looked around and saw about seven or eight soldiers passed out around him at the tables.

"Must have dozed off. Goodnight, gentlemen."

"A pox on ya," one snorted. Another gassed his pants rather loudly, his only reply. This reminded Robbie of his youth. "Mom, Johnny johnnied his shorts again," he remembered telling his mother about one of his brothers. Gone for over ten years now, they were. He pushed Private Nick Sweeney's leg out of the way, one of the snoring crew and managed to stand.

Staggering the wrong way to his bed he went behind a bush and let go a better part of a pail of suds and then suddenly remembered the inheritance letter and portrait of the deceased lieutenant's wife. His left hand slapped his right side of his chest. It was not there. He unbuttoned his jacket and pulled the seam apart. Fidgeting with the damn threads that he thought he had sewn.

Now this was a hindrance. What? *Wrong jacket!* The dead Lieutenant's jacket was obviously taken when he was in the hospital. When he enlisted he was given a private's redcoat.

Robbie turned and saw the back door to Noah's office was open. He was probably sleeping but because of the smell of cigar smoke he always kept the door open unless there were mosquitoes. In the back door he went. Stopping immediately, he saw that the old fart was asleep at his desk. His glasses were falling down to the end of his extended bulbous nose. Safe so far. Robbie walked quietly right by him into the supply room that was full of clothes in a bin and a few pairs of odd-sized boots. Shuffling through the pile of coats, he found the prize. The only redcoat with no holes and with finely brushed cloth. The buttons were missing so it was easier to pick out. Obviously someone saw the wealth of the buttons. Robbie remembered nothing of when the Sarge first met and interrogated him, flipping the golden buttons in his hand. Robbie reached in and secured his cache. He tore off the shoulder epaulettes that designated rank and switched jackets in haste.

Robbie heard a click. Turning his head around he saw a blunderbuss aimed at his stomach. One of the old turkey shooters full of brass metal shards or balls. Most of the militia used them. Sure enough probably a sport gun for him right now. *He is on a turkey shoot and I am now the turkey.* Before Robbie turned around he pulled off one of his buttons to his old jacket. Then turning to face Noah he held out the button and stated:

"I lost my buttons, I did. I did not want that mean Sergeant to be reprimanding me. I did not want to wake you. I also did not want to wait till after morning inspection. It is only four buttons."

At that, the head quartermaster let up. "Well I see you are not lying. You have nothing else. Grab the buttons you need. How goes it with you and the Sergeant? He's crazy." Old Noah put some thread and a bone needle on the table.

Robbie shrugged his shoulders and nodded his head and squeezed by Lieutenant Chapman to the door wearing the dead Lieutenant's redcoat. Noah was the only Jewish immigrant in North America. And the only one who could keep the books straight especially being under constant pressure himself from the ruthless and coveting sleuth Sergeant Percival.

"Get out of here. I never saw you." He dismissed Robbie.

Robbie looked at the small man, his back withered with age. He didn't seem daunted with his soldiering tasks. There was something for everyone in the Army – one big saving grace.

Robbie walked behind his sleeping quarters. It was usual for new recruits to be kept near the center of the camp so deserters would be seen. Robbie was sure he had the portrait of the beautiful widow and the Inheritance Authorization letter. She would not even know her husband was dead. He knew he had to deliver the letter. A few beads of sweat showed on his forehead as he pulled out and opened up the letter and scanned it for damage. Folding and replacing the important authorizing letter inside his new redcoat's lining he unwrapped her miniature portrait from a handkerchief and gazed upon her beauty. Lovely Whiltshire. Robbie sniffed the tiny portrait. He tried to imagine the scent of her perfume. She was about twenty. Full of life and energy and a blossom unfolding, ready to flower, to embrace.

Robbie placed the portrait on top of one of the water barrels and dropped his pants down to his ankles as he admired it.

Oh Lillian, your breasts. You would make a fine bed for a weary man. Maybe you will be my next love. We are both widowed it seems.

Robbie pulled his shirt and pants right off. He grabbed a scrub brush that was off to the side and dipped it into a pail of used soapy water. Robbie faithfully washed up every day when there was a rainstorm or when he was near water warm enough to dip into. He did not hear the Sergeant approach until he heard cackling.

With an important patrol on the plan for the next day, Sergeant Devil had trouble sleeping. The burly beast came out of the Barracks just in time to watch Robbie disappear around the corner into an alleyway and followed him in. Grabbing Robbie by the shoulders he spun the soldier around and saw the private with soap in his hand and covered in suds. The Sarge had a 'happy to see you' look on his face. Seeing the drawing on the barrel, the Sergeant grabbed it and pushed Robbie back so that he had no chance but to sit in that rather large bucket with disgustingly dirty water. In drunken shocked protest, Robbie stumbled out of the bucket and puked beer with noticeable sawdust contents all over in front of him. Sergeant Devil stared at the portrait. Robbie wished he could punch back.

"So what do we have here? A portrait of a beautiful woman. British I am sure. Very wealthy. Certainly not your wife. I would say you stole this portrait off that dead Lieutenant. Oh his lovely, lovely wife. Just like you stole the watch. So what were you planning, scabby? A party with jack?"

Robbie's head was clearing. But the beers had been too many. A headache was forming. Total exhaustion was enveloping him. The Sergeant noticed another paper from the discarded redcoat that lay askance.

The Sarge picked it up. His eyes lit up as if a prayer had been answered.

"What do we have here, Private Robbie? Planning on going to find her and take her for yourself? You dirty selfish dog. After all I have done for you. I make you a soldier and you do nothing but test me, boy. Damn you."

The jig was up. Further assault was coming.

Private Jim Murphy came out from the shadows. Robbie never saw the boot that flung him back causing severe neck trauma that compounded scarred tissue problems. The cold of the ground against his bare skin jarred the most. Robbie pulled his wet skin from the muck. He half ass-ed-ly took a dive for Lillian's portrait ripping it almost in half, both men holding a half in firm grips. The Sergeant and Robbie went down rolling in the grass and snow, the portrait gluing their hands to each other. A big and fat body rolled onto Robbie and squished him. Robbie could not breathe or be seen with over three hundred and twenty pounds of dead weight crushing the air out of him. All one could see was Robbie's boots. A few soldiers came out of the dark. They all laughed at the sight. They helped big Percival up and another soldier picked up a large handful of mud and partially covered Robbie's exposed privates. The corpulent Sergeant picked up and re-read the fallen letter.

"Of all the luck!" The letter revealed the release of a large fortune to a Mrs. Lillian Anne Whiltshire, wife of a Lieutenant Ian Whiltshire.

"You threatened a non-commissioned officer. And now I have you for possession of a murdered Lieutenant's personal items, theft of an officer's goods. After patrol, you will receive a lashing. Chuckling could be heard in the background. Robbie was coughing and gasping for breath. The sweaty smell of the sergeant being so close was terrible. That alone had made him struggle for air.

Coming to, Robbie in a traumatized state was able to say, "You do not understand. I have to take that letter to her as a personal quest. Otherwise, she may go home penniless and remain widowed and in poverty. I gave my word. Not just to the Lieutenant but also to myself. It is the right thing to do."

The Sergeant asked Robbie if he knew the allegations against him. That he could even be charged with murder of the Lieutenant if the right lawyers were brought to bear. Robbie nodded. His neck was stiff as a board. The taste of blood was in his mouth. He must have bit his tongue real bad during the melee. The Sarge was scheming with his eyes looking up and down the wall of the supply building. He could see Lieutenant Noah. All nervous and frail, Noah was looking out the blanket-covered opening which represented a window of the supply building. Best not to beat Robbie like a pumpkin with Noah as a witness.

They dragged Robbie around the back of the building where Quartermaster Lieutenant Noah Chapman could not see. Stripped and totally naked they proceeded to beat him bloody and torture him by throwing more dirt on him every time he started to pass out. After just a few minutes, Robbie bloodied and defeated gave in.

"Okay I have had enough," as if he was giving in to whatever the Sergeant was planning. He regretted mentioning Prince of Wales Fort off the west coast of Hudson Bay.

After the patrol, Sergeant Percival would exact further revenge. Maybe add to his plans that he was formulating. After a few more very quiet moments the Sergeant turned and with his head and brows high and eyes open wide and sneering ear to ear he had his plan.

"This is the deal, Private. You transfer to Prince of Wales Fort. I send this here Murphy here to sort of follow you and keep you honest. That way my control is absolute. You meet the woman in the portrait and you lure her out to get a few possessions left by her husband. His medals. I'm sure we can grab a nice redcoat from some dead 'un from around here. Maybe yours when you are done with it, Private."

Robbie pulled his head back in a start upon hearing the threat and worried the Sergeant would recognize the jacket he was wearing. "I'm not planning on ever being done with this redcoat." Robbie felt his neck snap back into place. He tried to move, feeling further pain at the front of his upper chest. It felt as if his collarbone was stuck outside his body. Oh still out. He felt six small cracks in his neck as he turned his head up.

The Sergeant resumed. "You lure her a mile from the Fort at least."

Looking at the Private, "Murphy arrange a spot to meet. She goes along with things and the girl goes free. We split it 50-50 this girl and me. I gets half the inheritance and then I release the girl with what's left of her fortune. Unless she wants to marry me. And I release you from your debts. No other way. No other deals."

Robbie could not nod in acknowledgement. He could not move his neck and his right shoulder felt higher and closer to his face than his left shoulder. This night was not going well.

They all broke for the evening. The next day's activities were soon to begin. They all separated for a few hours sleep or preparation depending on their nerves. The Sarge was repeating over and over as if reciting a children's rhyme: "Beat 'em both bloody and money, Beaten bloody and money. Da da da dada. Da da da dada."

Mrs. Lillian Anne Whiltshire

PORTRAIT GIRL SCENE ONE?

"M aggie, you must be pretty arrogant to call that a dinner table setting." The young and full-bosomed British beauty bent down and twisted a piece of ribbon around the bouquet on the table. "If we add a candle here and a name tag then they can be made into exquisite table centerpieces." Maggie nodded her head and resumed her party preparations. She raised her head to see the fidgety and nervous Major approach. At twenty-four, he was four years older than she.

Lillie waited till he had the courage to raise his head and had noticed her staring. He was walking hastily toward her in a determined fashion. When he finally raised his head his eyes were very intent on her cleavage, which she exposed as she remained bent over for his full view till he was close enough to smell her. Nervously, he wiped his mouth of dryness or spittle and swallowed. He removed his cap and knelt on one knee with his head down. "My lady."

"Oh what is it, Major Fredrick Mallory? And get up. You are making a scene. And please don't be so nervous. You make your feelings very obvious, Major."

The Major swallowed aloud and the reprimand brought tears to his eyes. In a high-toned voice he inquired, "May I ask you for a dance tonight at tonight's ball? Oh, am I being impolite?"

Lillian shifted uncomfortably feeling rather flushed. Maggie shuffled in her pose.

"Oh stop it, Major. Have you seen one? Major? A virgin, I mean. You know I am married. If I find word that my husband will not be returning you will be first to know, for you charm me. If you approach me tonight you will follow all the courtesies necessary in public. And address me as

Mrs. Lillian Anne Whiltshire, wife to Lieutenant Ian Whiltshire. And bow and stretch your hand to me. Take my hand to the floor for a dance. Not the last dance. That would not do. And we may share a glass of wine as long as we are always seen. And do not touch me, Major. I remind you again. I am married and waiting for my husband. And your good looks will not sway me from waiting for my husband to return."

The Major had his answer and a guarantee of a dance with the most beautiful lady there. He was quite the looker as well. Tall, blond, fair features and complexion, he was a young officer on the advance and a good prospect for a widowed woman if it came to that.

As the major was about to turn to his duties the evidence of his fondness was showing. British pants were white and tight. Lillian noticed his energetic protuberance with shock and awkwardness.

"We will not have any of that, Major. Not on the dance floor. You will have to control yourself." Both of them looked at each other. Both were red faced and embarrassed. Both were virgins. Both had hidden pumping urges of desire and lust. Maggie her maid took control and interrupted, calling Lillian away. There was still so much to do and plan.

HEARNE'S FIRST EXPEDITION
NOVEMBER 6, 1769

Lil Wolf became known as a quiet good labourer. However, when work was done he was always a loner. The group of Chachinahaw, Lil Wolf and a few stragglers arrived at Prince of Wales Fort burdened with many beaver pelts. Each would net a considerable prize for his master. Negotiations would start.

Afterwards, the main master of Lil Wolf signed up for an exploration mission to lands north and west to where the copper-skinned natives were found. They were called the Copper Indians and to no one's surprise they lived beside the Copper River just south of the Arctic. They were almost parallel with the strange Esquimaux.

This area and the Copper people had been so named not just because of their copper skin color but because it was rumored they sat upon a huge deposit of copper. This resource was only used in small pieces for charms. Most had disappeared over many years of scavenging by nomad people. There was no real use for copper in this part of the world at this time. Seems a white man of thin build wanted to walk there and back. Document it somehow. Look for a northern passage going east to west.

We get paid our 'guide money' in a good supply of ammunition and ball. We get preferential treatment when we go to the Fort in the future with our trade. We have a journey. Many did not want to miss the excitement of a newcomer who certainly would perish within a few weeks. He would never know what to expect. And neither did they. The journey was to start in November of 1769. The mighty Samuel S. Hearne's Expedition it was called. Something mystical was about to happen. Like a world event or something. As if this journey would be remembered in time for example. Or the accomplishments would be remembered or something like that. What did it matter? For Lil Wolf felt ashamed because he was a slave.

ROBBIE SAVES THE DAY

The weather was getting a little cold now that it was the end of September 1769. Sweating with all his gear on Robbie felt good being a soldier. Preparing for a patrol duty involved making sure one had the standard issue of ammunition, horn of fine powder and cartridge and shot pouches, two days rations and water supply and one blanket. Dress was immaculate. The British Redcoat brushed and standard brass buttons were polished. Boots were axle greased and rubbed to a shine for this special occasion. This was Robbie's first march with the troops.

Robbie confessed an early desire to be a good soldier. Let yourself imagine and try and feel what it is like to be a hero. Another confession was his love of the Regimental tradition. Being part of something bigger than himself. Something more important than oneself. To defend as well as represent. A regiment is something more important than an individual. To laugh and eat with and to fight for.

We first encountered an old French couple. They offered us tea and it was good. We said we would be back for more and tipped the man's wife well. One of the soldiers kissed her on the cheek because the taste of the tea made him feel like he was home. Not sure that she liked it, more scared than anything but it brought a chuckle and a more relaxed atmosphere. These old French people were settlers here from their youth. The first Acadian settlers. They could be no trouble. The men started their trek on a nice start. French tea had the tastiest of leaves. It must have cost a lot for those precious leaves. French coffee that had no equal was not so sorely missed when tea was served.

Robbie marched out to the side of the roadway and entered the heavily treed forest. His job was to alternately scout to the right side and in front of the patrol. Any noise or movement was to be reported. Robbie's neck was feeling better. He cracked it a few times to stretch it out. He took a deep breath and started shaking. Robbie realized that he was scared. Once into the shadows of trees he was alone and subject to a sneak attack from as close as a foot away. One menacing Cree could jump out from behind a tree and fell him in an instant. Before his knees noticeably shook, off he went, the movement giving him a feeling of a sense of purpose.

Robbie was proud to be a British soldier, a job his father retired from to become a homesteader with his English wife. Robbie in a way felt he was fulfilling his father's obligation to the army. Of course he would keep these feelings to himself. Upon judgment, Robbie declared a Regiment is a family, and the protection of the family is more important than the individual. Robbie felt over-protective of the bunch of guys walking down the roadway. Some curse, some are annoying and you can only tolerate a short while and some like to sing out of key but Robbie would risk his life for the men of his color patch, his Regiment.

He left the main pack. It was his duty to alert the main column by either shouting or firing. Once alerted the main pack would seek cover on the alternate flank into the sloped edge on the left side of the road. There were usually four good feet of the hill on the left flank to drop down to if the main body of the patrol got in trouble. Robbie's side rose on a good slope and was thick with pine, brush and other cover. It was difficult to navigate; needing to always cut a new path.

"Roll on over Mr. Robbie, another coming in. Robbie, here comes Private Fable," Sergeant Percival said. "Private Jim Fable off to your right, move it." Corporal Freeman doubled off the order and Private Fable and, with a scared look on his face, hunched his shoulders. He hopped a step and then veered off the main trail into the deep thicket of trees. Fable was not much of a soldier. He did what he had to and kept to himself. Word was he killed a pawnbroker. Seems he sold all he had and when he went back to pick his money up the guy refused to pay him. Said that after he took a look through the stuff that he figured he couldn't sell it. So he sold the stuff all together to a dumper.

"Only got enough to pay the transportation and storage. And the company has to get a cut." He said he was sorry but there was nothing he could do. Fable heard tell the guy liked to make up stories and decided he was trying to pull a fast one on him. Apparently, the importance of the money was to put food on the table for his mother and himself. Well Fable punched the poor man so many times and so badly that he said goodbye to his mom and volunteered for the Army to save a hanging. He came across to North America and here he was, smoothbore in his hand he saw Robbie wave him forward from behind a large rock just ahead of him.

The patrol had moved up efficiently on the road before sending in the second scout but Robbie had also moved efficiently through thickets and trees to be ahead of the column by at least thirty feet and then doubled back ten feet or so to wait and direct Private Fable. The musket he carried had an accuracy range of only a hundred and fifty yards. In the woods you could not see past a varying range of two to forty yards at the most.

The usual British tactic was to line up and fire en masse at preferably fifty yards away or rely on the speed of the charge with compelling seventeen inch bayonets. The smoothbore musket was the next step up from a turkey shooter. With an unusual thirty-nine inch barrel, the standard issue from India, the Brown Bess, a smoothbore flintlock musket, bragged a .75 caliber barrel. Any sized chunk of ball or missile padded with powder would do. The only rule was, the bigger the caliber ball, the greater the accuracy – an ideal weapon for skirmishes in the woods.

Fable tripped over the first fallen log obstacle then slipped on a moss-covered rock and went down, smashing into a bunch of brush going down face first real hard. His rifle held in front, saved him from serious damage. Robbie snickered. Not the quiet nimbleness necessary for survival. Ripe profanities were heard as Fable attempted to manoeuvre further. He found better footing and an old animal path to advance him down the line. Playing the buddy system, they took turns advancing while the other kept an eye out. They cautiously moved ahead and spread out. Francis took the low ground which was close to and level with the path pursued by the regiment; twenty-two troops in all. Scared as jackrabbits they were. Strict military march in the new continent was suicide, as hiding in the bush were native sharpshooters and people who were raised thinking nothing was better than to show off doing something daring in battle, or trick someone into a battle.

As a soldier, Robbie was now doing an Acadian Ranger's job only at half the pay. Less than a shilling a day for a foot soldier; two and a half for being a Sergeant. Robbie could not believe how far he had come from the small farmstead of his family, to family life with the Dog-Ribbed tribe with his wife and an adventure to Fort Niagara. Now he was a British Army Private under his Majesty's Service and wearing a bloody redcoat as well. Robbie took some pride in that. Spit and polish were not for today though. Wet, cold and mud. That summed Army life in Acadia. Robbie took the plume of his hat off and his collar that got in the way and rubbed more mud on the nicely buffed dead lieutenant's redcoat. No sense standing out, he reasoned. He had moved up higher into the hills. Moving much quicker and more quietly than Private Francis he was ahead forty paces and watching ahead for movement. The British patrol could be heard, their boots pounding on the packed ground. A billow of dust could be seen in the air above the column of soldiers. A large elevation of rock lay ahead on the left, narrowing the road and the group were marching toward it. Robbie saw movement. Three Cree stood naked with the exception of tiny loincloths and a few feathers pointing down from the backs of their heads. They moved down the slope in tandem, following in a row down a narrow wildlife path.

The soldiers were coming up to an area of soggy thick black loam-based muck. The road was not well constructed here. There were cedar roots to trip over and a few rocks. The going was slippery with more than one profanity heard after every new thud as another soldier went knee high in the black muck. A French soldier wearing a blue coat appeared just a hands throw from Robbie at the top of the hill to his right. He looked nervous. A branch hit Robbie in the face and made him startle. A bird could be heard in the distance, an eerie squelch. The French Captain had a revolver in hand and his uniform was adorned with glittering accouterments on his lapels and sleeves. Probably the leader and held at least a Captaincy ranking. He had the pigtails the French so favored. He went down the same path as the others. A few more natives followed.

Robbie held his hand up to signal the soldiers to stop. He wasn't sure Private Francis could see his signal well. *Where is he? Does he remember the signals I made him practice over and over?*

To Robbie's left with a rustle of branches and just ahead coming off the roadway through the thick side brush came Private Strutsenburger. He didn't last long. He went crashing into the brush and emerged six inches from a Cree warrior. The warrior swung his tomahawk and hit Sammy under the chin. Knocked him clear up in the air and at least a foot back against four thick intertwined cedars that blocked the action from the rest of the troops. Private Sammy Strutsenburger held the top part of the tomahawk's sharp point up under his chin. The four-inch tip had gone all the way in, through his tongue, entering the upper part of the inside of his mouth. as Robbie looked on helplessly, he realized Sammy had no time to think of bad things he had done in his life. No time to think of the kidnapped woman Laura he pretended was his wife but treated as a whore. Only death. The Cree whooped his victory cry. It was echoed by answering cries from his compatriots.

Robbie looked around. Sergeant Percival was out of breath, wheezing and unable to give orders. Robbie looked at Corporal Freeman who led the patrol.

Lieutenant Michael Noonan was coming up behind Robbie. Michael Noonan was a Lieutenant level scholar student; one of the new recruits being trained for officer status. His status held no power although his payment for commission was already made by his father. He was just waiting for the next Lieutenant to be killed and he was in the door.

The situation was already deadly. French-led Cree were dangerous. There were at least seven who had crossed just ahead, all in a flash. More were heard to the right over the ridge. Robbie took a few steps back and met up with the Lieutenant behind a large rock.

"Michael, go back ten paces and then to the road. Tell the Sergeant to turn to his right and fire a volley directly to his flank into the woods, immediately. Don't worry about Private Fable or what happened to Sam. We know to take cover. After they shoot tell him to seek cover behind the rocks on the left side of the road as best they can. Reload and wait for a signal."

The Lieutenant was sixteen. After two years of service he did not need to be told twice. He nodded his head in acknowledgement and with tears of determination in his eyes retreated back twelve paces and went back out onto the road.

Robbie sized up the situation. He glanced back at Private Jim Fable and called him back twenty paces by holding up both hands with fingers spread two times then pointing back the way they came. Robbie swung his hand and forearm around in quick circular motions as if to say 'hurry on.' Fable did not seem to understand.

"What?" Private Fable shouted, straining his neck to see Robbie.

Stupid! I showed you this signal. Robbie was beside himself. He clenched his fist.

The rustle of branches just ahead. Seconds now mattered. Grinding his teeth, Robbie repeated himself swinging his arm in emphasis. Francis stood there with a big grin. Robbie in frustration put his palm straight out and lowered it. Fable understood that and dropped flat to the ground. Just as he did a volley of fire erupted. The shots rang true and killed or maimed at least three of the off-road group of surprise attackers. Unless there was a distinct advantage in numbers or surprise the Cree would not continue the attack. That was suicide and they had no intentions of it. Their hesitation gave Robbie a chance to fire from above and take a warrior down. Robbie's shot from above spooked the attackers. No one wanted to fight from their rear as well. The remaining attackers vanished. Robbie shouted down to Private Fable, "Tell the Sergeant to hold fire. Tell him two are coming out."

Forty-five minutes later the fires were stoked and pork and potatoes were sizzling in the pans. Four were out on guard duty posted in a circle around the campfire. Camp was set up. The new moon meant total darkness if you glanced away from the fire. Other than the crackling fire, everything was quiet. We all took a duty at watch but no problems came in the night. The Cree had dispersed, as most natives not only preferred a surprise night attack but a distinct advantage in numbers or conditions as well.

The next morning dawned crisp and cold. As the men stood about nursing hot mugs of tea, they reviewed the previous day's events.

"They must have decided to retreat thinking it best being so close to the Fort," said Nick Sweeney, one of the Privates.

"Yes, most of us regulars have experienced at least two winters here in Upper Acadia," one of the other soldiers said, "Could have routed them all out."

"They definitely did not outnumber us or they would have attacked. Well their surprise party did get screwed up when Sam jumped out face to face with that Indian. Did you see any of it?"

"No," Nick said. Nick, the resident get what you need type of guy, wasn't cut out for the soldier's life. He got too excited and nervous. He was a constant complainer as well. Too much mud, mud on his boots, mud covering everything making things too heavy, too cold, too wet and the food was bad and too many worms in the bread were just some of his complaints. Nick found it hard to go through the changes in the action of a soldier's day. A bestower of people's wants and desires he felt it embarrassing and difficult to adjust from situations of extreme danger with fast and vicious bloodletting action followed by prolonged periods of extreme boredom.

Nick Sweeney felt it was not a good mix. "Ya can't just shut off your emotions," he would complain.

"Me neither." They all turned to Robbie who had already told the story of Sam.

"Too bad about Strutsenburger. Let me call the next skirmisher into the bush next time. It might help," Robbie offered.

The men exchanged glances. Not a one of them had anything on their minds beside Sam's young and plump wife. She was a cutie with a bit of baby fat and all.

Robbie did not notice. He was thinking, *That Frenchman. He looked so familiar. Why can't I place him? Why only one Frenchman and only seven Cree?* Just then Robbie remembered something.

"Sergeant Devil, sir. There were voices echoing in the woods besides the one Frenchman and seven Cree, minus the four killed by fire of course. Hard to tell but I did not hear any other accents beside the Cree shout. There may have been only one French officer. That officer with all that glitter I told you about. I want the buttons off that jacket. These ones here were badly tarnished when I got them. I can't make them shine at all. They don't even fit this coat." Robbie guessed the deceased Lieutenant had made the eyelets a little bit bigger than standard issue to accommodate the missing gold buttons.

Robbie was head to toe covered in mud earlier for camouflage and still had not cleaned his jacket. His hair was now cut medium short and his face shaved clean as he did every day. His clothes he washed regularly wherever he could. His jacket was always free of lice and was always brushed. Robbie had his arms and hands in the creek and was scrubbing when the jacket hanging on the limb nearby dropped one huge drying mud cake. A big piece of muck fell to the ground with a thud. Everyone noticed his always clean and brushed jacket totally soiled and laughed, even the Sergeant.

Watching Robbie, the Sergeant had a wonderful idea. He needed something more to pin on Robbie. An utterance of a threat to an officer could get ten lashes. Rum rations would mean a lot to some men but not to a man like Robbie. Robbie could take his drink or leave it and preferred his spruce beer. By the gallon on certain nights as long as duty did not call. No, the Sergeant needed something big to make sure his plans did not backfire. Robbie had to go to Prince of Wales Fort, that was a given. He would send with him Private Murphy and maybe Lieutenant, what's his name, Michael Noonan, the sixteen-year-old being trained as an officer. Get that cadet off his back. The Sarge was planning a devilish plot. He would get Robbie to lure the girl in the portrait out to at least a mile from the fort. Private Murphy with all his confidence would secure the lady and Robbie till he got there. Percival could leave in a month after finishing up some paperwork. The excuse to lure Lillian out of the Fort would be the legality of the trip, an unofficial non-authorized trip to expedite the process. If things were kept hush hush she could secretly receive her letter bequeathing her a large sum of money. Otherwise, months would be necessary to receive proper clearance to make a trip to her. It was all making such logical sense. He admired himself as he scratched at the burn wounds on his face. *Percival, you are a smart man,* he confessed to himself.

"A few months, gentlemen," he said to no one in particular, "and that beauty will be wishing to hell she stayed home in England where all sisters should go." He thought of his dead sister they blamed him for killing in that house fire so long ago. Since she had been born he no longer existed in his parents' eyes. Even though it was an accident and he didn't mean to do it he still felt good inside when he thought of the accusers tormenting him as a child.

She will either marry me and I will take all her inheritance or she can sign over just half her inheritance to me before I ... the Sarge paused in his musing. *... let her go.*

Percival Devil's first finger was twitching. Robbie should have done something to stop Private Strutsenburger from being killed. An act of cowardice while doing his duty. He should have fired and saved him. Even though it was known Sam had no chance and the fact the whole platoon was saved by Robbie's orders. *The threat of a hanging will make him bide by my plans,* the Sergeant declared to himself.

The way forward was clear of any intruders. There was no trace of the warriors. "Probably clear back to Quebec City if you ask me," Percival said.

With his growing confidence and admiring audience Robbie put them through a few drills and manoeuvres that were good for North American warfare. How it was necessary to hide behind trees and have a covering fire. How to jump three steps forward, crouch, fire, roll or duck behind a tree or other cover and reload as fast as it took to normally fire and reload but doubling up the motions. Making them understand it was not good sense for soldiers marching in column out in the open without scouts. They could easily get picked off by shadows in the trees. He also demonstrated how to properly throw a tomahawk and most importantly to wait patiently in the woods and turn into the forest itself. Until Robbie moved they did not see him. To him, these were children's games if you grew up here and had not much to do besides chores.

"I plan on showing you Brit troops how to sneak up on your prey and skirmish like the French and Cree do." Robbie realized his ability to take command. He had been able to remain calm under pressure. His natural skirmishing abilities he learned while growing up north of Acadia. Tall, strong and handsome, with a wiry build he found himself becoming more courageous, clever and resourceful.

Right as Robbie was loosening his neck stretching and relaxing his shoulders the two cohorts of the Sergeant came up from behind.

"How's your neck, Robbie?" Corporal Freeman asked. Before Robbie could turn or react the two were on him in a flash. The Corporal was almost as tall as Robbie with the same wiry build but not near as broad shouldered, while Private Murphy was well proportioned with a broad back and stood five foot nine.

"Bin digging graves most all my life, I have. Now it's ditches it is," Murphy used to say. Strong arms grabbed Robbie and put him down and tied him up real good. His wrists were hurting from behind his back but there was nothing he could do about it.

"The man saved my life sir, saved all of us." Private Jim Fable made a vain attempt to save Robbie from the Sergeant's wrath.

"You will both follow my orders as instructed," the Sergeant said to Robbie and Fable. "I am gathering charges against you," he said, pointing a finger at Robbie. He showed him the affidavit signed by Captain Knobbs charging him with utterance of a threat to a senior non-commissioned officer. There was one made up for desertion while on duty. A charge of cowardice while on duty was the most feared accusation.

"You should have fired upon those buggers as soon as you saw them and risked yourself instead of our poor boy Sam." The Sarge was building up to something. Truth was nobody liked ugly little Sam Strutsenburger and all were jealous why he could have a wife on duty when some could not. The decision to be allowed a wife was done by ballot, however. Sam already had an in because the Sergeant had set everything up to have his way.

And they were all covetous. No one knew how her being newly widowed would play out. They knew the Sergeant and his Corporal Maxwell and Private Murphy seemed to have the Strutsenburgers locked up in a terrible struggle of debt obligations. Sam had lent his wife too often to cover his gambling debts and drinking habit. This situation encouraged his drinking habit and worsened Laura Strutsenburger's own situation.

"You will be released with the instructions for your trip. Get that girl for me, I love her Robbie. A man needs a wife, he does. I am going to buy a new shirt. Wash me hair and all just for the occasion."

"What makes you think she will marry you?" Robbie cautioned.

The Sergeant just smiled and said, "I will keep the Inheritance letter and I will also give her a few things from her dead husband. He pulled out a button that Robbie recognized immediately. Even so long ago and so dark it had been those flashy gold buttons the suave Lieutenant Ian Whiltshire wore that were recognizable. If that French man saw that button he would crave the treasure for his velour of glitter. The buttons that were stolen from the jacket Robbie was wearing. A fine wool coat made from the Wiltshire's in Gates Bay by the shores. Only the finest craftsmanship was done at the Lords' famous tailor shop in Wickes. Luckily the mud on Robbie's jacket and the missing golden epaulettes gave nothing away. A charge of theft Robbie could not pursue. What was he to do? Go to the beautiful girl in the portrait that even he could not take his mind off of. She was a cultured young woman in her prime. Just from the portrait one could envision voluptuousness and passion, a sultry vixen, strong willed and stubborn, willing and loving; a complete package of what every man would want. Add her new wealth and power and she could command an army. And command many men's hearts and make them all pine for her till sadness had their soul. The bitterness felt in them for having to whimper for her aloof love.

Robbie was released right away after being read his new charges of desertion and knew his part in this fiendish plan. He had to go to freezing Prince of Wales Fort. Oh and on the way just happen to stop and get picked up handily and willingly by a supply ship in Cape Breton or thereabouts to finish the journey to the west coast of Hudson Bay after getting to Cape Breton in the first place. Then lure the maiden to Private Jim Murphy's chosen destination outside the Fort so that a hell of a man with a name mistakenly written down on his birth certificate by the drunken parishioner, 'Precious Little Devil' and in so doing put her in harm's way. The thought of that drunken fat bugger groping his hands all over Mrs. Lillian Whiltshire was too much to bear. *Bloody calling wedding bells he is. He wants to marry her for her inheritance money I am sure.* Robbie churned things over in his mind. Famine or frost a person could succumb to in this barren country. But a snake or the Devil himself could be a quicker death.

Robbie had lived with his wife outside Prince of Wales Fort for a few years. But even Robbie was not used to the extremities of the horrible weather of the north. Snow squalls that would blind you for hours on end so that one did not remember what was left and what was right.

What was on your left?

What was on your right?

If you stay in your bed

Don't let the bed lice bite.

As the children's rhymes went on those colder stormier days.

Cold that would seem to freeze you so badly that a fire and blankets would take hours to get you warm if you got chilled. It would have been extremely necessary as well for shelter. The wind that would send the cold deep into your body where all your bones and all your body felt cold deep to the inside would kill you in minutes. No open fingers or skin could survive the frigid cold in the middle of winter up in the barren lands. And it was nearly always winter here. The spring thaw still left snow in the high ridges and came back fully after only a few moons. That little thaw took away what little good loam was created and left barren rock and roots from frozen melts of the past.

The plot thickened. Robbie must find this widowed girl. The news of her husband's death would be shattering. Hopefully, he would be allowed to speak with her in private. She may have already have left for England. He must try and hold back his desires at the same time to explain in private of her newfound wealth and how to procure it. Of course, he would explain the dangers but that he would be there to help her and protect her. After all, it was because of her portrait he kept that the rebels believed Robbie was British and had beaten him. His dreams of joining the colonists in the south and bringing his family there were shattered. That was even before he knew his family were dead.

Robbie started to have guilt feelings over the woman he had to meet. It was too soon after the news of his wife's death to lust for another woman. Robbie shook his head to correct his thoughts and made the realization that his son was dead as was his wife. And a daughter he did not know he had. His wife's father would be dead from that group as well as a few other Dog-Ribbed people he did not know. The snap of a large branch close by in the woods brought him back.

"Must be a big caribou or moose running away from us just over yonder," said Nick. "Picked up our scent I think. Yes, you can bet on that just like them Cree. Scared jackrabbits they were."

"Yes sir, scared jackrabbits they was," said Murphy. The platoon gathered up for the march back.

HEARNE'S FIRST JOURNEY
- CONTINUED

Much can be made of doing something special in one's life. Whether in charge of a brigand, an Indian chief or a slave, one could have a memory of something bigger than themselves and their plight. One would for a brief moment in time rise above all and do or accomplish a great wondrous task that just might be remembered for all of humanity. Samuel Hearne's three expeditions had been just such entities.

With great fanfare and cannon fired off in salute for the group of Northern Indians called Chipewyans, a slave, six South Athapascow Indians, a sect of Cree, a white man named Samuel Hearne and his assistant they started their trek. No one really knew if we were to succeed. It was a mission which set up two further missions. Further supplies and different guides would be needed to be successful. On this journey the Athapuscow natives would be held in the same low regard as the three white men by the majority group of northern Chipewyans. The south tribe group were Governor Moses Norton's relatives, probably sent so the Governor of the Fort could keep some control over the mission and get some fame. The Hudson's Bay Company was being criticized for not enough exploration. The economic impetus to find a northwest passage through the top of North America was tremendous. Constant ambushes from the Orient, dangers across land and sea underlined the need for a new route. There were many idle British ships and seamen loafing around needing work to survive.

Hearne's arrival had sparked a flurry of new interest. When the group returned shortly after heading out they regrouped for the attempted second and then third journey out only better equipped. But it was on the eventful first journey that things got critical and different.

FOUND

Almost twenty six moons she had been alone and amazingly not in need or want. As she awoke again she just stared for many minutes. In front of her stood the tallest, biggest Indian she had ever seen. He spoke to her in Northern Indian. From her recent captivity she had learned a few native languages. She replied, fluent in his tongue. "My name is Kiwidinok. I am from the Dog-Ribbed Tribe."

She told him of her isolation living in her humble surroundings for what she believed was twenty moons since her escape from the Athapascow tribe. All alone in the wilderness, she did not seem to be in need or want of anything. Many months never seeing anyone or being with a man, she was quite nervous and shy. Where she exactly was she did not know. Somewhere she knew to the north was Clowey Lake and she was just east of the Slave River. Living isolated for many months in the northern wilderness was astounding. Taking time away from the necessary survival tactics of obtaining food and defending against the extreme elements, she had to apply herself to the constant threat and danger of the wolves and wolverines.

Very rarely was there a full night's sleep. The wolves prowled at night. The wolverines being used to burrowing into beaver dens would come from under the ground and get warmth off your body waiting for you to stir before they attacked. Putting vertical and horizontal stakes in the ground was a necessity before putting bedding down. Still she found time to make a rabbit-sinew fish net, and cute rabbit fur pieces mingled in her braids tied with rabbit sinews. Although she still wore deerskin leggings, they had numerous holes and their threads were bare, concealing little and providing no warmth or cover.

As the tall native guided her towards his tribal village, she wore her elegant rabbit fur stole with pride. The shawl was decorated with simple yet cute ornamentation. Although crude in construction the soft furs were very curiously gathered together and so judiciously placed as to make the whole of her garb very pleasing to the eye; giving a rather romantic appearance. Her beauty combined with her workmanship made her come across as very appealing. The way she ornamented her coat, her desolate circumstance and her attractiveness and allure made her whole aura very sensuous. The fact that she spoke Chipewyan helped as well. For no single woman caused as much excitement and lust among the hands of men who wrestled over her that night.

For it was the custom with these people that if you wanted someone else's wife you just took her. If there was an objection they wrestled over her with the winner gaining the wife. The camp would never be the same after this. As soon as the morning arrived the stares from the other woman and the threats were relentless. But they were not carried out for the men would retaliate.

NATIVE GIRL

The day the patrol was back at Fort Niagara there were stories to tell. The men ate well, consumed many drinks, sang and bragged and passed out. There were only a few arguments as most of the men were too plum tired.

Robbie held back on his drinking as the next day he would be on his voyage. Scheduled to part was a tall ship from the harbor. He would leave and beat these lecherous vandals to their affairs. It was for him to self prophesize and concluded, *I must seek this outstanding woman I am lusting for.* Robbie felt a pang of desire, his shoulders tensing, and a jolt in his loins. He could not help it. Just as he was off to his tent he noticed the same native girl. The one with the cute face and full figured body. The desire showed on Robbie's face. Staring at her soft dark eyes, eyelids half closed, lips half pouted and tilted head she pulled you in. His expression of liking what he saw was greeted with a warm smile. She brushed by him with her hips. She stopped a few inches past him spinning around with her long dark hair flinging around hitting Robbie in the face. Robbie shivered in reaction. She was something. Her hips were just slightly large and perfectly curved for comfort. Her bosom mostly bare was large and firm. She spoke in rough English and North Indian.

"I see you are handsome. I must see the Sergeant to clean the kitchen. It is my job. But when I am done I will come by this way to see you. If you are lucky."

Robbie's heart sank. The Sergeant. Egad, he could hurt her. He could beat her. Not the Sergeant. Robbie made a gesture but it was too late and she was off running. He felt at a loss for not knowing what to say. He felt protective of her. Her little tease humored him. Robbie smiled.

He was tired. Bed was his only option and off he went wondering why he had not thought to ask her name.

Lying in bed he thought over a few things. There was no escaping fate. The Sergeant would have his way. Maybe Murphy would not get on board in time. If he were to get caught then maybe he would be able to exonerate himself. Tell all of the wicked Sergeant's entire evil plan. That would be no good. *Not with the charges the Sarge has been building up. Desertion under fire. It is a lie. He has my father's watch. Of course I am going to get mad and say something to the belligerent toad. I can't believe it. No one would believe me and I am sure the Sergeant would get me before I got to testify. With that broad shouldered Murphy on my tail I have no choice, I must follow along. Get this over with and see what is to come.*

Once under way he would have no choice. Robbie wept for his family that night. He had little fight left in him.

DO IT IN THE MOR-OH-OR-NING

The Sergeant was in his office as the native girl arrived. She didn't know the Sergeant but the Sergeant had noticed her and had her summoned to him. To him, she was just a native piece of offal and she was reminding him of his sister with her petulant attitude. Playing coy and teasing him at the doorway. The Sergeant put down Robbie's assault charges and the new form for cowardice in action. He would get the Corporal to fill out everything in the morning. To help guarantee Robbie's co-operation these charges would be the insurance. The Sergeant would not have a clue how to write the words desertion or failure of duties and responsibilities.

The Sarge shuffled up to the hesitant and questioning native girl. His hands instantly grabbed her bosom very hard. She opened her mouth in shock and tried to step back. A large hand of the big blubbery Sergeant wrapped around the native girl's throat and he pushed her up against the wall. She started to struggle and found it difficult to breathe. Totally innocent at nineteen she was there to do house chores and certainly wasn't thinking of being hurt or sexually assaulted. She could see the warts on his hand when one went to cover her eyes.

The man's bad breath was repulsive when his lips gripped hers. He pushed with his big tongue to open her mouth, the sting of rum on her lips was repulsive. Pulling back he pulled off his undershirt to expose two massive drooping pectoral muscles and rolls of white and flabby flesh below that. Replacing one hand on her throat he wrapped his other arm around her back pulling her in. Sweat beading on his forehead added to the horror as his eyes looked with madness and hatred. As she started to pass out she saw the Sarge undoing his pants.

"No ..." slowly poured out of her mouth. The last she saw was a huge sausage finger pressing into her stomach when she started dreaming she had to relieve herself. For her dreams of meeting a husband and living at the Fort were being vandalized by more than just a sexual encounter. Her body was physically assaulted. She would pay for his sister's envy. The attention Percival did not get as a child when she was born. The hurt. The fire. One could only try to imagine his hate.

Whether he finished his lovemaking or not was not known. He strangled her to submission not knowing she was an innocent young girl. He had no shame. He had no mercy. Later he would go down to the mess and call out Private Murphy. He would carry the finished women down to the middle of town where there was a bench and some supplies kept. This was the dump site for the beaten native women that dared to get in the way of the Sergeant's wrath. Sometimes the girls would have enough left to be further assaulted by Private Murphy or the Corporal Freeman if they thought the victims would not die. Tonight would not be the case. Talented Hahaya Wehaya was too pretty to live. His sister would pay again. The Sergeant laughed and took another large swig of rum. Rum that was one of the soldier's rations. He took a lot for himself and some for his Captain. This kept the peace with the Captain. The Sarge had hit the girl kind of hard in the chin after the stomach poke and realized she was out like there was no tomorrow and fetched himself another flask of rum and some water to splash over the girl so he could resume his fondling while she awoke and hopefully screamed in terror.

Replenishing his supply of liquid but before he woke the girl for further punishment Devil picked up from the desk the portrait of the dead Lieutenant's widow. That made him excited. The native girl Hahaya Wehaya was awakening with a moan. Percival did not care. He kept admiring the woman in the portrait. The portrait lady was an angel. He smelled the portrait as drool left his lower lip.

THE ESCAPE

Robbie got up at midnight and made his way over to the harbor and discretely boarded the ship that was to sail in the morning and take him to Cape Breton. Robbie had only slept a few hours as he had to be under cover of the night. Hopefully he could escape the morning charges. He was not sure if the Sarge would press the orders now or hold them till he was done the Sarge's evil work. No sense taking any chances and maybe just maybe Murphy might not board the ship.

Robbie sorted through a group of items he packed to get him by and stashed them in a section behind the huge supply ropes in the lower deck, which were only used if a sail's rigging broke and became irreparable. In his gear he had packed some food portions of a few handfuls of dried corn, a piece of hard brick cheese that when melted in water or goat's milk made a creamy cheese dish and some jerked meat and a three foot flat package from Noah his Jewish friend that the Irishman Nick Sweeney brought to him. Looking onto the shores of Niagara the expanse was small for a natural port. Robbie was smiling and taking it all in being on a tall ship. To sail up the St. Lawrence River would be many a boy's dream.

Robbie started thinking about Laura Strutsenburger, the widow of Private Sam Strutsenburger. She was in great danger. The Sergeant and every man there lusted for her now she was a widow. A woman did not remain widowed long if she was an army wife. The next day she would be picked up by another. A woman had to be kept to be looked after. The awful Sergeant Devil would torment her for a long time before she would be safe and she may never get free. Robbie owed that young girl for nursing him back to health.

Robbie lay within the curl of ropes that made a fine mattress. A shuffle far in the darkness of the lowest deck and Robbie could hear the rats multiplying. It would be a long trip. A beetle was coming out of the half bun Robbie had found. Seemed there was four different species of beetle in every loaf as well as a number of unidentified bugs in the hard ship's bread. They provided extra nourishment. The blubbers would drown sure enough if they were soaked in water which was necessary to soften the ship's bread to make it chewable. The combination of seeing a pair of eyes lit up in the dark and thinking of Laura's plight left him restless; he could not sleep.

His early departure would be noticed and he hoped he would sail out before dawn before he was found. If he left the ship and went back he could help Laura and could still possibly make it back in plenty of time to re-board the ship without being noticed. If he was caught re-boarding? It was just better to wait till the ship set sail and had some distance between the impervious Sergeant Devil before he might have to report to the signing in officer. Robbie's mind was whirring.

In a flash up went Robbie over the rail, hand over hand down a tie line and slid to the dock with not a noise made. Not a sentry around to hear. All was dark and quiet tonight. Robbie looked around and made his charge.

At the hospital, Laura had just finished her shift. She was still alone in the office waiting for her midnight replacement. She heard a strange sound.

"Who's there?" she whispered as if someone was close. Her fear was compounded by the way all the men drooled over her. Only a few came over to taunt her. None of them gave any consideration of her recent loss. They only had one thing in mind. Have her young baby fat body under their control. When Robbie came around the corner into the office she was immediately relieved and with great joy she let out a big gush of breath and raced to him and put her arms around his neck and hugged him.

The perfume of her natural body intoxicated and consumed him. But, Robbie pulled her arms down and sighed. "I'm not here for that. You're a nice young girl. You are in great danger."

"I know. I have seen the glares and heard their comments. No one seems to care, except you."

"The Sergeant plans on splitting your time up between himself and a few of his cronies. He will not let you free. You will be his plaything until he gets tired of you. Then he will probably kill you or you will end up maimed and disfigured. I know this to be true."

"Oh Robbie, what can I do? If I had you to protect me," she bemoaned.

"No, you are too young." Robbie analyzed, *I'm twenty-five and she is not quite nineteen.* "Maybe in a few years." Robbie was trying to avoid a confrontation. He needed to escape.

Flattered, Robbie went on, "Laura darling, you're young and beautiful. You can still put this behind you. When the platoon went out on my first patrol we came across an old French couple just on the outskirts of town. They were very nice and everyone knows them and leaves them alone. They are one of the first true settlers here. They lost a daughter a few years ago to pox and probably would love your company. I had time to mention briefly your situation and they offered to help. You can stay there Laura and get a new life. What do you say?"

"Oh no! I can't leave. Sergeant Percival would skin me alive. As a matter of fact that is exactly what he threatened."

"You have only one chance, Laura. And it is now. On the way here I talked to Private Francis. He owes me one. Thinks I saved his life. Well he is on guard duty and will overlook everything and I can guide you to a new start. It is not far and I could make it back well before morning if we leave now. Wear dark clothes and here is some money, blanket and a knife. I know it is not much but you can have a new start. Put it all behind you and pack your things."

She took everything except the small knife. Laura did not need long to change her mind and as she was putting on thick woolens and sweaters when she heard Robbie say, "Laura you had better go with your maiden name Leblanc. It would be safer. They would remember Strutsenburger."

"Who wouldn't?" She puckered her naturally thick red lips and then smiled and her beauty shone with every sparkle of her teeth and tears formed in her eyes. She bent down and put on her boots with no sense of humility in front of Robbie.

Laura dressed with an army shirt on top and an overcoat and Robbie's blanket wrapped just so and disappeared with Robbie down the trail in the woods. Private Fable gave them no trouble at the gate and now she would be safe. The old couple would look after her. Everyone was in the mess getting drunk or passed out. Hopefully, the Sergeant was busy.

Dropping Laura off was a tearful hello and goodbye. On Robbie's return, Private Fable got his bottle of stolen rum from Robbie and a big thank you. The bottle had come from Nick Sweeney as a parting gift. Robbie confided to Nick because Nick was trustworthy. Extra thin in stature, and almost as tall as Robbie at just under six foot Nick's worst beef was 'Do not tattle tale.' He could get you just about anything. Funny what a few harlots and a barrel of wine will get you in the Officer's quarters. No telling how he had gotten it. Seems there were other things going on in the encampment that he was unaware of.

Robbie snuck back towards the tall ship thinking, *someday and somehow I'll let Laura know I'm fond of her as well. I don't know her well enough.* As well, Robbie's heart was set on the alluring widow Mrs. Lillian Whiltshire. Robbie concluded that Lillian was a year older and a much more mature woman. He did admit to himself of dreaming of lovely Lillian on occasion and felt guilty because of it. Her miniature portrait was very appealing.

Robbie thought to the future when they would have their first meeting together. At first, it would be awkward her finding out of the loss of her husband. But Lillian's gratitude upon receiving a promise of extreme wealth would hopefully be bestowed upon him. Both being newly widowed there would be a common connection. He might have a chance at love again.

Slinking along the back of the buildings hoping not to be seen he came across that smiling Athapuscow native who screamed in his ear almost deafening him. The mad warrior was still smiling. Maybe that was his permanent face. The warrior spat in front of Robbie. He said in a form of Cree, "I try and give your wife a baby many times." He closed his eyes and was about to do another one of his loud ear jarring screams when Robbie finally came out of his shell and hit him so hard in the throat that no sound was heard again except a few gargles before he suffocated from a broken wind pipe and an open gash in his throat.

Robbie had not known what he had done before his actions were complete. He dropped a small knife he had concealed in his fist. It was not planned to meet or kill the arrogant native. What was done could not be changed. Robbie wiped the sprayed blood from his face. His clothes had further stains he made good at cleaning off. He had to make it to the ship now. Charges of cowardice in the line of duty brought a hanging and he did not want to be around to see if the Sergeant was going through with the charges. Now add murder. Nor was Robbie going to wait for the Sergeant or Private Murphy to accompany him. He would get to the beautiful Mrs. Lillian first and explain the situation and save her. The Sergeant could not be expected to just throw the charges away. *He will enforce the charges just to get rid of me. Time to leave. Head out. See what is afar.* Robbie dragged the dead warrior into the shadows.

Robbie had just one more building to navigate past. Once there he would have to run to the water and board ship by way of the ramp. As Robbie approached the candle-lit interior of the building he saw true horror. He stood aghast, looking into the window at the nude and fat Sergeant holding what looked like the stolen, ripped picture of Lillian in his hands. He was muttering to himself.

The native girl was getting off her knees and just rising looking as if she was coming to. She stood and grabbed her deerskins in her arms and tried to reach the door. As she did, she banged the small table by her and knocked an empty rum bottle to the floor. The Sergeant turned. This time obviously excited to see her awake. Robbie thought he saw the Sergeant smile with affection. This time he did not hit her and just held her against the wall with his belly and it looked like he was going to start to finally have his way with her. She pleaded with him to stop. Her nakedness still in his reach, he made sure she did not move from the wall lifting her into a more fetal position for comfort. A moment more and he would have crossed the course of righteousness.

Robbie made up his mind in an instant. He knew he had little time. The Corporal and Private Murphy would be there soon to check in for the night or for their turns at the poor girl. Whatever held Robbie back before never crossed his mind. Pulling himself awkwardly into the window he knew he had better not be heard. What he contemplated would be treason – for a native girl's honor. In three strides he was across the room. An empty rum bottle appeared in his hands and a crack was heard as the bottle careened off the back of the skull of the Sergeant. Nothing happened. The Sergeant paused for just an instant. Without turning around he proceeded to keep trying to pull the girl a little higher for himself. Robbie grabbed the bottle with both hands and as the next hit finally registered on the Sergeant, the final blow floored him. The blows combined with the rum was too much for him. He urinated himself upon passing out and immediately started snoring, loudly filling the room with sour odour and abhorrent noise. Robbie dragged him out to the back lane where the soldiers on duty would go for their relief. Robbie dropped him face down in a puddle of mud and sewage.

The Sarge was so heavy he made a big splash when he hit the muck. Sergeant Percival Devil was unconscious and still naked. It also was coming up to the middle of September and the night was cold. Robbie in a few good blows would change his life forever. He must jump aboard ship now and not be found for certain. Then recruit to up north without turning back, get to Lillian and warn her of the Sergeant's evil plan and try and save them both.

The native girl grabbed her clothes and before putting them on approached Robbie and kissed him on the cheek leaning her bare warmth upon him. She did not speak any language he knew. Only a few words of communication. But she did not seem all there, as if she was not that comprehending. *She just went through a lot,* Robbie thought. *She probably migrated recently from one of the western tribes who came for money and adventure and ended up here.* Robbie hand motioned to go and he had to help her put her clothes on or she probably would have just stood there till the Sergeant woke up. Robbie then had to grab her by the elbow to lead her out. She was confused and not knowing what to do.

Robbie passed by a food table wrapping a tablecloth around a big flank of caribou, a handful of eggs, a few good meals of ham and a big fresh ten pound brick of hard cheese, wrapping them in a big warm blanket. He filled his pockets with ship's biscuits and a few berries from a bowl. Straps of two large flasks of goat's milk went over his shoulder. The fat Sergeant ate well. He did not spot his pocket watch on the table. He went back and re-corked an almost full bottle of rum the Sergeant had just opened. His coat pockets were almost full when he spotted on the floor near the Sergeant's clothing the portrait of the Lieutenant's widowed Lillian. After a thorough search, the inheritance letter was not to be found nor were the gold buttons or his father's watch. Before they huddled off arm in arm to the safety of the ship, pretty Hahaya Wehaya picked up one of the Sergeant's boots that he always preciously polished every day and scooped up some residue that one of the army dogs had deposited just outside the open doorway. She placed the boot and contents with the other boot. A big smile came to her face and she blushed as she ran off with her saviour. She was feeling better. Saved in the nick of time.

Robbie realized he now was in a predicament that he created. He saved the girls. He saved Mrs. Strutsenburger and killed in vengeance and hid the body of that smiling Athapuscow warrior. Trying to remember if there was anything else he recalled, he thought of the struggle with the Sergeant, the threat of lashes and the false charges of threatening a non-commissioned officer, which would now be a definite assault against a non-commissioned officer if the Sarge put two and two together. Escaping meant desertion and with cowardice in the line of duty, impersonating an officer and other charges against him he would be hanged. Murder and treason charges were not out of the question. The loss of his family had to be investigated and finished with. The need to set things right was upon him. So were his immense feelings of defeat.

The mad precious devil of a Sergeant lying in his own urine snored drunkenly. Robbie stepped over him, chuckled, raised his shoulders and brows in response to thoughts of getting caught. *The ship had better sail bright and early.* He knew he had a bit of time. But what about the girl? A real conundrum. Robbie had not thought past the paternal instincts of saving the distressed girl. Now she clung to him. When Sergeant Devil awoke he would be hung over and suffering a mild concussion. His demeanor would be foul. If he left her there she would be murdered. She was not totally clear headed and would be discovered easily. She did not confess to have an ability to be mindful. Robbie's respect for the native women and caring in general would not just let her stay and be killed.

"I can't leave you here. Do you understand?" Robbie's eyebrows were touching together with the look of concern. "Do you have somewhere to go?" Hahaya Wehaya shook her head side to side. She did not fully understand. Robbie went to walk away and her arm went around his elbow as if it was natural and they were off at this dark hour.

"You must be quiet when we go on board. I must stash you on board with me. We hide. When we are at the next port I will reveal ourselves and say I did not know what I was to do. And sign up then with the signing officer."

And give her over to officials there to take care of her until she is totally healed, Robbie mused. *And then let her find a home, a job or search for her family.*

His newfound friend started to communicate a bit better once she stopped being so nervous. Whether she knew enough to remain silent or whether she knew she was going to board a ship was unknown. He did not have a full communicative partner just yet. Robbie could tell she knew he was displeased with her. He needed time to think. Robbie smiled thinking about exacting revenge on the Sergeant. He thought, *As long as the ship sails in the morning.*

The dead Indian created mixed feelings. One of guilt along with the satisfaction from the release of huge pent up anger. This helped Robbie overcome his fear. The determined emotions of feeling bold and menacing followed by action.

Robbie picked up a broad axe-chipped board three and a half by five inches in dimension. The length was about four feet. A nice hefty club. He approached the lonely guard by the rope scaffolding hanging off the ship. Robbie thought, *Better for making beer than wasting this wood on this unknown man who will have a headache in the morning.* The guard was watching small bats fly in a circle above him. They would dip and hover for at least a few good hours into the night.

Getting the break they needed they carried their luggage onto the poop deck and then a short jaunt down a set of stairs to the lower deck. Further down still unseen they swung down to a lower deck where Robbie previously placed his stash. The hemp ropes cushioned their fall. It was cold. They were both smiling at each other as Robbie checked her over for bruises. They had only one blanket and bundled up together in the middle of one of the top swirls of rope where there was a big circular inner opening.

This gave them privacy if they were to lie flat as they were. High enough to not be seen by anyone walking on their deck level it also provided an adequate view for surveillance. After getting warm Robbie undid his ammunition pouch and powder horn. He placed his jacket beside them for more warmth if needed.

She was still fidgeting nervously and continued to look over her shoulder when she heard scratching noises. She pulled off some meat rather roughly with her teeth, a good piece hanging out of her mouth, passing him the caribou leg. She kept pushing it in his face and some of the juices were being wiped on his face. Robbie grabbed her hand to subdue her and pulled the meat down. She smiled showing big white teeth. She got him in a joke. They laughed together. They ate together. She grabbed a piece of cloth and wiped his face. Settling back she put a bare leg over his. They pulled his long wool redcoat over them and settled into their space. He put his arm under her shoulders and she curled and responded by cooing in a murmur and rolling into him. The softness of her pressed against him. The slight confinement provided warmth and intimacy. They shared a piece of peppermint stick she had saved and pulled out of her pocket.

It was still dark and you could hear the creak of wood as it expanded. The loons were out making their call. Robbie drifted off to sleep. Their shared sorrow, the close quarters, her nakedness pressed against him was so comforting. Eventually his needs and her caresses awoke him. As he started coming to he felt lust and desire rising deep in his mind. Ignoring guilt he was letting go of his timidity. From above him long black hair hung down and brushed his face. Her breath reached his face. When she leaned down and brushed her ample bosom across his chest Robbie could hold back no more. Automatic reflex made him put his arms around her with care and pull her into him as if he had waited for her a long time and wanted her with such a hard passion and wild desire. Their noses touched. Their lips brushed and met in equal anticipation. Her hands lightly caressed his forehead. Robbie pulled her even closer so their bodies were one and their lips stayed together for a few minutes. When they finally pulled apart she moaned in quiet pleasure.

DILEMMA

Being only eight going on nine Lil Wolf's burden of a full bag of powder and the heavy quadrant[3] was too much for him. The combination was fifty pounds on a boy who weighed no more than that. His master Conneequese[4] saw Lil Wolf struggling and took the powder and set off behind the others who advanced on the hunt. Samuel Hearne and the whole group were off hunting during their first attempt to locate Copper River. After a few minutes, the boy sat on a stump and started to cry. The humiliation was too much. To be treated roughly and half starved by his master was nothing compared to being a slave to this impolite white man. Lil Wolf refused to go on and sat only a few yards from where the hunters had started off. The half Indian boy's master saw the others had advanced too far ahead and he was not going to risk being lost or getting shot at. It was time to make camp. Conneequese and Lil Wolf filled their pouches with powder. They left the remaining powder where they dropped it and the quadrant and hastened south five hundred yards to sleep without fear of the hunters returning and finding their trail. They ate dried venison and got comfortable. They could hear musket shots in the distance and cheers of men as they drifted off. But not before Lil Wolf was bound to a tree.

At midnight they saw the white man Samuel Hearne arrive swearing and then a shout of laughter and joy. What the two sleepers overheard was that the hunting group had thought the quadrant taken and all their extra powder. They would have had a hard time getting home without the powder for they would not eat. They would have to go home if the

---

3   A special apparatus to measure location.
4   A real-life evil misdoer.

quadrant was stolen as they would not be able to document their progress or location.

The master Indian temporarily released Lil Wolf and kept an arm on Lil Wolf's shoulder and they gathered some more berries and had another meal. Apparently the white man had not eaten in a few days and was distraught at having to look for his goods of survival till midnight. If Hearne had originally gone back to where he left them his struggles would have been lessened.

Lil Wolf watched the hunters eat and leave before checking the camp for scraps of food. They now feared that they would be charged as thieves and did not know exactly how upset the white man Samuel Hearne would get. The decision was to head off in a new direction towards the fort and find some of his tribe. As they started off they turned and heard a smash of breaking glass and a scream. They went to investigate. Past the thicket and not far away the hunting group had set up the quadrant and the white man apparently left the quadrant on its stand and ate lunch. This was such a rarity to leave the quadrant set up and unattended but they were all so starved as to be totally unaware of the gusts of wind that started sweeping the landscape. In Samuel's diversion for some food the quadrant left undefended was blown over by a gust of wind ending their hopes of carrying on. Samuel's long search and worry at finding the quadrant he thought stolen was for naught, for on this moment the quadrant's little glass pieces shattered in a wide explosion when the apparatus toppled to the ground.

Lil Wolf looked at his master and giggled over the white man's awful misfortune. They would be heading back to the fort now as they had no measuring equipment. Master Indian suddenly smacked Lil Wolf to march him on and back at their small encampment. Master Indian tied him very roughly to a stunted Black Spruce so he would not escape and after tending the fire fell into a deep sleep sitting against a tree.

The small bit of rough treatment was common. Thinking about fighting back stirred up Lil Wolf. After sitting possum for so long he longed to be free. He had such rough treatment from this man. Lil Wolf wanted to punch Conneequese when he was not looking. Kick him. Work no nine-year-old should have to do. Lil Wolf was realizing a lot and growing up fast. He gnawed at the knot with his teeth. Conneequese was so tired after the last few days of walking that he was careless with the knot tying. Instead of pulling the two ends hard making a good knot he just roughly pulled them together. Lil Wolf already had the ropes undone. He stood over his captor and aggressor, a long knife in his hands – his master, a renowned warrior and killer, slept. Silhouetted with the fire behind and his master in front Lil Wolf debated on what to do next.

LILLIAN'S GALA

I am still undecided as to whether it was the hostess or the food that made us prefer tonight's gala," an older lieutenant remarked with a sly look. He was one of the few party participants still awake. It was an incredibly late hour.

"How flattering, Lieutenant. I see you have not lost your gift of complimenting in your so special way. May I say I agree with you, the hostess was sensational and I am also stuffed full of exquisite food," Mrs. Lillian Anne Wiltshire agreed. She turned her head and fidgeted in her seat. The candles had already burned out and she was exhausted.

"Mistress Lillian you were exquisite. The men had their eyes on you all evening, your splendor and presence lights up the room and every single man's heart who glances upon you. A marvel my dear, simply a marvel." The old Lieutenant leaned back in his chair and smiled benignly. The six or seven stragglers were kept awake by their need to not miss a few more moments in Lillian's company.

"It is late, gentlemen. I shall retire to my room. Good night." At that they all rose and she curtsied ever so gracefully. As she rose, she kept her eyes closed and her head up so the men would get a quick glimpse of her maidenly bosom, knowing she was not looking, sort of rewarding them for a wonderful night. That was only part of the beauty that she was, the attention she commanded and the lust she created in the men who were lucky enough to gaze upon her. Some men fought just to glimpse her.

At five foot two, with a body that was tuned and toned to perfection she had it all, including a low-cut dress as was the French fashion and ample bosom to fill it. She winked her left eye and turned and got about twenty paces when she was approached.

"Mrs. Lillian Whiltshire's official first party of North American High Society was most certainly a success," the Major said. "May I walk you to your dwelling, madam?"

"Of course not! Dickens, I hope no one heard you. You may follow me as far as the end of the rampart. Past that point we can't be seen. That is as far as I can allow. My honor is always watched as you know, Major Fred Mallory." She leaned into his shoulder and whispered, "And I would be quite obliged for your company, too many wild Indians creeping about. Scares me half to death."

Standing straight again and more loudly, "Getting cold tonight isn't it?" She was tired and decided to play distracted rather than coy. In a minute or two of silence they were at the separating spot and he watched her walk to her door and enter her apartment. She did not turn and give him a look goodbye. Someone might be watching and make something of it. A woman in 1769 could not afford to be seen alone with a man, especially at night, if it weren't her husband.

"Lillie, you must not cry after such a fine night," Maggie her cook, seamstress, friend and maid comforted. Lillian had gone into her spacious quarters, fell on the couch and was confronted with her loneliness.

"Oh I know. It is just that ..." After a good nose blow she continued, "I want love, Maggie. To be cherished by one man. Not the whole group of gaudy soldiers. Do you see how hungry their eyes are? I do not understand."

"You will, my dear. After your husband returns," the maid smiled.

"No, I want to be loved not left alone. I need to be hugged and appreciated. I need someone to notice my hair when I do it differently. I long to have someone's breath in my ear telling me he cherishes me. I need the fulfillment of my marriage. My loins ache. My thighs ache. Even my stomach aches and I can't take another day of those watchful eyes on me. One mistake and one of the old men would blackmail me into submission." A huge tearful bawl followed and then a she threw the couch cushions and an old ivy plant in a final eruption of childish frustration.

"I am sorry, Maggie. I pine so. I may be starting to like that Major. He does have a career ahead of him. And I know he likes me. He keeps throwing a sheep's eye on me. Nothing is definitely certain. Just a sly pinch here and a wink there and some other tinder tokens that may end in smoke after all. A girl will soon get a husband in this country.[5]

"Oh, what am I saying? Oh, what am I going to do?" In a depressed outburst, "Is my husband ever to return? Am I to remain a virgin forever?" When she said the word virgin her throat closed and tears fell from her eyes.

"Enough, girl. It will only make you sick worrying. If you must then, next month there will be another dance that you can have arranged. If no word is heard from your husband by then you have permission from your mother's authorization to let your intentions be known that you seek an active husband and relinquish your marriage due to it being unfulfilled. I know you will get lots of suitors."

Lillian's maid thought, *Things will be real messy if her husband is still alive and he returns. But go find true happiness, girl. A woman should not have to suffer with desire for such a long time.*

---

5   Quote from letters from Upper Canada illustrating the way they thought and talked.

FREEDOM

The moon was behind clouds as darkness enveloped the camp. The stillness of the air made everything surreal and immediate. The crackles of the fire pierced his ears, long shadows stabbed all around him. Lil Wolf was vividly exposed with a backdrop of fire. He stood there feeling sorry for his captor. He looked at the big warrior with his head back and mouth open. His throat was exposed. Beads of sweat poured down his brow. *What if he awakens? What will I do?*

His hatred over the last few months had grown. Beaten and starved, Lil Wolf was given all the chores he could possibly do. The worst was boys younger than him kept taunting and throwing rocks at him. Lil Wolf did not know how to react. He was a slave and punishment was always just around the corner.

He gripped the knife handle harder with both hands and stabbed down for his freedom. As the knife pierced the man's windpipe, the big bird awoke in a fright and pushed Lil Wolf off of him into the air. Lil Wolf was airborne but gravity quickly forced him down again. The Indian slipped with his outstretched arms as he was still in a sleepy fog and he grabbed only one shoulder of the boy. The point in Lil Wolf's right hand held true to its target. As Conneequese looked up Lil Wolf fell down on him.

He heard a small whimper as the knife sunk into his neck and severed the jugular. Lil Wolf rolled away. The big warrior pulled the knife out and charged Lil Wolf who by now had rolled away a few feet. Lil Wolf's master only made it two steps when all his attention turned to the blood pouring down his chest. The first plunge into his neck damaged his windpipe and prevented normal breathing. The second had sealed his fate. When the knife was pulled out in panic the damage was done. The skin had sealed around the knife so that when the knife was pulled out it pulled the flesh that tried to seal the wound pulling vein and skin alike. The warrior's anger was quickly squelched with his squirting blood.

Lil Wolf was now free for the moment at least. If the other Northern Indians found him or discovered the body he would be killed in retaliation. Sprayed blood dripped off of Lil Wolf as he remained crouched in shock. The fire died down and further darkness surrounded the tortured and traumatized young boy. Nine years old was too young to make life-threatening decisions. Survival at that age was not likely. Maybe he needed captivity to survive. He sat and wept for his dead captor. He did not know why.

CATCH A DEATH OF A COLD

The Sergeant was found by his buddy the Corporal. Maxwell had drunk himself to sleep and did not arrive till late in the morning at eight o'clock. Returning again after seeing the mess, with Private Jim Murphy, they looked at each other sheepishly and bent down and picked up the groggy blubber. Naked, his pure white skin and layers of fat made him grotesque and oh how he smelled. Mixed in his beard was his own puke and blood mixed with all the excrement of the last few years compiled onto that spot.

Sergeant Percival Devil sneezed. A fountain of spittle sprayed out in front of his face. He held himself up by a beam. He saw where he was found and became aware of his nakedness.

"Missed you last night, Sarge. Your lights were out. Early night?" The Corporal tried to make friendly conversation.

'Fetch my pants and shirt, you idiot." The Sergeant was putting it together. The native girl Hahaya hella. She was from hella, hella. He remembered opening the second bottle of rum and did not see it about. The Sergeant was very observant. After he put his pants on, Percival recollected his losses. He immediately went to the desk and unlocked a drawer. He pulled out the inheritance papers, a receipt for a watch repair and a stack of papers with charges made out on each. The inheritance letter that would make him rich was safe as were the papers for Robbie's demise. All the charges against him were there except the ones to be filled out. His quick thinking always saved him.

"Freeman, get in here and get these forms filled out. Murphy, give me a hand straightening it up in here. Grab an end of the table."

They went to work and the Sarge saw too much food gone and the bottle of rum was definitely missing. That girl was going to pay. After an hour, things were straightened out and the Sarge had his breakfast of most of the remains on the table. Still wiping stink from his body Percival started sneezing repeatedly, blowing his nose with his hand onto the earth floor. Spit hit the ground in a double shot, one a beeline and one of dribble. After a couple of more sneezes and a wicked shake the precious little Devil declared:

"I am sick. Really sick." Shivering, he put on his redcoat. "Where are my boots?"

The Corporal was off to the Captain to get the papers authorized and Murphy had gone to look for Robbie to go over the plan with the Sergeant again. Devil had to look for himself, not realizing the boots were where he always placed them if he removed them. Sometimes he needed to take his boots off to cut off a corn or wart or something.

NOW WHAT DO I DO?

Daylight shone on the horrible bloody murder. Lil Wolf threw up and cried for his mother. Lil Wolf realized he should have planned a better escape. Matter of fact, what he was going to do was not even a consideration until now. He started to gather rocks to cover him. Lost and alone he did not consider the consequences of his actions. There was enough dried meat to last a few days. The others had moved off quickly to the fort, leaving the sound of birds returning and wind rustled the branches of the Black Spruce.

I will stay here and just die.

SURVIVAL

She was petite and curvaceous with small cute features. She was not as big browed as some of the other native women. And the tradition of putting vertical lines on each cheek she refused to do. She had sensitive fair skin. The other women would rub powdered charcoal into their wounds and into lines that were made with an awl. A needle pushed crushed charcoal under the skin till they made the most unsightly black lines down their faces. Three to four black lines down each of their cheeks. She was an untouched rare beauty amongst the tribes of the north.

The first night alone with the Chipewyans the tired, scared and captured woman was wrestled and won over by at least a score of young warriors. Six months of torture with the Athapascow, many months of isolation and now to be again made a slave for this tribe's bidding. For Key, survival was all that mattered right now.

ALL OF A SUDDEN, CHAOS

After about thirty minutes, the Sergeant saw his boots where he always put them. Still shivering, Percival wiped snot from his nose that seemed to continually run to his mouth in a stream. Corporal Freeman came walking in giving an all good with his hands to say his job was done. The papers were signed. Murphy came in the other door and had his hands up in a gesture to show he had no clue about something.

"No idea, Sarge. Nobody seen him. Everyone was intoxicated at the fort except old Noah. What do you want me to do?"

Sergeant Percival Devil decided it was time to call the alert. Robbie might have helped that native girl. A bell clanged to announce the departure of one of the vessels docked at the shoreline. If Robbie was on that ship then time was running out. Murphy needed to be on that ship before departure. The wooden door swung open smashing into its frame. Private Fable came in.

"Let you know they are taking that Injun you know, down to the gravedigger. Someone knifed him pretty good last night. Fast and clean. He was found out back."

"What else do you know?" Percival screamed, inches from his face.

"Robbie and he didn't get along." Fable was going turncoat on his friend when confronted with the evil Sergeant.

The Sergeant remembered that just before his lights went out, the native girl from last night was still subdued. *She must have had an accomplice. Or she must have hit me.* Just then, Percival saw something under the desk. The portrait of lovely rich Lillian, who he planned on forcing to love him. As he picked it up he saw the picture had finally ripped in half and he only held a bunch of flowers on his part. Percival looked everywhere then smashed his hand down on the desk.

KIWIDINOK TELLS HER STORY

After a few days, Key felt a bit more comfortable. The northern group of people were on the move and it was refreshing to exercise. She felt comfortable enough to share her story. She told the group of women of how more than forty Athapuscow had ambushed her family and that when she was kidnapped they killed her father and then the rest of her family. They just laughed. No sympathy. She knew her life would be hard and she did not know if she would survive.

She continued with her story. After being raped over and over for days by many Athapuscow warriors she was finally given to a man who would treat her like a wife. She would have to help take care of him with his other three wives. She was not liked and was given all the worst chores and relentless hours of work.

BOOTS

The Sergeant sat his fat arse down on the bench just inside the door and asked Max to bring him his boots. The Corporal smelled a stench in the boots different than the usual rot smell but said nothing.

"Hand me my boots, Max. C'mon on, I don't have all day." Percival's head was throbbing and his sinuses were blocking up. A sudden sneeze made the Sergeant swear in pain and anger. Sergeant Percival put on one boot. He brought his leg up straight in the air till it was parallel with the ground with his knee bent. Pulling with both hands from each side of the boot and pushing his fat foot – it just fit into the tight new boots from Supply.

"My feet are cold. Where's my cheese? Anybody seen my cheese? My rum?" With his head still spinning from the froth from the evening before and from when he must have fallen and hit his head, he slid the boot up his leg to his knee. He noticed how his boots were polished to perfection, fresh from Noah – clean and polished.

Before he could change his mind or react, he saw something falling out of the boot. The quick glance did not register until he had thrust his foot fully in. What was it? A lump of wood? He pushed with his leg and pulled hard with his hands at the same time to make sure his foot jammed past the bend of the boot to securely be planted deep in its deep folds. Before he could react to his realization that it was a turd that fell from his boot and not a piece of black wood, he had already committed and yanked hard, sinking his foot deep into the soft mush of pooh.

117

"SHITE ... SHITTTE! SHIII-TTTE!" The Sergeant screamed louder and louder till his last scream could be heard half way across Lake Erie and then lingered to a bout of agonized wailing.

"I'll kill her and Robbie too! Just wait!"

BEGINNINGS OF HEROISM

The morning air was crisp and cold. Lil Wolf shivered on his first few waking breaths. He had slept where he had lain between his victim and the now dead fire.

"Chi china," he called. The rocks that covered him made no movement. His master was dead. The night of horror came back to haunt him. His mother taken from him made Lil Wolf feel saddened and lonely. He had exacted revenge last night by killing his captor. Never again would he allow himself to be beaten or become a slave. *I will learn to fight and become a rebel like my father wished. I will find my father.*

SCRUB A DUB DUB

Sergeant Percival yanked a stinking sock off his foot and plunged his foot into a bucket of dirty brown water. *First time I've had these socks off this year.* A bit of decayed skin flew into the air as the sock was flung away. A few lumps of doggy doo floated to the surface of the water.

Percival drew out of his vest pocket his half of the small portrait. A simple bouquet filled the half frame he possessed. He stroked the broken edge of the picture envisioning the bosom of his desire. *How I love thee. I will make you mine. Once you learn how to serve me you will know I am your Lord. I will take your money and you will serve me as my wife or I will kill you and Robbie.* Sergeant Devil thought of the busty blonde beauty from Britain and said aloud "I love thee." A few of the men snickered.

The Sarge was now controlled by his delusional desires. Mixing lust and coveting for her love he thought further *Her wealth and her knee bending respect.* Sergeant Percival Devil started shaking. *Now that is respect.*

THE MAJOR

"Not the same silly wood." Mrs. Lillian Whiltshire laughed at the Major over whether his cuffs were sewn the same length. He really was a spectacle. Around Lillian he was a clumsy oaf and in constant excitement around her. She confessed to herself that she secretly wished the Lieutenant she married would never return. Her emotion showed on her face. She shuddered all over. *Enough of that,* she told herself.

She continued to look out the window into the vast wilderness wondering what would come of her announcement next month while Major Mallory craned his neck to get a good angle to look at her.

"Quite right, my lady. If he cared at all he would have at least replied to you. I would travel miles to see you."

"The news does have to travel far here. Even so, by now he must have my letter that I have arrived. His delay would be necessary for Britain, I'm sure. And yes, I have fond feelings for you Major."

At that the young man stood at attention, bowed and exited.

He paused outside her door. His constant showing of his concern for her was starting to work. Possibly this missing Lieutenant may be injured, dead or not even show up till after it did not matter. He might be sent on a permanent journey west without anyone knowing. The worst case would be a duel. And he lusted for her so. He was a solid British soldier from a fine school. Admittedly, he was fresh out of school but life itself was a test of mettle just as much as any army experience. Convinced of his cause he jubilantly pranced away wondering why he could not think of anything to say as he left.

FRIENDS

Lil Wolf had walked almost twenty miles every day for more than a week and once stole a canoe and paddle and ran with the current for a long ways, probably eighty miles south at a very fast pace. He was travelling so fast he had no time to relax. After a few moons Lil Wolf was now some considerable distance south of Hudson Bay's famous Prince of Wales Fort. With most of the rivers freezing up he could traverse these and go in a straight line south to Boston. He finally found a spot to pull ashore and rest.

"Hello?" said a young voice from behind the trees. Or so Lil Wolf thought.

"Hello! Who are you? What you doing?"

Standing before him in the early evening fading light was a boy about ten years old. He did not see him at first as he was black in skin color and in dark clothing. He had camouflaged himself in with the bushes and was actually standing right in front of him blocking his path.

"I am Lil Wolf, descendant of a great Indian chief." He had forgotten his famous grandfather's name momentarily.

"What are you doing here?

"I never saw anyone with the likes of you before!" Lil Wolf exclaimed.

The thin black boy pulled his chin up and replied. "I ain't seen you around here. What you doing here? Thieving?"

Lil Wolf had been waiting to tell someone of his story. They both made do with their broken English. Munching on partridge, corn and berries that the boy named Cyrenius had in his pouch, Lil Wolf was gaining some strength. He explained his journey and lack of food. Living off berries and one dead animal that was still fairly fresh. His goal was to get as far south as possible before winter set in.

"Wanna come with me? We could both become rebels." Lil Wolf smiled for the first time in months.

Cyrenius looked at Lil Wolf with tears in his eyes. "My parents and brother were kidnapped. I have no one."

"Wanna hunt with me?"

"Sure!" Cyrenius smiled shyly and wiped his eyes.

And the afternoon was set.

HELLO ROBBIE

S ergeant Devil cleaned up everything including his boots. Then he got his men down to the docks on the double. The Inheritance letter and summonses for a multitude of offenses were in the Sarge's back pocket. He looked up and saw not only Robbie but the native girl too. Both were standing on the highest deck with the captain of the ship, his wife and a crowd of officers with epaulettes of gold and medals of bronze and silver all taking turns. The men were taking turns slapping Robbie on the back.

Robbie is deluding them, the Sergeant fumed. He could hear Robbie recounting the ambush story. There were witnesses on the crowded deck that could verify Robbie's quick thinking and how his actions prevented an ambush and many casualties. The charges would not stick. Not here and now. They were signed and still a legal threat to make Robbie execute his plan. He would not need to execute the charges. Not now that the stakes were raised.

Robbie will complete his mission under threat and be killed at the first opportunity thereafter. That bitch beauty will be on her knees begging to marry me before I'm done. And I'll have more money than I'll know what to do with. I may just buy all of the Hudson's Bay Company shares and change history.

In his demented state, the Sergeant had just elevated his criminal plot to murder.

TRANSPORTATION

Lil Wolf and Cyrenius walked with straight branches for fishing poles over their shoulders and a cloth bag tied to one end to hold their few belongings and marched south. The sticks would become play muskets when they were bored. Both child soldiers were full from a fish fry after their catch earlier in the day. They laughed as a skunk crossed their path and they did not get sprayed.

Upon getting to a shoreline of some size they came up to a barge with two friendly looking men on board.

"What do we have here? You two lost?" said a man of middle age who sported a large belly.

Lil Wolf, the more confident, replied, "We are off to join the southern colonists. I'm Captain Lil Wolf and this here is my recruit Private Cyrenius. Can we hitch a ride?"

The older of the two men smiled and glanced at the other, nodding his head. "Timing is right boys. Seems here we lost our crew. No one wants to flat bottom down rivers to Lake Ontario. Too much portaging they say. When winter hits, the boats make great sledges and by that time we surely could make purchase of one ox or horse. Then it is a straight trek south through the Opasquia and Wabakima river areas, east of the Huron and west of the Algonquins.

"If you want the land of new adventure and the thrill of opening up the wild west I can get you to the gateway of a new type of living. They call it democracy down there."

The call to adventure now had transportation. The boys grabbed a poling stick and jumped on board with their few belongings.

LITTLE ONE

Key spent six moons in captivity among the Cree before she was able to escape. After a further twenty six moons of isolation and then a few moons to get used to further sexual orgies among the Chipewyan Northern Indians, Key was finally able to talk about the loss of her daughter. She confided to the usual group of northern women about how her daughter died. She told her story.

"After about twelve night skies of captivity with the Cree I was allowed to wander the camp a bit. I'm not sure how long exactly because I was kept up many nights by many warriors so time was fleeting. On one such occasion while wandering in the shadows I escaped. Dashing through the the woods, I went towards where I believed I was taken from. This distance was a good two miles east of where I had been ambushed, not far.

"There was no threat of being overheard if I made noise. So I hollered, "*Ayashe!*" Running quickly another ten paces forward I called again. "*Ayashe!* It is Kiwidinok, your mother. I am here."

Key smiled at the memory. After only a few minutes of my frenzied behavior out from the woods came Layna, my midwife. She held Ayashe up to show me that she lived. By the time we closed the gap between us we both had tears running down our faces and my baby was crying. I burst out in tears when she saw how thin my baby was. Layna had lost a child only a few moons prior to illness and still gave milk. That and a few raw fish was all they had to keep them alive. Layna could not risk a fire …

Before Key could finish her story the group laughed and one of the young warriors took her into his tent. She would finish her story later and make them listen.

THE SERGEANT

The wind was blowing Hahaya's long black hair over her face making her laugh.

Robbie was leaning on the rail harbor side watching closely as two Athapascow natives boarded the ship at a lower level. And then Robbie and the native girl Hahaya simultaneously saw the Sarge staring at them from the shore. Realizing they were discovered Robbie spilled his drink as someone else slapped him on his back. Soldiers who were there during the ambush all started making a boast to drink over.

Robbie shrugged at his native girlfriend and turned his back to the sneering Sergeant. He'd noticed before that the burn scar on Percival's upper right lip would quiver when he was angry. And judging by the quivering Robbie had just seen, he was seething.

OH NO

As the Northern Indians finally listened to Key's story they just giggled and laughed. They seemed to be actually enjoying her story and her struggle to tell them.

"Layna and I were talking when we heard noises coming from the woods. I turned to face the biggest fear in my life since my family was massacred. My heart pounded in my chest." Key held her hand over her heart. "I gasped for air. I couldn't breathe," she continued.

"To my horror, out of the trees and brush came a group of about twenty screaming native women all with knives and rocks in their hands."

The northern women listened in earnest.

BRING ME STRUTSENBURGER

M urphy, me buddy. We've been over the plan," the burly Sarge
said. "You keep tabs on Robbie and make sure there are no slip-
ups. Meet me one mile west of the fort. Bring Lillian there. Tell her I'll
be waiting secretly for her with the power of attorney to grant her a large
sum of money. Tell her besides the Inheritance letter I have a few things
from her dead husband." The Sarge paused to make sure Murphy was
following his instructions.

"If she questions why she has to travel incognito and meet in secret
tell her I am unable to come to the fort because I have not arranged
clearances and that could take six months to a year and by then cause a
lot of unwanted publicity. Tell her she need not worry. Tell her she can
bring another soldier that is in both our confidence, a Private Robbie
Wolfe. I will be there for the meeting. Just need to clear up transfers and
paperwork and board the next ship. And tell her to hurry and not make
waste of my time as I am an impatient man. We meet again one mile
west of the fort in a few months from today. I have a lot of duties to get
back to or her money to spend," he laughed at his own humor.

The Sarge reasoned that Murphy was the perfect person to use as a
tail. Unassuming by his plain ugly looks and average height and weight
he did not stand out. Except for his natural straight and wide shoulder
stance and upturned menacing chin he resembled the type of person
who you would not notice in a crowd nor care what he had to say.
Murphy was also strong, only had to be told once and was smart enough
to figure things out on his own. He took and followed all orders well no
matter what they were. Whether it was helping Corporal Freeman clean
up the Sergeant's mess or killing an unwanted hero named Robbie he

would do his duty and do it well. And, the Sergeant figured, people liked to do things they did well.

The Sergeant continued speaking to Corporal Freeman, "We will be there about the same time Robbie and Murphy arrive."

To Private Murphy, "Set up a meeting shortly after that. We will all meet one mile west of the fort and go to the destination you choose where we can conceal one and perhaps two bodies. I'll bring Corporal Maxwell along to fill out the legal Inheritance Power of Attorney papers.

"You can leave, Private Murphy. Pack what you have and see the signing in officer at port. When I get there, there will be hell to pay if things don't work out," he warned.

The Sarge watched as Private Murphy boarded the tall ship. With him was Lieutenant Noonan, that pesky sixteen-year-old cadet and Nick Sweeney. Sweeney was struggling with two heavy duffle bags definitely filled with contraband and saleable accessories. He was coming from Noah's office.

The last the Sarge saw of Murphy was at the signing officer's station beside the gangplank entry. Deadly cold was an understatement for where Robbie and Murphy were going.

The Sergeant met up with the Corporal and after sneezing repeatedly and wetly, pointed to the native girl and mentioned that the Corporal could have her when they met up with them in a year or less, as long as she was dead when he was done with her and no witnesses. The stakes were too high.

"And bring me Laura tonight. She owes me money she does. Her dead husband's unpaid debts have interest accruing. I love this life I does. Make sure she knows I want double interest paid tonight, Max." The Sergeant pulled out a crumpled scrap of a picture showing blooming flowers. Sergeant Devil kissed the half of the picture Robbie had left. He would meet Lillian on the west coast of Hudson Bay. He would find out if Mrs. Lillian Whiltshire saw the other half of the portrait and if Robbie had shown her he would know Robbie had come by and taken a picture half. Then he would know for sure if Robbie helped the native girl in her escape. How else would he have lost the half of the picture? How else would they be together? The Sarge picked at a scab on the burn scar on his right cheek where the beard did not grow. He would find more rum for tonight. He might even offer Strutsenburger's widow a few swigs if she was subservient. *Mighty fine young girl she is. And she knows she's got it coming.*

DREAMS SQUASHED

Many moons passed as Lil Wolf and Cyrenius worked hard manoeuvring the shallow twelve-foot flat boat. The two men slept. The boys were to wake them if there was any danger.

Now, Lil Wolf took his turn at napping.

When the two men heard Cyrenius' story of possibly being orphaned and knowing of their planned adventure they had set Cyrenius straight. They explained that he could not join the rebels as they did not accept black people and he could be enslaved by them.

Cyrenius' heart pounded. His dreams would now not be the same as Lil Wolf's. He was at a loss for words. How could he tell Lil Wolf he could not go on? Lil Wolf was full of excitement and had a very adventurous spirit.

What am I going to do? Cyrenius wondered.

THE ANNOUNCEMENT OF
AN ANNOUNCEMENT

The tub water was hot and a drop of perspiration hit the soapy water. "Come in," Lillian replied to the knock on the door. Major Mallory stood inside the door and pushed it closed behind him. His look was menacing; he looked like he wanted something. She splashed some water at him and leaned forward in the tub but revealed nothing and laughed at him. Taunting a young man in heat could backfire. She decided not to get him too worked up.

"Oh dear, I got your breeches wet, Fredrick. I am sorry. Take them off and Maggie can set them out to dry by the fire."

At that, Mallory turned a deeper shade of red than the shiny apples on the nearby table. But still he stood at attention and did not say a word.

"Well, what is it? The water will be cold before you say what you want. And do not ask to join me. I am married, remember."

The Major shifted his weight and took a deep breath. With a bead of sweat running down the side of his face he announced his intentions. "Lillian, my love. I am a good soldier with a great career before me. We went to the same junior school together although not at the same year. We tease each other and you know ..."

"Enough, Fredrick. I cannot hear this now." She kicked the water, raising her shiny buttocks out of the foamy water for a second. "I have made a firm decision. If my husband who knows I am here does not return in one more month or I have not a word that he is still alive, I can have the marriage annulled by the captain of the ship on which I arrived. Then, if I am still in the right frame of mind I will listen to requests for courtship. And you, Major, know how I feel about you."

"Thank you, ma'am. That's all I need to go on. I'd best be going. It would not be right to be seen with you like this until we are betrothed."

The Major took one last look at Lillian's well-packed body on its small frame. He watched as that body rose with tightened buttocks out of the water to splash down again in frustration. As he turned away from that luscious sight he spun and took with him an expensive lamp with dangling lead crystals attached. The lamp smashed to the floor while the table rocked slowly back to its place. With a sheepish grin, the major turned, "I am so sorry."

She showed him out with a wave of her hands. "Away, before I have nothing left!" She laughed.

She was not sure of this young man with no confidence. She could not dream of him sweeping her off her feet. *I guess love will grow in time and I will become happy. Is that all there is in life? Am I to miss out on real love?*

She grabbed a towel from the rack and stepped out of the tub onto a sheepskin rug and dried off. She placed her towel on the couch's armrest and walked behind her dressing partition to stare into a full-length mirror.

One more month, she mused as she looked at herself in the mirror. Her earlier confidence was gone and she shivered in the cool air.

THE TEARFUL GOODBYE

Cyrenius and Lil Wolf climbed high up in an old stand of maple trees. There were branches off each that could be climbed. Cyrenius climbed as high as he could and swayed with the wind. Here he told Lil Wolf of the evil men do. That black men were taken from their villages in Africa and made into slaves in the southern parts of America. That it would be impossible to go with him and join the south. He could be enslaved or killed. The rebels in the south were the slavers and now they both knew.

"I'm sorry, Cyrenius. I didn't know. "What are you going to do?"

Cyrenius sighed. "I was told there is a community of black people down in Lincoln area. I'll stop there. The barge men said they'll help me find a place where I can work."

"Well, I have to find my father. He was going to become a colonist and then return for us. I need to tell him what has happened. I will continue my search for him and become a great warrior." Even though Lil Wolf had only white man features and looked like his dad the Indian blood and upbringing would follow him through his days.

They parted ways with both crying and sniffling.

ELEANOR FREELAND

The St. Lawrence River was green and frothy. With always a six knot current eastward, the trip was well under way when Robbie admired the morning sunrise and was approached by a messenger. A depth measurement was constantly being shouted so the messenger just handed Robbie an envelope. The contents revealed an invitation for dinner in the exclusive Captain's quarters. Only paying customers were so lucky. Everyone else's food had gone bad by day three or was stolen. Robbie went to get Hahaya Wehaya, hoping she was awake now.

To his amazement he saw that Hahaya Wehaya was lying on her narrow berth face down naked. She held no reserve.

"Hahaya, wake up." Robbie saw she was sweating and she should have been shivering. He covered her in a blanket. She smelled. She did not have the cleanliness of his Indian wife nor her communication skills. *She's actually quite stupid*, he realized. *One must be careful who one meets and makes friends with.*

She seemed distant and did not want food. Robbie left in anger. She was not making any sense. She did not appear emotionally stable, almost as if she were two people. Smiling and then angry, happy and then sad, benevolent and then vixen.

Robbie opened the door to the Captain's quarters and was assailed with the sensational aroma of beef, potatoes and carrots roasting. The room was crowded but afforded considerable warmth compared to outside. No one noticed when he pushed himself in and sat down.

A beef fat and potato sauce over cooked carrots with ship's bread and a full flask of wine was handed to him as toasts and introductions were made all around. Robbie moved and sat beside the Captain as coaxed.

The beautiful wife of the Captain sat beside Robbie and leaned into him pushing her bosom into his arm and resting her head on his shoulder demanding Robbie's full attention.

"I am yours, soldier," the venerable Captain's wife whispered.

Robbie was instantly aroused. Her perfume was intoxicating; a blend of lavender and vanilla. Her breath tickled behind his ear. Her knee crossed over and was on top of his thigh putting pressure on his leg. Captain Jim Freeland had seemed not to notice. He was busy talking to a merchant who did not want to pay some tithe to the Captain.

Robbie took a deep breath. In his cabin was a woman who had now become estranged. In Eleanor's grip he was being groped and felt her hands wander under the table. Dinner came and Robbie was saved. Mrs. Freeland sat back in her own seat and began grabbing food for her plate. Only once did she look at her husband over dinner and he was still in argument with that merchant. Her glances were only at Robbie and it was a look of want. Robbie only ate a few vegetables and put some meat sauce into a cloth napkin. Adding in two potatoes and some carrot Robbie grabbed his parcel and prepared it for travel. She leaned over and whispered into his ear.

"Soldier, my husband is very busy and does not look after my every need. Come to the port side deck. I will be waiting there needing you." At that she rose from her chair and left the dining area. Her husband never even noticed.

Fighting back fear of being caught, Robbie waited till he had counted to ten several times before rising and announcing his early retirement for the night. Faking a yawn and looking punch drunk from the wine he grabbed the remains of a wine skin and walked out to where he thought she was to be waiting. He did not think of anything wise to say. He did not plan on doing anything except talk to her and know her story and then get the food back to Hahaya. The sky was almost totally dark with a tinge of blue before black. Again he felt his breathing increase. Where was she? The hairs on his arm were rising. The cool breeze of the river was refreshing and cleared his head as he let the breeze blow into his face and hair. An arm came out and grabbed him from behind. A hand covered his mouth. A hand that felt as soft as silk as he turned to see her. He felt an urge of lust. She had undone her robe to reveal her forty-year-old nakedness. She was beautiful. A well trimmed body and a voluptuous smile. She opened her arms to him.

"Mrs. Freeland?" Robbie stammered. She took a quick step forward into the shadowy lamp light revealing herself fully to him. "You like?" She held out her arms in front of her.

"No, I just came to – you look so wonderful and beautiful." Robbie straightened as she approached him, wrapping her arms around his neck and looking up so expectantly.

Robbie was overwhelmed. In his haste he had not noticed the shadows behind him off to the left. They embraced and kissed for what seemed like an hour, their tongues exploring, breaking apart for the occasional gasps for breath. Their fervor was rising. Robbie could not believe his fortune. He pulled his shirt up to feel her nakedness on his own just as a scuff of a foot was heard on the deck beside him. The Captain was there with Jim Sloane the first mate and a few other crew members.

"Eleanor, are you all right, dear?" The Captain was red faced and snarling. He was obviously drunk and enjoying himself.

It was a setup. Robbie glanced back at Mrs. Freeland and she no longer was soft eyed and pucker-mouthed. Instead she was wide eyed and screaming.

"Rape me, he tried to." Covered up she was coming at him with a knife she must have concealed. He pushed her arm outward and shouldered her back to give himself room for an onslaught that must surely come. She fell to the deck, her robe spread out. The men paused to look on in the growing gloom. Robbie hit the Captain square in the jaw. No effect. He did the same to the first mate. No effect. Robbie was pinned down, cuffed and beaten then placed in chains after the brief scuffle. Seamen were strong, hardened men. They put him in the hold. Robbie cawed in pain as he was picked up roughly and carried off by the first mate to spend days in the bird cage until they reached Cape Breton.

HER DAUGHTER

Key, in recounting her story continued, "to my horror came a group of about twenty screaming native women all with weapons of sticks, knives and rocks in their hands. I was again kidnapped by the wives of my abductors who had followed me. My daughter and midwife were killed instantly. They were barbaric. They relished killing the other tribe's women and children, sometimes with their bare hands. I was taken into captivity for six months before I escaped again and lived alone on the land for several months.

MURPHY

Robbie was allowed out of his holding area for exercise and working some of the tow lines. He turned and saw his native girlfriend flirting with one of the sailors. She was half-naked as she liked to be and a big hand was fondling her ass as she laughed. No morals here. *I guess I got to leave her somewhere. I guess I deserve it.*

The Captain came up to Robbie. "I know my wife can get drunk and do the craziest things. But you should not have humored her Robbie. She is my wife." The Captain smiled.

Robbie smelled a setup.

Captain Freeland continued, "We have confiscated all your spirits and money. We found a pouch of gold in the lining of your redcoat and have taken that as well. You have nothing left except what the British supplied you with. We do not need to kill you. You're under house arrest under the guard of Private Murphy. By the end of the week all of you will be dropped off at Breton."

Private Murphy? Jim Murphy? Robbie shook his head. Things were not looking good at all.

Just then Murphy stepped out of the shadows. "Hello, Robbie. So being I had official papers made up before I left, I carry with me full authority to keep you under supervision. I can request an armed guard on you if you try to escape. Killing you for escaping is not beyond my power. So get in line with the rest of the new recruits."

Robbie lowered his head in despair. He lost the native girl, got caught messing around with the Captain's wife, whether set up or not, lost all his cash, gold and a bottle of rum, had a few extra bruises and now discovered he had Murphy tailing him around. He would not be rid of that evil Sergeant Percival Devil after all. Robbie stared at his usually clean but now dirty boots in dismay.

LEAVING YOU BEHIND

It did not take long to leave and board the next ship at Breton. There were no transportation mix ups here. No lost baggage. There was only one ship at port upon their arrival. Simple. The Captain's wife Eleanor had approached Robbie with an offer to be taken with him. Robbie flatly refused. He had no desire to get another beating or worse to stay in that hold any longer. At port, he put Hahaya under watch with the Indian Port Authority. They were just a group of natives who were relishing her but would seek out her own tribe.

Hahaya gave Robbie a sneering look that seemed to penetrate right through him. Maybe he was over sensitive. That was just her way after all. To be naked and joke around was natural to her. Robbie could feel he could not accept this girl for a wife. He compared his wife and her tribe who were always bundled up real good as it was cold up by the Arctic Circle.

It was true there was ruthlessness to their survival tactics. Most tribes shared or wrestled over wives. Some had wild drunken orgies. Not like his wife's tribe who were isolated and carried with them simple tastes and needs. Loving her and raising a family had been the only good things in his life. Simple things, simple desires and safety of home. Even though it had been a few years since he last saw her he missed them so much. Robbie tightened his stomach and closed his eyes over the home-sick moment. His only hope to love again lay in finding lovely Lillian and her liking him and escaping the evil Sergeant and his plans, Robbie thought moodily.

FINAL INVITATION

Mrs. Lillian Anne Whiltshire put down her pen and scribe after having put the final touches to the invitations for her big announcement. She put the final invitation down on the pile. The last was to Major Fred Mallory. She was still undecided on how she felt but she knew it only fair to invite him. He would be there anyway.

He will take it as an invitation for my love, she mused. *Am I ready to give it? What if he tries anything? How should I react? I'll tell him I need more time to think, that my heart is saddened. I'll just cry. That'll work.*

PERCIVAL MAKES IT TO THE FORT

Sergeant Percival Devil looked down at the shoreline and gave Corporal Freeman a tap with his elbow. "This place can rot to hell. We're going to get rich. Well I am. And you are my first man. Murphy too."

Maxwell smiled, his beady eyes showing his greed above his yellow and black teeth. He smoked another drag from his pipe.

It had been a good few weeks before Percival was able to sail out. The Sarge had to cover up his theft of goods and make things right with the Captain at Niagara. His supply of rum and extra food was cumbersome and required extra time to gather and load.

"We should make good time to the east coast. Almost non-stop it will be a bit more than a month, I think."

And again a tall ship to Hudson Bay would have the Sarge looking at his lust within another month and he was scratching his scabby face in anticipation. Little did he know it would be December 4th of 1770 before Robbie would arrive at the Fort, two weeks after the Sergeant and the Corporal arrived even though the Sarge left two weeks later. The Sergeant would wait when he arrived. He had no choice. It was cold this winter. He and his crew were forced to collect firewood on a work detail. It took seven to nine months of the year to collect the year's firewood at the Prince of Wales Fort. That and food gathering occupied everyone full time. It was really cold and gloomy as the Sarge lay in wait. He missed his Laura Strutsenburger.

YOUNG WARRIOR

Kiwidinok tossed and turned in her bedroll in the tent. The night before she was kept awake late as she was visited again by a young warrior. He was tall, thin and strong. She had no way to stop him. He could not get enough of her. Now that she'd been with the Northern Indians for six months since being found in her isolated spot some of the allure was finally wearing off and often she had time to herself.

That would be when the junior curious warriors would seek her out and be rough with her till she submitted. One at a time the youths would spend their late hours abusing her. Even that had worn off. Only this high strung youth would still meet her. He did not know how rough he was. Maybe he had scared the rest off. She was sweating and feeling a little light-headed.

Key had a knife in her deerskin leggings and planned to use it the next time this boy hurt her. She got up and paced the small tent. She would wait till he was at his most glorious moment and then thrust the shard up under his rib cage and into his heart or lungs. As he pulled away in amazement she would be ready to end his pleasure forever.

LAND

The ground felt grand underfoot, although it was mostly frozen over with tufts of green here and there. It was wonderful. Robbie had no further troubles sailing around the east end of the St. Lawrence and up the east coast of North America. The air got colder through the Hudson Strait and attuned them for the weather and dark days to come.

They were dropped forty-five miles southeast of the fort due to high winds running the ship aground. Ship repairs would take days. The rest of the way they would have to trek by foot. In all, there were eleven soldiers including Lieutenant Noonan the cadet, Nick with his goods, Murphy and Robbie. Good recruits by the look of every one.

One other recruit stood out in particular, a rather large blond-haired man with a beard who wore a deerskin jacket. He was in perfect athletic shape, built with wide shoulders, a big V back and strong arms, shoulders and upper chest. *Someone to watch out for in case he has an attitude,* Robbie thought. They were all glad to be standing on solid ground.

Armed with a knife, musket, bayonet, a three foot throwing tomahawk, compliments of Noah, powder horn, cartridge bag, triple round of 37 shot of lead ball, all standard issue and one extra flannel shirt and socks, a flask of almond milk and a brick of cheese curds they would not need anything else in the world besides their rum rations.

The land was flat and white. Not much here. No life here, everything seemed simple. In the distance Robbie could see specks of black on the landscape. Was it men approaching? There was only one small gathering of trees, not what one would normally call a woods or a forest. But the thought of being under cover in case of enemy fire was dominant. They moved out as a group. Robbie waited for Murphy to take command.

Private Murphy had some papers and the charge of authority because of it. He was not taking charge and it was clear he was unsure what to do. Lieutenant boy, Michael Noonan was there. Would he ever grow up and become a soldier? Nick had more pull than a team of oxen. What that man would pull out on some nights. But he never liked soldiering. Could not get used to it. Robbie knew they only had to register at the fort and someone would assume command there.

As they trudged on, Robbie thought, *What do we know? Most of us are just freezing. It is mandatory to have fur hat, heavy gloves and wool socks. Tell all immigrants!*

They covered two hundred feet in haste. The troops assumed two man cover behind the stand of trees. Robbie called to Murphy and pointed to himself and then went into the trees. Private Murphy nodded his head and along with the rest of the group held back not knowing what to expect. Robbie moved into the thicket of miniature pine, poplar and elm. Tangles of bramble bush made walking almost impossible. There was still enough green to help in camouflage. Heart pounding silence followed.

Waiting was worse than action. But waiting might save their lives.

Nick never could get used to Army life.

REALLY?

The floor of the hut was dirt. Hardened and brushed with pine branches. The vomit hit the floor and bounced six inches off in a splash followed by another bout of dry retching. Trying and trying but still not another kernel of corn. All wretch and no prize. The young native boy had come in the middle of the night. She was too sick to put up a fight. He was quick and left looking ashamed. *Maybe he won't be back,* she thought. She drifted off to sleep and had dreams of her daughter and son, rolling often in the night. After awhile she awoke and put two and two together, *Oh no!* Key realized her blood had not come for two moons.

Staring at herself in a bowl of water she looked into her eyes. This fact accompanied by the morning vomiting the last few days became warning bells that rocked her head. Was she really with child? It would have to be a Chipewyan father. Only the Northern Indians were with her for the last twelve moons. She would not let anyone know about this. She would just be sick after all. Maybe she would be real sick.

IVOR

Rage. An uncontrollable anger usually accompanied with a surge of restless energy. The first time Robbie felt this he experienced a loss of mindful things. The bread needed to be purchased, the hole in his spare sock needed mending and the girl in the picture all disappeared for this moment – this moment of possible fatal trauma. Certain brain processes were elevated such as being acutely aware of everything around you, every sight, sound and movement. A slow down of reality where it can seem you can think creatively and have time to react in a mannered way. A time of anxiety and fear that required mustering fierce boldness and rage to be let loose in a cacophony of energy. That was what Robbie was feeling and a monster he was to become.

The Indians approached not suspecting his vengeful explosion. Robbie was in a ten foot opening with a tree at his back. A warrior started to scream insults Robbie did not understand. A stream of vicious savagery was about to be unleashed. In his heart, Robbie felt a need to seek vengeance for the loss of his family. These unsuspecting warriors would know Robbie Wolfe's wrath.

Robbie leaped in three soft landing steps yelling a blood curling scream. Three warriors were slashed or gashed with his bayonet in an impressive display of riflemanship. The first was gashed in his lower stomach and fell immediately to Robbie's feet. A second was rifle butted unconscious with a vicious upward move that knocked the warrior's head back so fast he never knew what hit him. The third warrior was not so lucky. He ran past to get around and was stabbed deep in the lower back. Robbie ran back to his original position eight feet back in front of the tree.

He knew from his time with his wife's family that a tomahawk can cut a fine half inch gap in the flesh of a man easily two to four inches deep. If the blade is stone sharpened to a fine edge and wielded correctly it can slice through a torso and not get stuck in the enclosing flesh of the wound. Robbie wielded Noah's weapon with a menacing glare.

Another two warriors closed in. A two hander moved the three foot tomahawk in a wide circle cutting open the throat of Robbie's fourth victim. The resulting follow through cut deep into another man's forearm only to be stuck there temporarily till the man shook it off and started running off screaming and spilling blood everywhere.

Robbie had a few moments to gather himself. *Call up the troops? No, that would put them in danger,* he realised. There were maybe thirty more coming through the woods. Ten more were coming in a bunch. Robbie had no time to scream.

His smoothbore would be loud, alerting, blinding with thick, white smoke and make the air smell horrible. It just might buy him some time. Robbie hesitated. The warrior was one of the handsomest natives he had ever seen. Strong chiseled features, big jaw, nose, brow and a strong well developed body. With a youthful looking face that showed a large amount of intensity in his eyes he was confident until shocked and angered till saddened; it was almost too painful to fire. He had no choice. The blast hit the warrior and he fell a few inches in front of Robbie. They were both crying over such a waste of a young life. With the lead assailant down Robbie reloaded. He could fire off three rounds in about two minutes but he only had another forty-five seconds at best. The hammer was pulled back to half cock. The fine powder was trickled into the pan and the pan was closed. The rest of the powder poured down the barrel. The ball was placed with a bit of cloth down the barrel and a brass ramrod was pulled out from under the barrel and used to ram the propulsion into place. After refitting the rod Robbie pulled back the flint while raising the weapon all in one motion and was again able to inflict punishment from a distance. Robbie's shot hit a second warrior in the arm and a third in the face. Just glancing blows but limiting shots nonetheless. Both warriors would turn and retreat for recovery.

Robbie realized he was no longer scared. He had forgotten being afraid as he was executing a thrashing. The next mad warrior slipped and fell at Robbie's feet. Robbie stomped on the warrior's fingers that were holding an eight inch curved piece of sharp iron, making him release it. He then stomped on the man's head with his soldier's boot. Then kicked his hand again and then his head. That was all he had time for.

Three braves ran off far to his right probably going to sweep around and flank him from the rear. There was still the immediate danger of three more advancing braves whom had seen him leaping toward him. The first warrior pushed Robbie back with a spear into the side of the tree. Robbie was supported by what felt like a shoulder to correct his fall. A gentle shove put him back in place. Robbie shoved forward without looking around and got the large brave who tried to push him to the ground. A bayonet carved into the warrior's belly. He held the spear no more.

The next warrior was pierced much like how a pitchfork would grab a bale of hay. Robbie turned and saw to his surprise that the big soldier in a deerskin jacket he had noticed earlier, had picked up the next warrior in line with his rifle's dagger and was having trouble shaking off the big bird. The last attacker was right behind the speared lobster. The big soldier fired through the first hitting the one behind. The first warrior looked down at the smoke coming from his belly and up again in shock. His eyes wide and his mouth wider, no sound came out, only hissing air from his lungs.

"Thanks, mister. Don't think I would have recovered if I hit the ground; too many of them," Robbie smiled a big white-toothed smile at the big blond man dressed in deerskin and white cowboy hat. Robbie only came up to his shoulder.

"Not a problem. I am Ivor Jennings from Amsterdam. Pleased to meet you." They clasped forearms briefly.

"Explains it then. Viking blood. A big Dutchman," Robbie said out of the side of his mouth. He was watching for more aggressors.

"We dekken jullie."

"What?"

"I got you covered," Ivor Jennings boasted.

"Lot of English words originated from the Nederlanders like Hallo, Vaarwell and Blunderbuss/donderbus meaning pipe/tube box which shoots a bunch of small bore lead balls."

They continued to fire off two more rounds and one more native dropped and one other was definitely hit but continued on. All the rest escaped. The remaining Indians realized they were outgunned or against crazies worse than themselves and ran off.

"How did you join, enlist? Robbie asked.

"Impressment. I was working on a Dutch sailing vessel and the British seized everything and made us take an oath to the Crown. They were afraid the French would use the ship against them. Didn't mind really. Get to travel and meals are paid for and I get to shoot some wild savages. Beer and rum rations make it quite enjoyable."

The one warrior who Robbie knocked out started to come around and was being questioned now by Lieutenant Noonan. The troops arrived just in time to scare off the three braves who were attempting to flank Robbie and then secured the area.

"Private Murphy, Robbie you got to hear this. Fellow here speaks a bit of English. Seems they were following us to exact revenge on that dead one back at the fort. Two Athapascow tribesmen came on board and met some friends on shore and gathered others for their cause. Don't know how they got so far ahead of us. Didn't even see them leave the boat. Guess they jumped ship before we got here and scooted on ahead. Seems a few people want Robbie killed for something." The Lieutenant was fresh with excitement about having uncovered something.

"Ask him what happened to my wife!" Robbie retorted.

LEFT FOR DEAD

K ey knew that in northern areas where isolation, famine or weather were at the front of everyday existence, if a woman could not carry her own gear and her husband's, the stored food and the children then they would be left to fend for themselves. If they were old or could not feed themselves or were delirious or extremely ill they were left as well. Sometimes they were just too old. They would usually be left with a bit of water and food, enough for a few days. After that, fatigue would work on them till they would be so weak the wolves could eat them alive, a painful and shocking experience during such a personal moment of dying.

Key had never thought about what happened to them. It was a tradition and was just accepted. Key was very sick that morning. She showed no signs of childbearing yet and swallowed blood from a partridge that was saved for a sauce to calm her belly. Partridge blood came out of both sides of her mouth and drooled down her chin to the ground. She screamed and held her stomach in disbelief and defiance. She would not admit she was with child. She admitted only to a poisonous stomach ache and fever.

She did not clean the fish or do any of the chores and when it came time to move camp she just laid there. A few of the women began to talk of her illness. There was talk of leaving her behind. Key had no strength. Retching and retching she laid there in her stew. Food would not go down. She knew her strength and life depended on rising and eating some food. She could not move. She thought of that big young energetic warrior and knew.

WHAT HAPPENED TO MY WIFE?

In retaliation for killing that Indian at the fort?" The facts were registering with Robbie. This group of Athapascow braves were out to ambush Robbie and had been foiled from killing him. How did they know? Must have been rumors from the Sergeant at Fort Niagara. The two natives who boarded the boat in Niagara? Murphy? The body must have been found.

The captured warrior was one of the ugliest humans on the planet; fierce looking with heavy eyebrows and cuts all over his face.

"And my wife? Did he know her?" Robbie paced in a half circle around the man clearly intent on killing him.

After a bit of difficult communication and an argument Lieutenant Noonan's guide got his information.

"Seems like they did know her. When they kidnapped her she was given to a warrior. She was to serve him as his third wife. He took care of her. She returned his kindness by running away six months from when we kidnapped her. Said she could not live with a tribe that killed her family."

Robbie shook his head at the news. *She lost a dad, son, daughter and uncles and cousins. She had also lost her modesty after many abused her. My poor Key.* "Go on, what else?"

The guide and warrior talked as more information was exchanged. "When she had escaped after only two weeks of captivity she had gone to fetch her daughter who was hiding with a mid-wife. Her daughter and mid-wife friend were stabbed many times and their stomachs ripped open. Key was in shock and remained in total silence for a long time after that. It was only because of the beatings that she finally responded to doing chores."

Robbie could only imagine the horror of the vicious desecration.

After further back and forth translating the Lieutenant went on.

"After six months of captivity the tribe realized she was missing one day. They sent out a search party. They found her after she had been raped and then they saw her killed by white rebels."

They all heard huge weeping sounds from Lieutenant Noonan's left. Noonan put the wounded native under armed guard for his own protection.

ONE MORE TIME

Freezing, dehydration, starvation or vitamin deficiency would weaken you till the wolves were biting on numb and weakened limbs. The throat and stomach would be attacked next. They were big and strong and attacked in individual attempts till they sensed weakness and blood. Then it was everyone for themselves at getting a piece of the pie – a rip of an internal organ or flesh that would satisfy the hungry cunning canines. They would stay out of sight and wait.

The tribe marched away in groups. Everyone carried a heavy load. They were taking some of their tent supports for sledges and future huts. No one complained. The excited young Indian warrior who had beaten and raped Key continuously came up to her.

She was in morning sickness and had beads of sweat slide down her face. If this young warrior wanted her she could do nothing except hold her belly and rock back and forth to ease the pain. The boy dropped a deerskin water pouch beside her. He patted her head softly and left. He would be the last northern Indian she saw, for winter was fast approaching.

After a few hours night came and Key was sitting up beside a small fire she had made to try to keep warm. The tribe had ceased being heard for a long time. She was alone again. Isolated. Only this time she was with child, no doubt the young warrior's child. She wept for her lost family and dozed off.

In the brush, a young boy warrior came back for his one last time with her.

MOSES

It took over an hour to make the final trek to the fort. Upon arriving they were all questioned. The Governor of the Fort came into the Headquarters' cabin.

"Moses. Moses Norton.[6] I am in command here." He glanced across and picked out Robbie. In his interrogation on him he found out Robbie had a native wife who was presumed dead. The Governor was fuming. He did not allow any European or White man to fraternize with the native women. He himself was part native and part French. A Métis. Moses had six beautiful wives. He did not allow anyone to even glance at them without a fight.

Robbie thought, *This winter will be cold and long.*

Robbie was dismissed from his interrogation and went to find his barracks. On his way he spotted a group of natives who resembled the Dog-Ribbed tribe in appearance. Same light skin color and thin bodies. Robbie quickly started conversing with them in their native tongue. Robbie knew quite a few words and slang.

"Yes we know the story. A group of seventeen from another camp had journeyed out on a death walk and had been massacred. They walked to ten miles south of Clowey Lake to leave two elders to die. Two females and two children were in that group."

Robbie was certainly convinced of his loss now. "A baby daughter?"

There was no other information. The tribe did not go investigate because the territory was so hostile and there was so few of them. They never learned of this till many moons later.

---

6   Moses Norton was a Métis who was given power at the Prince of Wales Fort and resided there many years as a hard ruling Governor.

ONE LAST TIME

Before Key could react the young warrior was upon her. She tried to tell him she was with his child. He did not care to listen. He was convinced that she was left to die and that was that. If he had his way it did not matter. She was going to die anyway. She was still very beautiful even with the scars from the beatings. Her not too prominent brow, straight nose and subtle features came with a nicely proportioned small frame. This gave her quite an appealing petite look. One brief encounter with her and you were sure to be mesmerized and dreaming of being with her again. She would surely be missed.

It did not take many slaps for her to allow him to do his bidding. Afterwards, he beat her with a branch and she did not feel anything because she was unconscious from the first blow. With broken bones and bruises she lay in her blood weakened condition which substantially put a doubt on her ability to survive. Night came and the soft pat of paws on the snow were all about her.

OFF TO THE GOVERNOR'S

That evening everyone was into their rum ration to keep warm. Murphy was not there but everybody else grouped in the bunk house all bundled up and drinking. Ivor was extra jubilant and gave a good reason to drink beer, "Ya don't want me to get scurvy now would ya?"

As Robbie was watching, Nick pulled out a pocket watch. Robbie asked to examine the piece. The watch was his and it worked. "Where did you get this?"

Eventually it was sorted out and Robbie found out the Sarge had given Noah a watch to fix. Being a retired Jewish watch repairman the spring was rewound and the watch fixed easily. Nick gave Robbie the watch. More hugs and cheers blessed them all for the barracks was full on this winter's night and the ale was fine.

Robbie was handed a written message requesting his presence at the Governor's headquarters. Reluctantly Robbie threw off his blankets and got dressed.

"Off to the Governor's is it?" remarked the big Dutchman.

Robbie admired the big man and again thanked him for his help.

"Not a rescue, just help. Ass saving help though," he added.

"I think the Governor is going to give me one of his wives," Robbie chuckled.

Ivor Jennings raised his brows and added, "Find me one too would you?"

"If you do not get a woman I can line up a girl or two when we get to the Fort," Nick Sweeney said between slurps. They laughed. Robbie, Nick and Ivor had become good drinking buddies especially ever since

Nick was packing extra rum rations. Robbie grabbed his redcoat and headed out into the cold biting wind.

Walking behind the Governor's building would bring one to the front doors of the Headquarters' building. In the dark, Robbie did not see the four Indians approach. Robbie did not know Murphy gave drink to these four and told them of Robbie's murderous acts on their tribe. They sought revenge. All four were big and armed. The first native whacked Robbie right on the top of his head with a club, a staggering blow that knocked him to the ground. There was no time to recover before they all were punching and kicking him. His head was bouncing off the ground like a rubber ball. One of Robbie's eyes closed shut. And then there was nothing.

Robbie came back to consciousness and heard them talking. He knew some of what they were saying. He braced himself for another blow and spoke his question in Cree.

"My wife, what happened to her?"

One of the group turned and said, "You killed her husband, the one who looked after her before she ran off."

"What? Impossible. Who?"

"The brother you killed at the fort was your wife's man. She was given to him to look after her. You repay his duty with murder. And you shall be killed as well."

The realization started to sink in on Robbie. "Did the rebels kill her?"

"No one knows what happened to her. After she escaped they did a good look about. Killed by the environment, weather or the wolves got her. She would not have survived this long. The story about the rebels was only made up. We don't want a war with the white man or other tribes. They concocted a story about how this woman and a small family of travelers had succumbed to the beatings, rape and killing by traders who were white rebels. We trade at the fort. We did not want the governor angry with us because we trade furs with him. We did not want the Northern Indians or the white man to be upset with us. So it was decided to blame some rebels."

Robbie had his answers. The knife he had on him was still in his belt. Obviously, he was only out for an instant as they were still figuring out what to do with him. Scrambling to his feet he lunged with his dagger.

The first brave was caught off guard and looked only when he saw movement out of the corner of his eyes. It was too late. Robbie sunk the knife deep into the back of his neck. The blade stuck there.

Grabbing the club from the drunken native he slammed home a big hit to the next and the next opponent. The last started to run off. Robbie caught him with a push and he fell to his knees. The man struggling over a nest of cut branches snapped his knee as he went down in much noticeable pain. Out of breath from the exertion Robbie did no more damage. The three he felled were dead. The fourth would get his one day. For now he was immobilized.

Robbie saw the lamps were off at headquarters and no one was inside. Resigned, he limped back to barracks with a massive headache. Just another drunken brawl gotten out of hand they would say in the morning.

ONE WITH THE WOLVES

Ascratching at her legs drawing blood awoke Key. She was so beaten she could not stand. Her legs, swollen and blue from the attack of her aggressor, were now bleeding. A long claw scrape curved down her calf. Focusing she saw a furry blur jump back at her movement. To her right, a growl and a big show of teeth only a few feet from her head started to inch forward.

"Whooo!" she bellowed at the big wolf. Immediately it backed off a few feet and then to her surprise leaped at her. She had nothing but her deerskin water flask beside her. She threw it hitting him in mid-air. It was just enough for the big beast to falter off to the side and keep running. The first wolf in front of her growled and jumped forward grabbing her leg with clamped jaws. The wolf started to drag her by her leg. With all her might she kicked with the other foot hitting the nose of her killer.

Letting go, the wolf gave a high pitched shriek of pain that held its echo. Another wolf grabbed her loose tunic and pulled her onto her back. The third wolf had now changed direction and was watching the events. Whimpering and running the kicked wolf ran off out of sight. The wolf holding her tunic was surprised by Key's fight. She bear hugged the wolf and dug a finger into one of its eyes. Yelping and squirming, the fur flying, it attempted to run away. Enough was enough.

The wolves would return tomorrow night to feast on their supper, patience being the better part of valor. They scampered off into the dark, their fangs still white and their mouths still drooling. Key ripped a piece of cloth from her tattered clothing and dabbed at her fresh leg wound.

She was eventually able to stand with the help of a branch she found. She raised her head to the moonlight and tightened her throat. "Aauugh-oooo," she howled to the moon. "Aauugh-oooo," she repeated over and over. For she had become one with the wolves and the wilderness.

There was nothing more to fear.

EAVESDROPPING?

"Oh I have dreamed of your touch, you make me swoon. Take me." Lillian whispered to her mirror and to the person walking in her room. "Oh, Maggie, you scared me." Lillian blushed brightly.

"You must not talk too loud, they will think you are either loony or a ... a lady of the night," Maggie replied.

Lillian laughed in embarrassment.

"I am only practicing. I am still a virgin you know."

'Yes and your dreams are of the young and wild. Nice to be twenty." Maggie was forty and had been through a lot with Lillian.

"Let's make up the bed and go over your checklist for the party tomorrow. Your public announcement of the annulment of marriage based on it being unfulfilled is going to liven things up. Do you think every soldier in the Hudson Bay area will be crooning?"

"I wonder. Just the thought I am going to be throwing myself out to someone has me vibrating. My knees buckle thinking about actually being with a man. My stomach aches. I long for a man's touch ... Maggie? Is that so bad?"

At that the door closed and standing behind Maggie was Major Mallory.

"Hello Major. I see you have been eavesdropping again. I hope my private confidences have amused you. I am a wanting woman, Fred. But, I do not think you are enough of what I want. We will see. I must prepare for the socialite party. You are coming, Major? Major?

Flushed and flustered at her knowing he overheard her embarrassing outburst and showing no confidence at all, he looked at the floor tiles and said, "I will be there and be the first to ask if you would like

165

a drance. Uh! Ah, I'm sorry." He meant to say dance but did not have the courage to shout out his dreamed desires and just stood there with nothing else to say. He looked at her very briefly seeking pity, hoping she would come up to him and say everything was all right and that she was his. The thought of him actually having a real chance now that she had an announcement of an annulled marriage was extraordinary and he could not think with his heart racing so fast. He stared at her with lusting eyes, a look of unadorned want in them.

"A poor display, Major. Please, leave." She threw a cushion from the couch at the door after he closed it. Maggie looked on in wonder.

SON OF A GUN

Lil Wolf had travelled a lot further south. He never saw such a wonder as Niagara Falls and its thunderous water dropping hundreds of feet to a white broil of froth, a never ending magnitude of water pouring forever over the higher to lower landscape.

Lil Wolf got a job as a cabin boy aboard a ship sailing south. He was now nine years and four moons old this February of 1770. He was mature for his age. Having to undergo such hardship and trauma either destroyed you or made you strong. Lil Wolf was already showing signs of being a capable and energetic member of the crew. The lines were in and the crew was waiting for the last few sails to be set. The top masts would be lifted once manoeuvred to the Seneca River. Boston was where Lil Wolf was headed. He would figure directions out on the way. His father was to join the colonists there to barter for land and opportunity.

Son of a gun. I will do the same. Following his father's footsteps or intended footsteps he just hoped to find his father.

CONNEEQUESE

Robbie had one more group of Indians to talk to. The Northern Indians were arrogant and rude and always complaining about their deals at the fort, wanting more and crying of starvation or being treated unfairly. This group, he would approach cautiously. There was a tall thin white man with them. It seemed he was organizing them. Robbie approached the white man who seemed cocky and rude.

"Sergeant? I thought for sure you were walking around as a Private earlier?" He displayed mockery and arrogance.

"The Sergeant stripes and one and a half shillings extra per year. Just got 'em for going with you."

"Doubles the salary then."

"And a bit." Robbie admired his stripes for a bit. "Suicide missions are always more giving. Probably would have got at least a Lieutenancy if I went to Cuba with no commissions attached." Robbie waited for the man's reaction.

"Malaria and disease versus frozen, starved, death then. As a British Royal Explorer I am quite aware of both I'll have you know. I have extensive experience in ship warfare and in astronomy from my good friend William Wales.[7] I am known as a talented snowshoe enthusiast. I have survived tests out in this wilderness already. I have eaten just berries for days or nothing. I have learned to love venison and partridge. I have eaten raw fish or birds for survival as well. And most importantly, I have

---

7   William Wales majored in Astronomy and stayed at the Prince of Wales fort in 1768-9. He taught Hearne to use nautical equipment and the stars to calculate positioning. See footnote on Longitude under Author notes.

learned to survive in the wilderness probably better than anyone alive. I will not die Sergeant ...?"

"Robert. Robert Wolfe. One of the first families of settlers in Niagara."[8]

"Moses is upset I will not take his blood for scouting. Moses would get further acclaim."

Samuel Hearne[vi] favored the Northern Chipewyan's as guides over the Athabascan Cree.

"Bloody Hell! Conneequese[9] and his slave had run off with the bloody Quadrant[10] on an earlier attempt and had caused all the havoc to start and our immediate return. We would have died if we lost all that powder." All the indignities and frustration over the measuring device falling and shattering contributed to his outburst. Hearne was visibly upset at the failure of that expedition. He did show a determined will to succeed.

"There are no more openings for volunteers. Maybe on the next trip," he said.

"I, you mustn't. Please. You are passing by where my wife's family was camped and ambushed. I would like to inspect the massacre site."

Hearne thought for a moment. "You can wait outside the Fort. We always pick up stragglers along the way. You will not be officially recorded as being on this documented journey but I will get you clearance to go and it will be a journey of journeys. You may accompany us, Sergeant."

Hearne relayed a sympathetic gesture.

---

8   Surnames McGrath and MacDougall were recognized as the first settlers in Upper Acadia with large families near the Niagara and London (Lincoln) areas.

9   Conneequese was a real villain of a man. He was responsible for much hardship on Hearne's journeys and was blamed for the Quadrant mishap and did go missing.

10   See section titled Longitude in Author Notes.

AAU-OOO

Key awoke from her slumber and pushed back the piece of deer skin covering she had found and rose to the weak sunrise. She raised her head tightening her throat and started to howl again. "Aau-ooo, Aau-ooo-ooo." In the night, they would respond to her but for now she was just marking her space.

She held a piece of iron in her hand, a small piece that she had put in her hair for ornament. She put it between her knuckles and began to stalk for prey. She had no stores of food or firewood. She would not survive the winter with what she had. She would become a wolf; a hunter from a forager was a big leap.

COMING TO MARRY YOU

There was another task at hand. Robbie was looking into the lady-ship's quarters. Flowers and shrubbery, herbs and decorative plants adorned her entranceway. One of the soldiers had built a wood picket fence around her quarters. She had tiled the dirt floors and had applied ship paint everywhere. There were ribbons and bows tied to the small shrubs and a few oil lamps for evening light. Just her surroundings were intimidating to Robbie. He went to the small white gate and jumped over it. He was a good hurdler and a very fast runner – traits that were good for skirmish fighting. Robbie jumped over the railing of the porch and opened the door, he entered without a sound. The interior was gorgeous for a log cabin in 1770 on the coast of Hudson Bay.

There were two levels and elegance everywhere. Potted plants and painted decorations hung everywhere. Robbie did not know that this was a special social event. These decorations could have been everyday décor for all he knew. The ribbons gave away a possible festive event as did the sign 'Lillian's 2nd Socialite Gala party. Special Announcement night.'

"May I help you, Sergeant?" Maggie stood indignant at the unannounced newcomer. "You cannot come into a lady's quarters without permission. You were not even announced."

Scrambling for something to say Robbie blurted out, "I am searching for a lady. The lady in this picture. I have important news from afar. Most distressing news I am afraid." His battered look carried with it no credulity at all. Just a dusty windswept soldier at the doorstep. Maggie did notice his rugged good looks under the bruising and dirt.

"Wait here and I'll see if she can talk with you. Is it about her husband?" she inquired.

Robbie gave nothing away. "Please, I must see her," unable to hide his impatient desire to see the lovely sultress of the picture.

He was ashamed to admit his want of her when he was going to bury his dead family. She would not have seen her husband for longer than he had not seen his family. Almost three years since Robbie left coming up to the second of December 1770.

Robbie had dreamed of things to say to her. Advanced were his thoughts on what it would be like together because of his incessant machinations over her picture. Love would find a way. The good news about the money would surely win her over.

Robbie felt warm around his collar. Straightening up he saw her for the first time. Just like the picture she was a magnificent bundle of fresh and bouncy, young and energetic sparkle of joy. She bounced down the staircase with a smile and expectant eyes and was everything he imagined she would be.

A bit of natural blush about her cheeks, her femininity enhanced by how she held a weak wrist added to her appeal. "Madam Lillian Whiltshire. I am pleased to make your acquaintance. And you are …?" Her innocent curtsy unconsciously revealed a bit of generous cleavage.

Robbie was smitten. "Robbie Wolfe madam. Ah, madam, the times I have talked to your picture for inspiration for carrying on. The trouble your picture has gotten me into. Rebels thinking I was your husband and wanting to tar and feather me because I had your picture. Another beating by the Sergeant and his cronies for the discovery of the picture and thinking I stole it."

"Slow down, Sergeant. You speak to a picture of me? Where did you get it?" She grabbed it out of his hands.

She looked up with tears in her eyes. "This was for Ian. His eyes only. How did you get it? Have you word of him?" She got right into Robbie's face looking up at tall Robbie and her just over five foot frame tensed.

"I am sorry to bring you sad news. I was with your husband when he was shot in Niagara. He died heroically. He asked me to search you out. I looked at your picture every day and it gave me strength to carry on. I lost my only family to an Indian raid. I grieved for a few years and have come back to bury my dead family. I am sorry. I know it is not the time to let you know this – but I fell in love with your picture and that gave me strength to be here. I may have come with bad news but I also bring a promise of new love."

"What! Are you insane?" Lillian was bright red in the neck and her eyebrows were raised in total dismay.

"I am sorry, Lillian. I know I am assuming too much all at once." Sweat dripped from his forehead and Robbie grabbed the curtain behind him for steadiness.

Lillian started to walk in a circle passing the inner confines of the room shaking her head as if she had been taken for a fool.

What have I done? Robbie realized he had spoken too much too soon. "I have other information to tell. There is a delusional Sergeant who is coming to marry you. You must prepare for it." Robbie had to step back for room.

"I have heard enough. I will be leaving in two weeks for England. My family misses me. I am surrounded by handsome soldiers who want nothing more than to bed me. Get out! Get out before I call the guard!"

Robbie was shocked. Her reactions were certainly not what he had expected. Her reaction was nothing short of mean.

She continued, "Let me get this straight. You come here and tell me my husband was shot and killed. And then you have the audacity to tell me you are infatuated with my picture which shows my breasts in close up. You probably stole this picture in the first place. He would never have given you my picture. You villain – you probably killed him. Get out. Out!"

She raised her head and put her arms across her breasts and let out a gasp. After expunging a huge puff of air she allowed herself to be culled into his arms as he comforted her, his concern for her grief sincere. His hug around her shoulders was tender yet strong and warming.

"I am having a party here tonight, Sergeant, ah … Robbie?

"Robert Wolfe, one of the first born in Upper Acadia. I have to leave for a mission in two days. Tonight might be my only chance of seeing you again. I hope our paths are not going in separate directions. However, I fear they are. I have but just a few obligations that would take a year to complete. I would like to know that I could find you when I am an officer and gentleman."

She swooned at his kind and affectionate manner. A shudder went through her body like a chill or warm strength. She straightened her back lifting her two assets up below Robbie's chin in flirtatious coying.

"Tonight then, Sergeant. Tell them your name at the gate and your name will be on the register."

"Thank you madam. I know you make the wisest choices and I commend you on your willingness to take a chance. In a few days I will be heading out to possibly a starving or freezing death. The warmth we share can warm us both till we complete our obligations. Certainly trouble will not find us in the few hours before I go. Tonight then, I am honored." He bowed to the lady as he left, his usually short hair falling down in front of him.

RE-ENLIST

Robbie was beside himself with excitement again. *She* was what he wanted. Lillian was as he had hoped. Robbie still wanted to question the group of Northern Indians and he had to pack and be ready to leave by seven in the morning in two days. He would re-sign with the army in exchange for a bit of leave. He had done his mandatory training and would sign on for five more as a Sergeant. They allowed his job of escort for the Hearne journey to be included as part of his tour of duty. Things were so much more compliant in the barren north. Everything was simpler. Survival was at its heart. Bending the rules of regulation and circumventing other formal steps would not be beyond their interpretation of Army regulations.

FOOD

The flower arrangements were on the tables. Maggie gave Lillian a wink. Some choir members were assembling and creating a music area and musicians were practicing scales. Flutes going "Oh ah ah ah ah," penetrated the ear higher and higher in pitch and down again really fast. Penny whistles and flutes provided most of the dance and amusement. A Scottish piper would soon have everyone prancing to a Scottish reel. As the fiddlers began their warm-ups on Scottish jigs and reels the rum barrels were uncorked and spouted. The men laughed as if they did not have a care in the world. For most of the time it was difficult being a man in this day, a farmer, a soldier, a beggar, thief. Usually a poor immigrant hoping for land.

The journey alone would kill a lot of them. The hours each day spent on obtaining food and cutting trees for the next year's supply of firewood were numerous indeed. The lack of necessities created the hard work. This could only be justified after many years of hard work when one could sit back and postulate 'I am free, my own man.'

As someone had written, "A mind easily amused and abstracted from gloomy thoughts is a great enjoyment indeed. Most new settlers discover loneliness, a sinking feeling of the heart and a longing for potatoes and buttermilk from home. But as comforts increase, he becomes reconciled to his lot and finding his independence makes him happy and realizes that he really is in a paradise to himself."[11]

---

11   Quote from the Authentic Letters of Upper Canada. This book was an invaluable source of information giving detailed descriptions of the times, conditions, state of minds, needs and costs of coming to North America.

Cooking in the huge frying pans was savory pork, potatoes and vegetables known by the indiscriminate appellation as sace.[12] Plums, pickles and preserves rounded out the menu.

On the long table there was wine, spirits, raspberry jam, vinegar, tea and coffee. Almond milk, which is a good substitute for cream in coffee, was in three large pitchers. It would be good to remember substituting on any long voyages.

Water was boiled for the teatotallers. The French make great tea and coffee and French Canadians make them great too.

"Maypole or maple syrup is a sugar from sugar maple trees. They are not grown in England. Mix maypole with plums and heat to a paste. Makes a nice jam," one of the confectioners said. And a table full of Bamble pies[13] attracted a number of bees.

Potted flowers of red and orange marigolds adorned everywhere. Everything was set for a new romance to blossom. Lillian had placed a small amount of rouge on her lips. She ever so distracted continually looked around for her handsome messenger who seemed so charming and confident. Her heart would not stop pounding in her chest. *Is this what love is like?* she wondered.

A gentleman broke her daze, "Drink, madam?"

---

12   Sace: This was the name for a main dish of the times. Simmering in a pot all day would have been potatoes, pork and vegetables. Condiments such as pickles and preserves would round out the entrée, along with bread.

13   Bamble or Bumpkin Pie: apples, maypole, pinch or two of cloves, glass of whiskey, makes mighty good eating. However the Whiskey was like ditch water in the 1800's in Acadia.

BOSTON

Lil Wolf jumped off the wagon he hitched a ride on from the dock and finally made his way to the outskirts of Boston. Church spires popped out over the landscape of many shops and residences. Colorful flags were blowing in the wind. There must have been twenty thousand people. Lil Wolfe admired the many buildings with detailed ornamentation. The whole area was active with everyone doing some choir or job. Quite a difference from his home in the Arctic..

Lil Wolf walked up to the first man he had seen and sticking out his chest exclaimed,

I'm here for land and opportunity. I'm looking for my father. He was to get land. I want to do the same."

The startled man scratched his grey beard and thought a moment before replying,

"Well now around here you have to have money to buy land. You need a job to make money. Go see Mr. Mason down at city hall. He might still be there. Off you go. And tell him to get you a new pair of britches, those have plum worn off," the old worker said. It was a bit of a walk but one could traverse and see all of Boston in a few hours. Lil Wolf scurried off.

IN MOURNING

"Do not let any single person have thoughts that there might be single women available. There are about as many single women as there are spare boots here in North America. And that answer is none. On the other hand, the prospective female immigrant should expect to meet a gentleman within a few months and that is considered as being proper." The local parishioner tried to explain the natural order of things in America to a gathering.

Lillian sat in the corner her head down. She realized after announcing that her husband was dead she would need to be in mourning instead of being single and available with an annulled marriage. They would feel sorry for her.

The crowd went silent. With deference they shied away. Even Major Mallory was quiet and did not look at her, preferring to drink with the men. What she had done was announce her integration to a required or expected state of mourning. For this she would perform the proper etiquette of the time. All because she announced her husband's death instead of her eligibility. Oh! Further torture. Further setbacks in her desires. Where was Robbie? Did he stand her up? Was there no respite for this despairing little virgin?

SAUSAGES ANYONE?

Robbie packed and was ready to meet the band of explorers. Just as he was eyeing the gates of the Fort he spied those same Northern Indians who were with Hearne. Not knowing much Chipewyan, with its high bird-sounding gargle he did what he had to do.

"Ah-Hee?" It was a struggle communicating. The Northern Indians would just laugh and laugh the more they learned of the demise of his wife. He had to find out what they knew.

Robbie shook his head. A tear started the downpour. Crying while watching them laugh.

"Oh God, the pain and torture she must have endured," he wailed. This is the way of the barren north for humanity was tested to its limits here and there were few rules. The Indians laughed at his plight. It was one thing to be disheartened by his troubles but to laugh at him? There were a few of them watching him when he sprang into action. The closest loudmouth laughing piece of sheep turd got it first. Robbie threw a lunging punch to the temple and then kicked his groin as the man now rolled into a fetal position face down in the dirt, moaning loudly.

"Laugh now would you?" Robbie snorted.

Robbie hit the next one running with a haymaker that close lined him – cutting off his breathing temporarily. But then the rest circled him and started poking him with branches and throwing stones at him in a circle shoot. Two jumped on Robbie and were struggling to hold him down. Another was laughing. Robbie's ribs hurt and his old leg wound was hit, making the bones in his right calf ache in paralyzing pain.

"Cut open his intestines and feed them to him as he watches."

"Before we cut his throat open," chirped another. The hateful and mean warriors were in no mood for pity and wanted to make a quick end to it. Robbie could not understand. One of the Indians ran his hand across his lower belly and then mimed pulling out his intestines and then put his hand to Robbie's face as if he was handing over a string of sausages.

Just then someone stepped over him and said something. A very large native stood over Robbie. The gang went running off.

"M ... F. B. I."

After a moment Robbie started to respond, "Well I don't think—"

"M for Matonabbee. FBI for Faggan Big Indian," was all he said as he thumbed his chest.

This man was huge. The biggest Robbie had ever seen. Even his new friend Private Ivor Jennings was not as huge although about the same height. Ivor had an athletic lean body with big shoulders and a V back. Matonabbee was twice in width and stature. Sergeant Percival Devil was also big but he was accompanied by rolls of fat and his bigness came from hugely proportioned hands, forearms, chest, belly and rear. M was solid as a brick house.

Robbie squinted out of his good eye and tried to focus. *With this big lug I may never get to see another sunrise.* To his surprise the big man helped him up.

To his dismay, Robbie found out that this warrior was part of the northern tribes and was ambassador to all of these, declaring himself a leader of all northern native people. The Dog-Ribbed and Esquimaux were not included. Mostly the Chipewyans and a few northern Cree settlements. Matonnabbee was about to embark on a trek with this Mr. Samuel S. Hearne. A second objective would be diplomatic relations with new tribes he would meet. Join together and become strong was his motto. He claimed he wanted to unite the northern people and work as a group trading with the Fort instead of all the constant fighting.

"Thank you. They would have killed me. Thank you again," Robbie pressed together his swollen lips.

EATING SQUIRREL

"May I walk you home Lillian?" The old Captain of the Guard offered. Six very intoxicated people were resting at the last active table. Most of the guests were off to their prospective beds. Others had passed out where they sat or lay. Major Mallory was snoring quite loudly in the hall and if someone had not rolled him over I swear Lillian was going to kick him hard. Six guests remained awake including Lillian.

"No, Captain. It is just a short walk. Tomorrow I must mourn. Mourn for a love I never had." Lillian was at a loss of how her situation had changed. *Well at least I don't have to face the Major. What an obnoxious drunk!* Certainly he would need taming. He would continue his flirtations soon with a pinch here and a pinch there. And then maybe, just maybe she would give in and surprise him. *Imagine him if I just kissed him,* she giggled. She did not regard the Major bold enough to get her attention and to be actually quite boring. He did have a respectable means of survival, was considerate and somewhat kind. *Oh where is Robbie?*

At that thought she rose from the table of old men. They all loved her. She walked around the building to the outhouse to complete her nightly chore of getting ready for bed. It was dark and at the back where she could not be guarded or seen. She would use the back entrance to avoid the old men's watchful eyes and in tears and sadness she would return to her quarters an old maid, leaving the behemoth of a party to broil down at the Headquarters building.

Lovely Lillian mastered the corner, her wine-filled bladder ready to burst. And to her surprise she saw a dark figure hiding in the brush. Her heart was thumping. A drunken native or soldier. *Oh god, I hope he's not going to instigate something.* She was very afraid of the drunken prowlers and of being molested. There were so many stories. She hurried past the unmoving figure leaning against a log. She hurried on and was about her business. Robbie was asleep, his bruises swelling.

When she came out she saw his hair and recognized him. "Robbie, you stood me up. Where were you? Was it too much for you to come and see me? Not even a note?" Then she looked more closely and saw his swollen eye and lip. He was starting to come to and struggled to talk.

"Quite a lovely dinner table. I helped myself earlier. No one saw me." Robbie admitted.

"No Robbie, I haven't eaten. I thought you were not coming." She reached out and held his jacket open and saw blood stains. "You're hurt, come inside and I will look after you. Quickly, we mustn't be seen."

Inside, Robbie lay on a floor mat and groaned as Lillian helped him remove his outer clothes. She inspected him where he instructed and cleaned up his wounds, gently dabbing with a damp towel.

"I did not think you were coming. I had given up. I'm a mourner now. Not single and available Robbie. You know that? Can you believe that?"

Robbie relaxed in her care, wincing only as she wiped some blood off a tender area of flesh. Definitely his ribs were sore and one calf. His swollen eye seemed to respond to her placing a tuft of snow against his face.

"I was an Acadian Ranger, looking for southern land. I ended up becoming a British soldier after being beaten when the Sergeant found your picture and thought I had stolen it from your deceased husband." Robbie winced as she cleaned a gash on his arm.

When the rebels saw your picture they confirmed me as a Lieutenant and not a civilian and said you were so British looking that I had to be a Brit to have a girlfriend that looked like you. I was beaten twice and had a near death experience by tar and feathering – all because of your picture. I constantly thought of you. I promised your husband before he died that I would find you and bring you your inheritance letter.

"I too have lost family. I am widowed too. I thought you would need sympathy as I. I'm an idiot when it comes to love. I ..."

They both stared at each other.

Lillian broke the silence. "Look, you are wild, Sergeant. I am high society. I like high society social parties, talk of politics, world affairs. You live in the wild as a soldier. You are just as happy sleeping in a tent or rolled up in a blanket against a tree. I, on the other hand, would demand luxury. I have been educated in piano and theatre. I will buy pheasant and will have a French cook to baste and spice. You ..." She was still a woman with a bit of wealth even without her husband's money.

"Still can't get used to eating squirrels though." Robbie stopped her with that and they both laughed.

Robbie's smile showed his straight white teeth. "I've never gotten used to the inch thick rolls of tobacco that colors most men's teeth. Nor the awful cigar smell that comes with it. Chewing tobacco and snuff are also taboo for me."

Lillian closed her mouth and smiled, pulling back her lips which were thick and rouged and showed her perfectly straight white teeth. She looked Robbie up and down stopping, at his hands and noting the cleanliness of his nails and the strong rugged texture of his hands.

"You are handsome under the dirt. Maybe you could make a good stable hand," she chided. Lillian pinched his cheek lightly. "Where did you get your scar?" she finally questioned.

Robbie looked at his small letter 's' just below his shirt line under his right collarbone and replied, "Hit with a cattle prod in exchange for my life I guess."

Brushing off the topic Robbie compared high-strung Lillian to his usually reserved and stoic deceased wife. Lillian did show a lot of confidence and spirit though.

"Your presence here shows your adventurous spirit. The lifestyle here is definitely different. Everyone from the Governor to the housewife pitches in. No one is beneath picking up a shovel or joining a bee[vii] to raise a barn," Robbie informed her.

"I can assure you I can do just about anything any woman in Upper Acadia can boast. I will adjust," she said disdainfully. "My status requires an officer's position for marriage."

"I will make an officer. I will do more than they ask," Robbie promised. He glanced up at what she was wearing. A most beautiful low cut gown with lace and a bodice and colors. The bottom of her dress was now soaked in mud. Obviously, when she was tending to Robbie's wounds she knelt in the mud and never said anything.

"Sorry about your dress, Lilly," he smiled while trying to press his lips together.

"Looks like we both need to scrub up. Maggie has been preparing hot water for a bath for the last hour before midnight. Ever had a bath, Mr. Wolfe? A hot bath?"

Robbie stood up slowly, wincing as he put pressure on his twice wounded leg. They continued back to her interior rooms avoiding any windows in case they were seen.

On the way, Lillian spoke up. "You listen to the colonists. May I call you Robbie?"

"To be sure! Most do, thank you. So you feel the demonstrations in Boston have merit do you?" Robbie said. "They have the right to have representation if they pay tax. What should be done with the money and how fairly it is collected should be discussed. Instead, a new tax is levied as soon as the British can think one up. What for?"

"The British have need of large funds, Sergeant," Lillian was showing her inbred heritage.

"What for? Louis XV, Cuba, India, Spain, Portugal? What about expansion in Niagara, Quebec and here in the northern wilderness? So far, the Hudson's Bay Company has not fulfilled its obligations of further exploration. That is why Hearne's journey is funded. They have to be communicative in coming up with new taxes. Not just say 'here is the Paper Tax, the Tea tax.' How about standing up to tyranny and imposed magistrates? It is the voice of reason objecting because England is so removed from America they do what they want and get away with it. Quite the contrary here, where British rule remains prevalent and in numbers."

"It is true the British government keeps borrowing and borrowing. They will never have enough to assist us." Lillian was getting into the American spirit. "It is lovely enough in Acadia, land of opportunity."

They entered the room containing the bathtub and change area just as Maggie was going to fetch another bucket of water.

"Oh! You startled me, Lillian. See you have a late night visitor. I'll be fetching your clothes and clean them up Sergeant. I'll bring towels. I put your red evening robe out with your wool sleepies!"

"Yes that will do. And one other thing. Do not mention we are here. If you know what I mean?" Lillian shifted uncomfortably.

Maggie turned her head away from Robbie to conceal a smile and a wink to Lillian as she walked away with the water bucket.

MR. MASON

I am almost twelve." Ten-year-old Lil Wolf defended his claim of age and demanded to be enrolled in the American forces. "I claim independent citizenship in America. To hell with the Brits."

"Well now lad we do not have a separate country down here. Not yet anyway. Philadelphia alone has many British supporters and we have only been meeting for a while. We have no regiments or government but we have ideas. And boys with strong wills like you we want. I will send you into Boston to observe the British movement and see what new type of taxes the Brits are putting on the table. Any information can be useful. We shall become independent if they continue to try and rule us with no regard to our rights. I'm talking too much. Now off with you. I will give you a name to report to in Boston before you head out. See the kitchen and fetch some vittles first. And ask the lady there to give you a new set of clothes and to burn yours."

Mr. Mason[14] was an intelligent man full of ideas. It helped that he was wealthy and had a group of intelligent people to discuss political developments with. *A democracy,* Lil Wolf thought, *for the people by the people.*

---

14 Mr. George Mason was instrumental in starting the State of Tennessee.

PAYBACKS

I don't think so," Robbie was reacting to placing his hand in the bath water and found it pretty hot.

"Yes, Mr. Robbie. Here is a towel and you place your clothes there. I will have your jacket cleaned and brushed. Nothing like a clean and well outfitted soldier. When you are done call me." Lillian walked over to the partition and stopped at Robbie's comment.

"This water is used!"

"Yes. My water from earlier. It is still a whole lot cleaner than you. If you promise to soak for twenty minutes I won't use a scrub brush on you." Lillian almost broke out in laughter on that comment as she turned away.

Lillian was still dressed in her mud-soaked dress. She grabbed the night clothes she was to wear and placed them at the end of the couch where she could reach them from behind the partition. She walked behind the barricade to strip off and observe.

She discretely watched the bloodied and muddy Sergeant strip down, after having some trouble with a sock and balance before finally managing to get a leg into the tub.

"I usually bathe from a bucket or in a stream or any cold water location. This is simply amazing and so soothing," he commented from the steaming tub.

Maggie walked in unannounced and Robbie created a big splash submersing himself in a hurry with a muttered curse. Maggie roared with laughter. Standing beside the tub she poured the bucket of water she was carrying over Robbie and he, red-faced accepted the punishment and slid under the bubbles. Maggie took this opportunity to grab his clothes and scoot out the door.

Robbie knew he had been duped. His clothes were gone. *Fine, I will do the same to Lilly.* He quietly snuck out of the tub and tiptoed over to her clothes pile on the couch and grabbed them and hid them behind the tub. Adjusting a small mirror he then snuck back into the refreshing warm water. Robbie waited. The ends of his fingers were going wrinkly.

After Lillian had pulled off and thrown her apparel toward the door for Maggie to pick up she sat and brushed her hair and used perfumed oil on her skin. There was a partition separating from where she dressed and the bathtub, which put her just out of sight.

"You will feel so much better Robbie once you're clean. Was that Maggie? Maggie?" The door closed loud enough to hear. "I will give her the rest of the night off."

"She has already left." Robbie stood in the tub and tried to reach his towel.

Maggie came in with some men's dark pants and white shirt. Another curse and splash.

"Mister Wolfe, here is something to wear till morning. Then I shall personally return your clothes mended and cleaned."

"Oh I guess it is not maid's night off?" Lillian giggled, aware of Robbie's predicament.

"Oh yes dear, I am weary. Thank you. Goodnight then." Maggie left.

Robbie was not facing Lillian when she sneaked behind him and stole his freshly laid clothes. Paybacks could work both ways.

Lillian after returning to her position came out again from the front and wrapped in a towel squealed, "My clothes, they are *gone!*" She was standing where Robbie could see her. He was already wrapped in his towel and looking around unbelieving.

"I swear I saw her put down some clothes right here. You stole my clothes too?"

They both laughed. Lillian could see through the cracks in the partition wall and Robbie could see in his mirror. Both childish pranks but the same joke. Still chuckling, Rob reached down behind the tub and handed out her clothes. Lillian pushed her clothes off to the side.

"Robbie, hug me. I need you," she pleaded.

"Your image consumes my soul, my aching thoughts," Robbie confessed.

She whispered against his lips, "Robbie, my body is yours, take me."

He held her close and their foreheads touched. Their eyes met. Lost in desire they kissed, arousing them further. Moving to the couch in between kisses they dropped their towels and resumed their touching and exploring and asking what each other liked and got lost in the episode of love. A final climax to the night was hours away as dawn approached.

INHERITANCE

A breeze of cold air woke them both as they lay naked and shivering. After pulling over a warm wool blanket they cuddled and kissed. Lillian laughed and was at last feeling truly a woman. She purred in his arms showing her pleasure.

Robbie was a splendid gentleman. He got up and got her clothes bundle and put on his freshly washed and folded clothes. Maggie must have come back later that night. They both squirmed at that thought.

He left her alone to sponge bathe and dress with Maggie's help. Lillian put on a most seductive garment that only partially concealed her body. A most fitting sort of garb that was a tight-waisted dress in a light muslin material, concealing yet revealing shadows in appearance. Maggie installed a *pannier* – a whalebone cone under her dress to fluff out her gown and highlight her corseted waist. Her flat and muscled waist did not need a corset; French fashion dictated her apparel. The front neckline laced appropriately in a 'u' shape revealing pressed cleavage fourteen inches across. The length of her dress went to just below her knees on a cross angle so that one side went down to her ankle. An evening or casual night dress a woman might wear if in silk.

She could see that Robbie loved it. Every little thing she did her man appreciated. It was like every move she made a rose petal would fall and adorn everything around with tenderness, happiness and contentment. She never knew love could be like this.

Having breakfast in the room two days before Robbie had to head out was tense. In the confines of her room they would not be discovered. Maggie brought in ham and some leftover potatoes, and rice cakes.

Maypole syrup covered them. Sipping French coffee Robbie confessed his story.

"At our first meeting, I told you that there is a Sergeant who is coming here and he wants to marry you for your money. You need to be prepared for his arrival as I will not be here."

"What in the devil for? How would he even know me?"

"He saw your picture and borrowed it for awhile."

"For money? What money? I have some but not a lot."

"Your inheritance. He wants to embezzle you."

"What inheritance? You gave him my picture?"

Robbie shrugged his shoulders and then dropped them letting out a pained gasp. Explaining everything he could recollect he tried to calm her down. Robbie explained about when he was talking to her picture and the Sarge caught him with his pants down and admitted it sounded strange. He continued on telling her about how he got the picture back from the evil Sarge, omitting Hahaya and her struggles.

The Inheritance Authorization letter from Lieutenant Ian Whiltshire, her deceased husband, and the Sergeant Percival Devil slash Horace Wartnabbee's evil plan to extort money from her by marriage or extortion was detailed. A woman of the day had no rights to inheritance, property or money if she was married. It was part of her dowry when she married. If she married Percival she would lose her inheritance. But the Sergeant had the authorization letter. A situation was developing.

Robbie had signed up for Hearne's third expedition. He would now leave on the seventh, one day after Hearne marched out on expedition. It was December 5th, 1770.

If the Sergeant did not show up in the next few days she would be on her own to deal with him till his return, which might take a year or more. It also meant she stayed in the Canadas.

"You lost my inheritance letter? You're conspiring with I don't know who. I'll call the guards. How dare you withhold this? You seduced me. How much do you want?" Indignantly, Lillian threw down her fork and moved to the window trying to let everything sink in.

"I'm really super rich?" She sqeaked in a high-pitched voice.

"Beyond your imagination. But only if we can get that letter. If the Sergeant comes after I am gone hire an armed escort. Be careful though.

If the Sergeant is aware that you do not come alone he threatened to eat the letter."

Robbie didn't know the Sergeant had arrived at the fort much earlier and had been out doing firewood collection for the last few weeks. The Sergeant and his sidekick Corporal Freeman were together scheming over the plans again. Murphy was at the Fort but just stayed out of the limelight. Like Robbie, Ivor, Nick and Lieutenant Noonan, Murphy had only been at the Fort a few days. Murphy had left early this morning compass in hand. He had left to mark off a meeting area for the Sergeant and Lillian. The fight was on.

Robbie left for inspection and vowed to revisit her at eight that night. She would keep dinner warm. They still had much to talk over.

BOSTON MASSACRE

*T*he Boston Massacre, known as the Incident on King Street by the British, occurred March 5, 1770, where British Army soldiers killed five civilian men and injured six others. British troops had been stationed in Boston the capital of the Province of Massachusetts Bay since 1768 in order to protect and support crown-appointed colonial officials attempting to enforce unpopular Parliamentary legislation, specifically the Townsend Act. Amid ongoing tense relations between the population and the soldiers, a mob formed around a British sentry, who was subjected to verbal abuse and harassment. He was eventually supported by eight additional soldiers, who were subjected to verbal threats and thrown objects. They fired into the crowd without orders, instantly killing three people and wounding others. Two more people died later of wounds sustained in the incident.

The crowd eventually dispersed after Acting Governor Thomas Hutchinson promised an inquiry, but reformed the next day, prompting the withdrawal of the troops to Castle Island. Eight soldiers, one officer, and four civilians were arrested and charged with murder. Defended by the lawyer and future American President, John Adams, six of the soldiers were acquitted while the other two were convicted of manslaughter and given reduced sentences. The sentence that the men guilty of manslaughter received was a branding on their hands. Depictions, reports, and propaganda about the event, notably the colored engraving produced by Paul Revere further heightened tensions throughout the Thirteen Colonies. The event is widely viewed as foreshadowing the outbreak of the American Revolutionary War five years later.

"Jesus, Joseph and Mary! They fired on us!" someone shouted in terror. Lil Wolf was in the front of the crowd because he was small and had squeezed past everyone. Lil Wolf could not believe things had got so far out of hand. A moment ago a single redcoat was discussing politics and taxation with a gathering of colonists. When the discussion got heated more British soldiers formed to total eight and, with four Loyalist civilians and an officer, held back the baying crowd.

Lil Wolf could feel the tension in the air and the soldiers looked nervous. One of the civilians with the soldiers was in charge of collecting some of the British tax. A piece of garbage flung at the redcoats splattered refuse on them. *This is really not going to end well,* Lil Wolf thought. Sure enough, one of the soldiers, indignant and protective of British authority, fired an unauthorized musket shot. Two more soldiers fired in reaction and well-dressed men with obvious wealth and influence fell. Crispus Attucks a runaway slave was first to be killed. Lil Wolf ran away as fast as his legs would carry him.

The crowd doubled in size the following day, Lil Wolf reported to Mr. Mason, and forced a British retreat.

THE JEALOUS MAJOR

Alone, Lillian came to the realization that she must wait for Sergeant Devil. She had to report to him or he would eat the letter. She must delay him for a year or more till Robbie got back. She must get a hold of the inheritance authorization papers. She looked down at her hands, which were shaking and clammy.

"I hate you, Lillian! I knew something was up. I can tell." Major Mallory was livid. "I know I was drunk last night but my men kept filling my mug. There is no one more sorry than I, today," he finished lamely.

Taking a more aggressive stance, he demanded, "Are you being courted by another man? There is something different about you and I want to know what is going on."

Lillian did not have the experience to thwart his questions. She could not talk to him straight with all her problems broiling in her head. She did not want to divulge her whims either nor hurt Fred's feelings. "I am … I am in mourning. I am sorry, Fred but I must have a year to grieve the brutal death of my husband."

There was an extra coldness to the morning chill and neither spoke again. Both rushed off with duties, his to his soldiering and hers to her patient wait for the unknown devil of a Sergeant, Sergeant Percival Devil.

TOWNSHEND ACT

*H*aving the Townshend *Act* repealed was what they wanted. *R*epresentation was what they demanded. *F*air treatment was paramount.

At the end of the critical moments of unauthorized indecision the British Governor Thomas Hutchinson promised an inquiry, which dispersed the crowd. Paul Revere commissioned an engraving plate of the horrible historic event where colonists first stood up to the British authority. Lil Wolf was learning first hand some of the problems in the American colonies.

SARGE IS BACK FROM WOOD GATHERING

As luck would have it Sergeant Percival Devil and a group of soldiers struggled into Prince of Wales Fort with sleigh and oxen. At least three full cords of firewood were ready for stacking. The Sarge came in, saw Robbie and came right up to him.

"Ya got it all wrong. I wants to marry her I does." The Sergeant attempted to sound sincere and all.

"You're an evil man, Sergeant. She doesn't want you."

"Oh, put a cork in it," the Sergeant retorted.

Smack and whack and Robbie was down. He didn't know what hit him. The crew put a moribund Robbie in a bundle of gear to be shipped out with Hearne on the sixth. It was still the fifth of December. He would wake up to a big surprise. If he woke up.

DIPLOMACY

Before Lil Wolf turned east to Boston he dropped in on a group of businessmen and merchants. They were called democratic organizers. Mr. Mason was presiding and they were noisily discussing the latest taxes. His voice was heard over the crowd.

"The Stamp Tax is too corrupt."

"Sons of Liberty in Boston!" shouted another.

"Nobody paid duty on the Molasses Tax. Nobody paid the higher Sugar Tax. The Sugar Act was repealed and replaced with the Revenue Act of 1766, which reduced the tax to one penny per gallon on molasses imports, British or foreign. They try to trick us with a lot lesser tax so we will start to pay."

Products covered by stamp acts included playing cards, patent medicines, checks, mortgages, contracts and newspapers. The items often had to be physically stamped at approved government offices before being dispersed and only after payment of the duty.

"No taxation without representation," the chanters grumbled.

One man stood and held up his hand for silence. "We have no representation in the British government. It is a denial of our rights as Englishmen. They've made no attempt to sit down and discuss our concerns."

Another jumped up, "They think too highly of themselves to allow the riffraff of American colonies to have any serious opinion and thus any proper representation."

"Respect our ancestral heritage and accept British rule without question is their stance," said another. "Maybe in India or Spain but not in America where the land gives freedom for hard work. Land that makes men honest and proud and patriotic to themselves. Men with common hardships making a bond. Well hogwash to them. Times are about to change! They'll have no one but themselves to blame when we fight for our independence!"

A cheer went up as the men stood and clapped each other on the back.

Lil Wolf had asked around about his father. Word went out for the young boy because he was well liked. Word would spread with word of mouth by travellers; horse-drawn wagons making deliveries would have inquiry notes included with the mail. Someone had carrier pigeons and two of the birds went west and returned home with their messages. The search was on.

I'M GETTING MARRIED
IN THE MORNING

Lillian had no chance. That same day Corporal Maxwell Freeman simply overpowered her into submission. Lillian was young, athletic and had a powerful physique but her short height proved she was no match. She was easily shoved around and submitted as soon as he slapped her hard across her cheek.

"You're coming with me. I need to take you to the Sergeant, you wench." Maxwell responded to her errant kick to his midsection. It would do no good. Maggie was off with her captors and everyone was busy preparing for Hearne's Expedition. No one would see him take Lillian away tonight.

It was already going dark.

One mile out from the fort at the compass settings agreed upon Sergeant Percival Devil stepped out from hiding. A crock of ice-covered trees, bush and rock hid him till the last moment. Both Maxwell and Lillian's horses were startled. The Mustangs were from the Assiniboine, a Manitoba tribe that ventured east for adventure and trade, Hahaya Wehaya's tribe.

"Madam Lillian Whiltshire, I presume." He held out his hand to assist her down from her saddle. The *pannier* had been discarded and she sat side saddle with a fair amount of leg showing. Her bonnet once tied so carefully was tilted and she looked in disarray at the rough treatment and the difficult journey in this wilderness. One of her cheeks was red and puffy. She looked on with a stern set to her face and slid down to the ground with the Sergeant hugging her around the hips to prevent an ankle sprain. Her gown rose to a height that revealed way too much.

Percival breathed faster, eying her up and down as spittle drooled out of his mouth. He pulled out a half picture she recognized immediately as the other half to her miniature pencil drawing. Percival had the flowers half. Her bosom was relegated to Robbie's copy that lay on her dresser. She directed her question point blank.

"Where is my inheritance letter, Sergeant Devil?" She tried to sound composed and in control.

Percival laughed, spraying spittle in her face. She turned away in disgust.

"You won't be returning home, ma'am. Maxwell you will have to dispose of her when I am done." He started to undo his belt. He cuffed her behind the ear with his outstretched palm, sniggering at her angry look of defiance. His big right hand grabbed at her breast barely missing, making her lose her balance. He pushed her to the ground, his belly suffocating her with his weight. His mouth hovered over her face. He started to kiss her cheek. She couldn't breathe and almost succumbed, passing in and out. He lifted himself to one side and kept his hand on her neck, firmly holding her in place.

"Corporal Max and Private Murphy are next. They want to give you some exercise," the Sergeant grunted.

Lillian had never been subjugated to rough treatment. Being brought up in a high society all-girl school and being protected all her life she crumbled. She always had a fear of irrational men. There were so many drunken Indians and soldiers about the Fort.

"What do you want? My inheritance?"

"That will do my lady. I shall marry you and we will live rich ever after. You will do my bidding or die here and now. I love you. I craved your picture. I kissed it every day till Robbie took it. Here—"

He held out a gold button from her husband's jacket. "A keepsake for you. I took this off your husband's jacket when we threw him in the death cart." His lie unnoticed, he pulled out the inheritance letter and held it out in his hand.

Lillian having received further news of her husband's death just closed her eyes and wept quietly, waiting for him to do his bidding. Nothing was happening. He was just staring at her waiting for her reply. *I must stay alive until Robbie can get to me. He'll be home for dinner by eight tonight before he leaves on the seventh – forty-eight hours before he is gone for a year or more. Maybe only twenty hours to find him before the wedding and ...*

"Very well. If you allow me to announce you tonight in the dance hall things would be appropriate. I need a husband. Take me back, let me refresh and we can re-join at eight thirty tonight."

"We be getting married tomorrow afternoon then. That should allow enough time to get a clergyman. There is one in every town." The Sergeant was taking no chances and acting as if a light just turned on, "The Governor will do it."

Swindle her out of her money. She had no choice. He refolded and patted the letter and put it back into his back pocket.

"Uh, twenty hours before I am married," the incumbent virgin lamented.

The Sarge, all enlightened, helped her up and they headed back to the fort. Percival could not believe his luck. Turning to his rejected mates he said, "You can have the native girl when we catch her."

That night after announcing to the few patricians of the dance hall her engagement and quick marriage plans she went to her room to prepare for the next day. All Lillian wanted to do was crawl into bed and sleep. But first she would cry. She saw no escape and did not think she could keep it all together for the torture to come.

Maggie was livid.

"She doesn't know what she is doing," Maggie gasped in amazement. "And Robbie didn't show, which has only added to the poor girl's distress."

Robbie was still unconscious in a pile of supply bags.

MINOR PENALTIES GIVEN

Lil Wolf, sporting a new pair of brown wool britches and boots and an off white shirt, was getting his information.

"Lil Wolf, did you hear the news? Bloody soldiers got off." Mr. Mason was with a group of organizers. The news had just come in. Six soldiers got off. The remaining two soldiers and four civilians got off lightly, a simple branding on their hands to show their involvement.

"I know if I was accused of shooting a soldier I would get hanged probably before the trial." Lil Wolf's informant threw a piece of apple core out of the window. Lil Wolf thanked him and went to see his contact in south Boston.

"Things ain't finished yet. More trouble will be brewing. Lil Wolf, we are going to need good communication here. Make this place your home and make friends. You can still stay at the Mason's farm when you visit. Your job will be to keep a tab on developments and report back to me. Be our ears and eyes. Refer to the men of Boston as the Sons of Liberty. His contact was one of the Sons of Liberty.

LILLIAN'S EMBRACE

The next morning Robbie woke up with a sore head. He had slept really well. He cracked his neck to ease the pressure. How long had he slept? Lillian? He realized with a jolt that he was cold and seemed to be somewhere near the docks. He could hear the water close by. Staggering to his feet, he tried to remember the events of the previous day.

"I thought it might have been you Sergeant. I guess I was wrong." Major Mallory looked downhearted upon Robbie's return to the Barracks. If his head had hung any lower it could have been used to sweep the floor.

Robbie knew something was up. "Major, may I ask what's going on, sir?"

"Lillian is to be married in the afternoon to Sergeant Percival Devil," the Major spat out. "It was a very sudden announcement for a woman who just informed me she was in mourning for a year."

Robbie noticed her quarters were well guarded. He saw Murphy at the front gate. No doubt Maxwell would have the back entrance. The Sergeant Devil could be having his way with Lillian right now. Robbie tried to think. He had his Sergeant stripes. That should get him through the gate. Robbie marched right at him.

"Murphy, stand down, Private." Robbie had walked up and ordered. Murphy did not move.

"Got me orders, Sergeant Wolfe. No one allowed in. Security before the big high society weddin' and all." Private Jim Murphy pointed his rifle at Robbie's midsection.

Robbie's reaction surprised even him. He grabbed the rifle and yanked Murphy on top of him. This time Robbie, with reserve to think, punched the heel of his right hand into the nose of Murphy as they went down. The musket didn't go off. Either it wasn't loaded or it misfired. No one was the wiser. The scuffle was not brought to anyone's attention yet.

Murphy was blinded by watery eyes but still held his rifle with both hands. Robbie was learning the hard way about hand to hand combat. Murphy recovered fast. The rifle butt came up quickly.

He's got me, Robbie thought, leaning back as far as he could while still holding the barrel of the bayoneted musket. Robbie slid his right leg behind Private Jim Murphy's forward leg. A subtle movement forward and an Indian leg throw flipped Murphy over and exposed his flailing head. Robbie wasted no time in subduing one of his major menaces. Bloody mouthed and with a crushed nose, Murphy lifted his head for the last time that day. Robbie's final blow hit him so hard in the jaw Murphy's mouth lay slack and out of position. Robbie winced at his damage.

With time running out he leaped up the steps in two strides. Inside the hall entrance Robbie could hear screaming. It was Lillian. Sparing no haste he entered the room just as the Sergeant had her partially naked and held up against the wall in his arms. He was just about to heave her onto his huge stomach for support when he heard her scream with a scratchy voice "Robbie, *help!*"

Turning to see his attacker, Sergeant Percival roared for the intrusion as spittle sprayed in a line from his mouth across the room. Just in time to save her, Robbie recalled Percival drooled whenever he sniffed Lillian's picture.

Robbie took in the scene and tried to think. *He's so big and covered in blubber. How to hurt him? Certainly he cannot be pushed from his feet. And if he grabs me with them sausage fingers I won't be getting away.*

Sarge: A dreadful rogue

SAME RANK

D amn you!" Lillian grabbed at the top of the big Sergeant's hair. He had a curly bush of it like his beard. Trying to hold him from turning his head she really did not know what she was doing. He dropped her to the floor and she went down hard on her rear. Her legs went up in the air. Her spine hit the corner of the doorway and she screamed in pain. Lillian kicked out with her legs, hitting air.

Robbie was not quick enough. The big Sergeant Percival Devil could now exact revenge on him. He took a step forward, widened his arms as if to swallow him. Robbie rushed in. At the last minute Robbie darted right and slammed into the wall. The diversion only stopped briefly the Sergeant's puffy and massive big left hand from grabbing a bunch of cloth and skin in a tight grip. Squirming, Robbie hauled back.

"I can hit you now Percy. I am the same rank." At that, Percival glanced at Robbie's coat sleeve allowing just enough time for Robbie to slide out of the sleeve and escape the tiger grip. The big bugger guffawed and shook his head up and down. No man had beaten him – Robbie was his. Kill him and say he was a jealous lover who was willing to risk his life foolishly. Everyone knew of Lillian and Percival's unbelievable wedding plans.

Robbie looked at the hardened dirt floor. Would his instincts save him? *I am in extreme danger here. God help me.*

WIFE'S DISCOVERY

The caribou were being herded by a group of men and women walking them into a large V-shaped entrapment area. They were making loud whooping sounds and scraping brush on the ground to keep the nervous animals moving. Prior to the hunt, the men made a thirty foot horizontal V of tree limbs and branches. The young boys were flinging arrow after arrow into the panic with their mouths watering, anticipating the fine meat to come. Some of the deer got caught in entanglements. Traps would be hung. The animals would get snared and on the other end of the rope would be a heavy log or a long thick branch. That would stop the prey long enough to be shot.

The Dog-Ribbed hunters were far from home when they found Kiwidinok. She just lay there in disbelief. These were her people.

LATRINE DUTY

Robbie was able to get a few quick and direct punches to Percival's head. After about four hits, Percival let Robbie go and took a step back appearing briefly stunned. Robbie reached out and swung hard with a haymaker. Percival was not that hurt and responded by taking the jolt of the blow and then grabbing Robbie by the neck and tightening. Percival's arms athough thick were of short length. Robbie was able to exact the same stranglehold with his left hand. Both landed a few blows but both were unable to breathe and were losing energy. Robbie hit out with his boot. Percival responded by squeezing harder than Robbie thought possible. The day darkened. The cause was not clear. The tiredness came and their lights dimmed.

"Out like a candle flame in a breeze. That is how we found you both." Major Mallory was trying to figure out and explain what happened at the same time. He pulled out a one inch roll of tobacco, stuffed some into a pipe and struck a contemplative pose.

"It appears you both pounded away at each other till you both passed out by strangling each other." Percival was coming around. They both had bloodied faces and swollen eyes along with bruising at the neck.

"Arrest that man," Robbie shouted in a hoarse whisper. "He has been trying to extort money from our dear Lillian. Quickly bind him. And get that inheritance letter from his back pocket before he can destroy it." Robbie coughed, his throat raw.

Lillian composed and dressed had scurried out and got the Major and a detail of guards to cover the situation. She grabbed the letter as the Sarge rolled over to get himself up. She had her letter. *Dear husband.*

Dear Robbie. Dear Major Fred Mallory. Dear Grandpa Whiltshire. Dear Acadia!

It turned out to be a grand day. The Sarge was too groggy to put up any further resistance. With his plans in disarray all he said was, "Ya threw me under a horse cart, ya did."

Corporal Freeman and Private Murphy were scuttled up too. They would be doing time in the brig and digging and refilling the latrine trenches as their duty for most of their stay. Time spent filling in the smelly trenches using dirt from a new trench beside it. As soon as one started working the heavy breathing would suck in the foul stench of decay.

Lillian's spine was okay. She had a bruise on her arm but showed no effect from her abuse. Robbie would recover and would meet lovely Lillian for dinner later that day after the Hearne mission headed out. Major Mallory while walking off was all smiles. He left the red rouge mark on his cheek for his pals to notice back at the bar. Puffing his pipe he hummed a jig tune that stuck in his head from the pipers earlier in the week.

REPORT FOR DUTY

Robbie gathered his belongings and reported in for duty. This morning's march was cancelled because of today's expedition. No one needed any more snowshoeing practice. Down south, horses were cheap at about sixty pounds for a good stable pony and saddle. Up here though, snowshoe and sleigh and canoe were the common modes of travel. The cannon were being brushed off for the big send-off of Samuel Hearne, the first great white explorer who would perform the honorable task of covering vast miles of northern barren lands on snowshoe as high up the latitude lines as the Arctic. Robbie, with the final day off, rushed to Lillian's side.

THE END

Dinner was wonderful. If you want me to kiss you later do not give me any more bamble pie – I am punching out at the shirt buttons." Rob was stuffed to the gizzard.

It did not take long for them to resume their lovemaking. Her hero had saved her and would now be rewarded. Love was in the air. They spent the evening and night in passion, getting up twice to eat dinner and then again for some leftover ham and some plums. Maggie came in once. Showing her soft side and relief after the ordeal she brought them both some wine, bread and a fresh water jug. The latter part of the night the lovebirds had slept in loving splendour, blissfully unaware of their separating ways to come.

The next morning seemed tense. Robbie was packing his gear. Lillian was heating some leftovers on the pot stove and was absent minded, having had little sleep and an energetic night. He had said she was the best lover he ever had. She smiled. Even though jealous she still wanted to know if she was up to his standards.

"I leave today." Robbie said over breakfast. "I have to catch up to Samuel Hearne outside the fort. Hearne's Journey will take over a year. I do not expect you to wait."

"I have a fortune to collect in England. Come with me."

"I will not be able to cancel. They will arrest me and take my stripes. I seek an officer's position. Even you told me I needed that."

Lillian lowered her head in thought. She had covered herself in a robe and was to bathe and dress before the day's duties would call. Walking over to the cold bath water she swiped her hand hard across the top spraying water in a big wave at the space in front of her.

"Money is the most important thing. I must return to England. We do not have much in common. I do love the high society life in England. My family will receive me and I shall spend my time with loving family in a high lifestyle. You want this country. I have had enough. I will return home." If he did not want to stay with her and go to England and live with wealth then she did not want him.

"Go on your stupid journey. I won't stop you," she challenged. Lillian was hurt. Not just because he would not follow her, which was impossible, but also because of the realization of the probable end of their romance.

At that, Robbie held her hand and they both cried forehead to forehead. What was to become of them? She would go back to England and he would return in a year and she would not be there. Alone.

"Can you not forget the money? You have a dowry and some of the major's salary. More than enough for a new start here." Robbie tilted up her chin. "One would only need one hundred pounds to secure and clear land and buy what is necessary like oxen and yoke, some tools and pay for the help in raising a barn and cabin. A cabin could be put up by eight men in thirty days at fifty pence per day per man. In two months even the inside would be done.

"Oh, what am I thinking?" Robbie shook his head. "This is no place for a woman alone."

The sun was low on the horizon. There would be no full daylight for another moon at least. Winter winds crossed the land and entered every crack. Even through the cabin walls a chill could be felt right to the bone. Robbie did not explain what he wanted her to do. Lillian did not see him off.

HEARNE'S THIRD EXPEDITION

Everything arranged to perfection the next day the expedition members did meet without too much agitation. So on December 7, 1770 the gang of Samuel Hearne, his guide Matonabbee and his six wives plus his one young twelve-year-old and a few scouts carrying supplies met up with Robbie and lit out for the Coppermine River to search for copper and possibly discover a northwest passage to the Orient.

To be used as ballast for the return trip home, copper had few viable uses at the time. The Royal Navy had tried sheathing the hulls of some of its ships to protect them from the corroding effects of salt water but with little success.

Hearne certainly broke the boredom of survival up a bit. His attitude was so snobbish and rude. He thought he was better than everyone. He expected the Northern Indians to be his slaves. Carry this and that. But they showed him. They went ahead as hunters and killed all the game. The ones who carried dragged up behind went hungry, including the white man Samuel Hearne.

They were a long way out when they finally ran out of game and dried venison. If one was to record the events following they would have been empty if food or dinners were to be itemized. For five days they ate nothing but frozen bark and dried frozen berry stems except on one of those days a partridge was killed, one that did not give everyone even a mouthful. Hearne did not get any and was pouting.

They endured the cold and snow. Only Matonabbee and Hearne had tents. The others were never invited in there. One day the winter storm covered it all. They only had their sledges as a one sided shelter and stayed huddled together from the biting wind and bone chilling cold. They did not have time or materials to construct any proper shelter as the storm hit suddenly. The sledges had the few branches used up. Where they were at there was only barren ground and a few pines and poplar; pelting snow blinded their vision past a few feet.

Well M, also known as Matonabbee was sitting with his wives in his tent all cozy like and eating. It was quite out of their power to make a fire, which even in the finest weather could only be made out of moss as they were near one hundred miles from any woods.

They endured and made it to within ten or twelve miles south of Clowey Lake. Matonabbee took Robbie aside. Matonabbee knew where the massacre site was and promised to show Robbie when they were close to Clowey Lake.

One day he came to Robbie, "It is time. We shall take a day and go to the burial site."

At that Matonabbee and Robbie set off on snowshoes a short distance to the massacre site of his family. Robbie was jumpy and edgy. His nerves were getting to him. *How can I endure this?* He cut out the mental images in his mind. Clearing his head he tried to keep up to the great M. A toenail fell off from this trek and his foot was very painful the rest of the way. In his mind he thanked the man in charge, Samuel Hearne for his leave of absence.

LIVE THE LIFE I WANTED

The dust was a continual problem in cabin life. Dirt floors could be stomped on till solid and swept clean. Maggie worked furiously wiping down the walls, shelves and table. Lillian was going on about how much money was rumored to be in her husband's inheritance. She was authorized to receive it all.

There would be legal squabbles with cousins, uncles and aunts. The courts would tie up things for years in legal wrangling. Lawyers had to get their share. She would be given a tidy lump sum and income checks every month till things were settled. She would buy one of the Duchess' country homes and entertain guests every day.

After not much thought she turned to Maggie, "We shall sail on the first ship out next year. We will be home in two months if the winds are favorable."

"What about Robbie?" Maggie stopped cleaning. She could not bear to look at Lillian.

Caught in Robbie's rejection, she turned it around.

"I have a new life now with responsibilities, Maggie. Money. Enough to live the life I have always wanted." Lillian's mind was set and she went about picking out what she would take with her. With her letter concealed in her carrying bag she needed no other possessions except some clothing and some food for survival. She would buy new whatever she needed once she was there. Wait till Aunt Adelaide saw her. She would be so surprised.

RAISE THE STAKES – SCALPING

Scalping: Slice a six inch semi-circle across the top of the forehead. Dig deep enough, about one inch so that the scalper can get three fingertips into the incision. Grab with your free hand and push with the other hand down his nose or jaw if he is dead or unconscious. It only takes about thirty seconds to do. A small snippet of skin or hair stuck to the remaining scalp may need to be cut to speed up the job. Slice, pull and tear.

It really can slow up the advancement of troops when they had killed many enemy for they had to endure the wait as the natives would spend extra time scalping, beyond the usual looting.

Most of the time the victims were still alive being just grabbed or clubbed or knifed into submission. While hearing the killer's shrill scream would make your back quiver, your head was secured in a head-lock position so that you could not move and the pain would be horrible and the terror of the realization of what was happening unbearable. The forehead and scalp bleed profusely. The loss of blood and immediate infections would kill him in days if not hours.

The French's Iroquoians had a history of ambush, whack, swoosh, scream and scalp. Most tribes were confrontational and liked to revel after an attack. When a Dog-Ribbed Indian Chief went out in the dark to be sick and relieve himself he made a nervous young man of fifteen shake in great joy and garner much respect from his friends. The boy, a native Southern Indian would take his first scalp ever and his first of the day as well. For one Indian sweep of the leg put the man face down into his own vomit. And then he struck with this wicked L-shaped war club held with two hands, which came ferociously down onto the elderly victim's head. With one heathen blow he stopped the heart forever – the father of Robbie's wife. The blow only grazed his head and shoulder but the shock and age factor took its toll for his wife's father was now dead. The wise elder who was listened to by many for all his experiences at survival would be sorely missed. His word was followed because he was usually right and his blood had ruled the tribe.

There are facts proving that the native tribes liked to have an advantage when they attacked. If they could outnumber their adversaries it would be best. Attacking in the dark while the opponents slept was a ravaging strategy that worked well. They did not know the group of Dog-Ribbed Indians were mostly old people on a death march to leave their elders for dead. They did not know until every last one they could find was butchered.

MASSACRE SITE

I f he was able to find her bones it would be too late to cover them with rocks. The wolves would have eaten the carcasses and the bones and clothing would be scattered. Possibly the freezing weather would retain a lot of flesh for identifying. *What if they were wrong and the wolves were low in number that year?* Robbie mused.

He had a new mission to accomplish, to seek the remains of his wife, children and family and bury them and send their spirits to the Gods. He planned on saying a prayer to her Sky God and Wolf Mother and one to the Lord for her father and mother. It was quite a few years since he had said a prayer. *Will I recognize the foul lumps of death?*

Approaching the approximate area the ground was frozen as it would be most of the year. A few months of thaw, if at all. There were still noticeable marks of travelers from the past. Possibly marks from his wife's tribal march of death. Robbie shuddered. Looking around he did not see clear traces which led anywhere. Matonabbee suggested trying further west and south. It could not be far.

Scalping: Sometimes included with the act of scalping, the cutting and mutilation of tongue, ears, intestines and sexual organs was performed and often the specimens bagged in leather pouches for later display. The scalp was always treasured.

Relief was finally felt when they found an old campfire and then saw the desecration. All the family was strewn out where they had been resting before the attack. All had their scalps removed and their bodies stripped and mutilated. The wolves must have not travelled this far. The cold kept everything intact. The stakes were raised.

"Help me set a fire and then we will bury the destruction." Robbie talked as if in a trance. Matonabbee held his gaze and nodded his head slightly in acceptance. Being a leader and chief of the Northern Indians he was not used to taking orders. He just responded with picking up a few pieces of dry wood and set about making it warmer. Both were quiet. They both were thinking of the destruction and sadness that had taken place, something so common in the barren north.

Matonabbee, the great leader, was raised at the fort when his parents died and learned English and the white man's ways. He was the greatest diplomat and explorer of Indian lore. He risked his life going to other tribes and nations to bring them together as one, going into unknown and hostile territory to meet the nation's leaders and befriend them. Many times threatened and often in a small tussle he survived and went on more than one journey to meet these people. A true brave soul.

They warmed by the fire and Matonabbee offered, "Count the bones of the bodies. We will know how many are here. There should be how many?" Matonabbee questioned.

Robbie blinked and stopped looking at the images in the fire. His son's face reflected in the reddened burning elm had him frown with an open mouth, his jaw sagging in remorse.

"I think seventeen."

All the bodies were scalped. Some were burnt, defaced or disembowelled. Most held together from the extreme cold, decaying just to the ripeness of producing nausea.

"The site will be called the Forgotten Burial Site. No longer the misfortunate name of Massacre site that I have seen here. No longer will I speak of this. It is done. Your Indian way is cruel," Robbie said.

"No different than white man's suffering and tendencies. Your history has many examples of man's evil that is beyond my thinking and power. Count the bodies of the adults and children. I shall gather rocks to cover them. Hurry before it gets any darker." The sun was below the horizon this far north.

Robbie was counting the bodies. He recognized the similar appearance in his tribe's dress. Then he spotted them. There was a slight woman's garb and bones and a baby's bones together. His wife and a daughter he had never known. It did not register on Robbie. He continued counting and not till he was done did he return and see the wooden and human hair little doll Key's father made. They all had them at one time. This was his daughter Ayashe's. He learned of her name from the Dog natives he had talked to at Prince of Wales Fort. Ironically these dolls were to ward off evil and to ward off scalping.

"I am sure. There are no bones of any other smaller persons, only adult bodies." Robbie was confused and in a poor state.

"Then we must look around. They dragged him off and then killed him. He would not be far. Your son would be young and naive and caught easily in his sleep," Matonabbee encouraged.

After doing a scout about they found no other traces. They came to one other conclusion. Seventeen out marching. Boy missing. Sixteen bodies left right? No, fifteen adult bodies and one baby. The mid-wife must have been taken slave. She was still nursing and they would want to keep her for food or novelty.

"It is possible your son escaped but at such a young age of eight he would perish."

They finished their work and spread out the sticks on the fire to let it die down and in the cover of darkness started their trek back to Hearne's expedition. They did not talk for a long while. The weather was excruciatingly troublesome. A freeze came about from the north and covered everything in ice making for terribly slippery conditions and slowing their progress. The icicles on the stunted trees were pretty but also became dangerous daggers from the sky.

DIPLOMATIC MISSION

It was not just kindness that brought Matonabbee out to help Robbie. Matonabbee was a mediator for all the northern native tribes. With Governor Moses' blessing, Matonnabbee declaring himself Chief knew of a tribe close by he wanted to approach. He approached the one hundred huts with Athapascan and a few words of English.

"We claim all land. We do not need excuses, our hunting parties go far and wide. There has been a shortage of deer this winter," the elder told Matonabbee.

Trying to bring peace to the tribes was a dangerous and difficult task. "Tell them of the fur trading at Hudson Bay. They will also take your wampum and give you food in exchange," Matonabbee advised.

Robbie's sore toe was blistering even worse after he was made to follow Matonabbee on his diplomatic job. This was certainly a hostile group. White man Robbie was kidnapped and taken to a man's tent. As Matonabbee struggled with their acceptance he decided enough was enough.

He went into the tent and pulled Robbie out. "Enough I am leaving. And I am taking my slave with me."

"So now I am a slave?" Robbie said, chagrined. Matonabbee stood his full six foot five and spread out his wide frame.

"You can take me now or let me go. I am big and strong. It will take three or four to take me down. Three or four will get hurt. Or, you can let us go and I will return again with a few more trinkets of iron for you to consider the thoughts of trading and joining all the bands together. Strong we will become."

His boasts did not go well with the chief who would prefer segregated individual authorities instead. At that, Matonabbee and limping Robbie exited rather quickly back to the burial ground and then in the direction of the expedition's encampment.

A short ways out from Hearne's crew Matonabbee wanted to set up camp and eat. After eating M said he had more to say.

"I know where your wife was left. I was the one who found her in her isolation after her internment with the south natives. She was left for dead after one year with us. She had the morning sickness. I think she was with child."

Robbie was beside himself. "Why did you not tell me of this before?

"I saved your life. You will not kill me now," Matonabbee said and smiled.

Robbie relaxed his shoulders a bit and tore off a bit of flesh from a piece of rabbit they had captured earlier and cooked. The sky was overcast and his eyes were doing funny things with the sparkling snow, giving him temporary snow blindness. His eyes usually dry from the cold wind were wet and sore. He could smell the smoke from the fire and his nose dripped when it usually would have been dried up by the smoking flames.

"Everyone lusted after her. The camp was changed after she arrived. All she talked about was her daughter getting killed and of her family massacre from before that. She was a survivor, no doubt about that." Matonabbee tilted his head slightly looking up to the smoke of the fire and smiled. His thoughts were of his time he had with her. He did not tell Robbie.

"I can show you where she was left and you can look for her remains. There is a chance your wife is alive. As for your son we only found out now his bones are missing. You don't suppose …?"

"Let me get this straight. After she was ambushed she was taken captive and that woman's bones with my daughter would have been the mid-wife Layna. She spent six months with the Cree then six months, no, over two years in isolation and then one year with you and the Northern Indians. That is why the Northern Indians at the Fort did not say anything. They were in on it. They were the same men who wrestled over her for many nights." Robbie shook his head in new understanding.

"She was left with nothing in the middle of the winter. She would not survive. She had no food, water or provisions."

A wee ray of hope showed in Robbie's eyes. He breathed quickly out of his nostrils in a huff. There was more to this madness. More to this horrible trip of discovery.

Matonabbee told Robbie about how on the first few nights he was not participating in the orgy involving Key. There were many young warriors that Matonabbee with his size could have defeated for his turn at the new woman. Instead, in his older age he sat with one of his wives. Matonabbee told how his wife had chided him in front of others about not being able to even take care of his own wives. Matonabbee explained he was prone to violent fits of temper, one time stabbing a man who complained over being homesick for his wife after M had stolen her a few days before. One of M's wives embarrassed him so badly he had lashed out and pounced on her, inflicting serious injury. She succumbed to those injuries a few days later. The whole thing a rather odd mess. Everyone at the camp was smitten with Key's influence. Even he admitted he was influenced only in a different way.

"Why did you not tell me all this?" Robbie was shaking his head in disbelief.

"I was waiting for the right time. Before, you might have killed me. You must stop your revenge now that you have buried the dead. It is not good for your thoughts. It blocks the soul from peace. You plan on killing them all? Even if you did your soul will not rest well. Your health will not be even. Your thoughts will consume you. Conflict is the native way. Accept that life is not always fair. And here things go on. You are one of the lucky to know what happens after a kidnapping. Be content on burying your dead and console your soul."

Matonabbee pulled out a roll of tobacco. He ripped it apart and mixed it with some leaves of herbs and jammed the black tarry goo into his peace pipe and signaled Robbie to sit beside him. Robbie complied and smoked the pipe with his companion.

Matonabbee continued with some repetition and emphasis. He found her. She had been isolated for two years and two months. Never seen a man in that time. They kept her alive instead of killing her because she knew a lot of their language. They took her back to the camp and took turns wrestling for her. She would know many score of young warriors on that first night. She was beaten a lot. She got sick and was left to die. She had no food, shelter or weapons. She was not eating anyway. Maybe no water was left. She would have lasted only one night or two at the most. There seemed to be many wolves around camp. A small ray of hope kindled in Robbie's heart. *She could not have gone far. I might find her bones.*

ESQUIMAUX

In search we came across twenty unsuspecting Inuit. This Esquimaux killing became known as the Bloody Falls Massacre. It was here an Inuit young girl grabbed the white man Hearne's leg. She died begging for mercy. Hearne was so upset the Northern Indians were querying him to see if he wanted an Eskimo wife. Samuel Hearne was visibly shaken and never seemed the same after that.

At Copper River we found it was not navigable. A four pound lump of copper is all that was found. There were just too many years of pilferage.

There was no northwest passage found to the Orient. Over two hundred and fifty thousand square miles were observed and recorded over frozen water and terrain. Vast areas of uninhabitable wilderness were charted in nothing but bitter cold and starving conditions.

Legends were made of the atrocities and unbearable hardships on the human condition. Unbearable inhumanities, unrelenting unbearable weather and famine beyond anything known. Hearne also lost toenails on his return trip to the Prince of Wales Fort. Even though this journey would discover no copper at the rumoured Copper deposit and no Northwest Passage to the Orient his achievements of survival in uncharted territory in terrible life-threatening circumstances would in themselves be regarded as remarkable and his written memoirs a fascinating read on human endurance and survival. His drawings and descriptions of newly discovered wildlife and fauna were met with equal joy and astonishment.

"We will regroup at the fort, get supplies and go look for your wife's remains, which are not far from the fort off the Hudson. Bury her with rock. Everything will be frozen so we will not be able to dig. We will find her body." Matonabbee stood and made ready to continue the journey home.

THE STORM

On day two aboard a ship headed for England, Major Mallory came down with the worst of fevers. No one knew if he had the cholera or not. He was quarantined on a lower deck. At least no one had to hear him retching anymore. He put up little struggle. The food had gone bad by the first week and what was left was stolen.

Meanwhile, Lillian enjoyed the Captain's refreshment of wine and berry juice. There was no ice but the glasses were put in a pail of snow to cool and frost. The beverage soothed the throat and warmed the belly. The tingling rush of alcohol reaching from the loins to the fingertips gave her a rush that spun her head.

"Enough of that, sir. Maggie will have to carry me if I drink another of those." She smiled the most mischievous smile at the Captain of the tall ship that was sailing them to Britain.

About three and a half weeks into the travels during a luxurious dinner for only the captain's paying guests, Major Fred Mallory came out looking rather well. One could tell he had lost some weight but the necessary rest had taken away the weariness in his face and the absence of tobacco and alcohol surely helped. Maybe it was from want of some tobacco that gave him that craving look he showed all of the time. That look was missing and replaced with a most brave smile.

In his most chipper voice he asked, "What's for supper? I'm starved." The Major smiled from ear to ear. With a motherly touch she had him sit and put his head on her lap while she fed him pieces of hard cheese she had in her pocket. The ship's buns were pushed before them. They were watching for another beetle to crawl out from the opened crust. No one dared to take the first bite.

"Seems there are worse things than squirrel." The others did not pick up on her private joke.

"You are a true friend, Lillian. My heart is still yours." Fred Mallory looked at her with weeping eyes.

Lillian Whiltshire wondered what Major Mallory would do once he controlled her money. Marriage would do that. He had so much maturing to do. And that awful tobacco and his drinking! Would he be worth it? It was just then that the Major started his little pinching game. If he pinched you he got to do it again. If you stopped him he said he would not try again. Then he would pinch Maggie's behind and she would giggle.

Then, while pretending to be preoccupied with Maggie he would quickly lean in and pinch Lillian in the nipple very hard. It would hurt and hers were especially sensitive and no matter how she covered her bosom he would still find some of the half inch tip. She admitted his grin was cute but he had to progress beyond his childish ways of trying to get attention. Maybe she should make the move to bring him up to her idea of a relationship. Bring him up past a level of a friend and actually let him have the satisfaction of kissing her. He would be rough.

"It would be like kissing my brother. I don't think ..." Lillian blurted it out too quickly and no one understood what she was babbling about. She remained quiet and kept on the alert for Mallory's creeping fingers. She fought back with a wicked pinch to his cleavers and she heard him gasp in pain as he rolled over.

The sun came out briefly before the clouds closed in and then the rain turned to snow and light became dark and no one knew where the wind came from. The ship started heaving to and fro. It was time to bunk down for the night.

"Tomorrow then Major, goodnight." Lillian leaned on Maggie and they disappeared into the corridor of the ship late into the night. The Major followed in a slow stagger in his recovery.

OLD FRIEND

On the journey back to the fort, the natives were eager to get back to their wives and their comfort. The pace was quick.

On one such meal stop Hearne in his typical sarcastic way said, "And the raw fish was as little relished by my southern companions as myself." He was commenting on having to eat raw fish as there was no wood or moss to burn.

It was unbelievable. There ahead on our journey was the golden fleece, the emerald and gold glittered blue French jacket. British racism was big against all French. There was plenty of reason for it. The two had a history of marauding each other's shores. Louis XV's wars were costly affairs. A natural hatred was instilled in the army as well as their sons and daughters.

Robbie advanced quickly through the small pines and willows. Holding position he dropped to one knee and fired off three rounds. Scattering were two Iroquois probably in Louisiana by now. The Frenchman had no such luck. He fell back against a small pine and hit the ground, his back hitting with a thud. Robbie approached the man who had escaped him in the ambush while he was on his first patrol. He couldn't believe his eyes. He recognized this man as his childhood neighbour who lived on the next farm over.

"I was recovering from injury for five long months. While mending for another four I assembled a force of Iroquois from some who nursed me back to health," The dying man wheezed.

"Montcalm is dead. Quebec was taken ten years ago and Niagara just before that," Robbie informed him. News didn't travel fast but it did travel.

"I know. We are scouting for food and wealth. Maybe find a French settlement. We have been lost for a while."

Robbie's friend held up his hand full of thick blood. His belly pumped out quite a rush of it.

"I am so sorry," Robbie was beyond grief. He was overtaken with regret. He didn't even realize his childhood friend was French. They had schooling together with Robbie's mother. They often ran off together when they wanted to skip chores. Cholera and Pox swept the land and there was nowhere to escape to. The diseases took their toll and moved on. Robbie had moved north after losing his family. The gravestones told the tale. Many complete families of various ages were etched side by side. Even though the first Census[15] in Acadia registered some 3215 non-native people in 1667, in 1767 it was easy to lose touch when there were no communication systems other than mail packet. And most journeys were long treks to other settlements. Robbie knelt and was saying a prayer, wanting to reverse the course of events.

"Next time, look before you shoot. Hello and goodbye old friend."

At that he keeled over and let out a last gasp of air and stanching spittle.

Robbie had killed the man in the golden French jacket. In so doing he killed his childhood friend.

"This is so senseless fighting over politics. Europe should leave North America alone. There is enough land here for everyone. Everyone knew both sides could be ruthless and bloodthirsty. Revenge and abduction were common themes among the scribes recording the history. Robbie added another feather to his cap, another knife stab deep into his heart. He tried to cry but the loss of his wife and now an old friend overwhelmed him. He returned to the troops with the ornate jacket.

---

15 The first Census was actually done in 1667. Native people were not counted.

MAJOR MAKES A MOVE

"No. The answer is no, Major. I am tired. Please, do not persist in this."

The quite bashful and polite young gentleman was trying to get into their cabin. Maggie was listening inside behind the door. After a few rash words and in his weakened state he apologized and said he was still sick and delirious. He had thought she wanted him to follow her. He hoped to kiss her in the shadows. Lillian thought of life with her aunts and cousins. She thought of waiting for the Major to come around to her and making a home for them. Was he to spoil it in one evening?

HEARNE'S CELEBRATION

The agony of a bowel problem that ended in death was a painful experience indeed. Governor Moses Norton succumbed to his affliction after weeks of suffering. He was such a jealous man that when one of his six wives was being comforted by a Lieutenant by holding her hand he noticed and in his almost dying breath cursed his revenge on both of them as soon as he was feeling better. Such was the man who held control over so many lives. During his tenure he was not past using poison to ward off jealous husbands or controlling fathers. There was not much love lost over his departure. The Fort would be under new leadership. A job Hearne had an eye for. He would be most suited for the job.

Many knew of Hearne's travels by now. Many wanted to meet the strange white man who could not understand we did not want to do his bidding. No one wants to change their ways. He expected us to jump to his orders. We laughed when he suffered, a native scout had stated. Samuel Hearne was in shape and his thin stature and strong will and need for few nutrients on his travels bid him right to be the first explorer to traverse north of the Arctic Circle. Most outstanding was his ability to cover such vast distances by snowshoe, sleigh and on foot. A lot of his geographical measurements were inaccurate due to many factors not created by him. It must be noted that at the time one of the greatest preponderances was the scientific dilemma of finding a way to measure longitude.[viii]

Other considerations to be deliberated and be sympathized with was the realization that many measurements were from hearsay. It meant relying on encounters with natives from which to calculate some of the distances across a lake or a measurement from an incalculable altitude. Certain areas one could not reach and were best left alone and judged.

Hearne traversed over five thousand miles, (8,000 km) and explored more than 250,000 square miles (650,000 square km), a remarkable feat in itself. The people at the Fort were all excited, as were the weary travelers. Cannons celebrated their return.

FOOD

Several moons with child, Key was sporting a large belly, which really showed on her small frame. She cried when recounting her story over food and herbal tea. A hut was erected around her and they ate well, stuffing themselves on fresh venison and stomach contents cooked inside the stomach lining. Simmered to just a warming or sometimes eaten raw, it was a delicacy to someone adjusted to the wild.

OLD FRIENDS

The welcoming cannons were firing inside the fort because of our return. No one could believe the vibrant and snuffy English gentleman would return after a year and seven month final journey.

A believer in human rights and equality and recompense for the Dene, Robbie watched in horror. As the troops came closer to the Prince of Wales Fort a young native girl was to be run over by four oncoming dog sledges. Robbie pushed aside a rider and jumped on a dog sledge from the Fort that had come out earlier. The man laughed as he fell and slid to a stop against a snowdrift. Robbie got to the young girl just as a few more dog sledges came towards both of them. The girl was crying and visibly shaken from the near miss but doing fine. He kissed her on the cheek and gave her a hug and she responded with a small shy smile.

Robbie set her out of harm's way, almost not showing how tired he was. The last few steps to the Fort were the worst. Every tendon stretched and muscle taut with blood from exertion, the pain multiplying when trudging the last bit of the journey. Ivor was up ahead holding up a keg of beer and someone had already handed him a mug for his effort. A flask of spruce beer was coming his way and Robbie thought how much impact the broth would inflict when he was so thin, dehydrated and starved. *I am going to order pork. Pork roast and potatoes. And a brick of cheese and Maggie's homemade buns would be good too. Lillian, you young beauty.* She was so wonderful when she teased him, Robbie thought.

The guilt feelings over his affair were not as strong now. Enough time had passed. He admitted to himself that yes he was infatuated with Lillian's youthful fully developed body and her willingness to laze about the afternoon with him. Frustrated and edgy he dismissed any idea his wife was still alive. His heart had already been punctured by unbearable events.

Robbie did not see the young native girl sitting on a log bench outside the fort walls. The girl kept her head down and did not give notice of her satisfaction at running into her hero who mistakenly had left her with her native Assiniboine Tribe at Cape Breton. She would surprise him. She had a leg of lamb and a knife if she was refused. Hahaya Wehayaha had travelled and endured a lot to have a chance at his love again. She would not fail even if another woman was in the way. She had earned the right. He was the only man who was tender and loving to her. A caring attitude was not something common among the warring tribes or callous prejudiced white men.

With Hahaya an injured warrior sat listening to her story. This Athapascow warrior had a bad knee and walked with a limp. He needed a walking stick to get about. He wielded it in his mind as revenge blistered in his soul for Robbie's beating and killing of his Cree brothers and for maiming him earlier at the Fort. Mocaunse was his name, meaning young bear, with a nickname Moe.

Private Murphy, who proved himself an innocent bystander, sat on the other side of Hahaya with a blanket disguising his whole figure. The trio were starting to boil while showing no movement to expose themselves. They would wait for revenge. The Sergeant would hear of Robbie's return. The Corporal was being released from latrine duty right now and the Sarge was yet to be tried for his espionage and was held in a dank cell. As no one was hurt his charges would not stick here at the Fort. He was a British soldier and above suspicion among the settlers. His release would coincide with the Corporal's real soon.

Robbie was pleased to be at a place he could call temporarily home. Food, beer, friends, warmth and Lillian. She would be there for him. Give him strength to carry on.

OFF TO THE FORT

Key recovered over the next few days. The fact of being among her own people was just the tonic. More luck than she could believe. Her baby would be welcomed to strengthen the tribe. She had to endure.

After much debate, the elders elected to return to their hunt and take Key to the Fort to deliver her baby. The distance to the Prince of Wales Fort was a considerable trek and she would not be able to walk the last weeks of child bearing. There could be no delay. Key would have to carry her weight in supplies but they would not overtax her.

LATRINE DUTY

I t was not long before Robbie had the news that Lillian had left without leaving a note or message. Everyone suspected their attraction to each other and of her luck at receiving an inheritance. He had left with her sitting quietly by the window. She was lost in thought and Robbie felt it was best to just leave and not have a tearful farewell. Thinking in hindsight he knew now it was not a very good idea. After unpacking, Robbie walked back to the front gate to report in for duty with Lieutenant Noonan who held a register at the gate.

Inside the fort the small pot fires melted snow for water and except for the fresh excrement from the soldiers everything else was frozen. Earlier, Sergeant Percival Devil had complained about being sick, dizzy and that he kept smelling burnt toast. Sergeant Percival Devil was on latrine duty hanging onto his shovel watching Nick do some work. Nick worked the wheelbarrow. "Wheelbarrow Operator," he boasted. Nick had a truncheon to protect himself when he was out from the ranks and had latched onto the safe stinky job. To avoid debt he had signed up for five years because he did not know he only needed to sign for three. Nick always complained. He would rather dig latrine trenches than go out on patrol. Everything is damp, heavy and muddy he would say when out on patrol. He was right.

Certain duties required digging with a shovel through frozen ground to make a new privy hole. To save duty the freshly dug trench would be dug close to the full refuse trench and the freshly dug earth would be used to cover the stinking mushy human waste. During a throw of dirt the shovel usually held a large heavy clump of frozen ground that usually needed peeling off with the hand. When thrown into a puddle of ooze it would hit with a thud and stick but the residue would splatter all over. And so it did. The Sarge was wiping off his beard with a piece of newspaper with a soft stringing piece of goo attached. Such an awful sight.

Robbie passed by him with his head down and off to the barracks for needed rest. Neither spoke to each other. Nick, caught sucking up to the Sarge by assisting him, didn't say anything either.

HAHAYA

Corporal Ivor Jennings was sick of stacking wood. After Robbie rested a bit he met up with Nick and Ivor who were sporting a table full of spruce beers in front of them. Ivor lifted one up to Robbie. The whole room cheered. There was much to celebrate. This was big news and a big event. Robbie went out to relieve himself. *Ivor is great,* he thought. A big drinking friend and always one to tell a joke. He would always say the joke twice so you would always get the joke.

Around the corner where he had met Lillian that fateful night another encounter was to happen. The native girl Hahaya approached Robbie, her shoulders and loins were covered this time. Her chest was bare, exposing his prior lust of her bosom.

His forward momentum had them on a collision course. He held out his arms to protect her. She responded and wrapped herself around him. Their lips met briefly. Robbie tried to pull back. Hahaya resisted, pushing her lips to his. Robbie grabbed her arms and tried to stop her. She twisted away. A narrow-eyed look of spite went his way. She knew now he did not want her. She had travelled so far to find out.

What did I do? Hahaya asked herself. *He will not get away so lucky taking my innocence away and he really did leave me.*

"I hate you." Hahaya wanted Robbie's life. A moment before she loved him. And now in her anger she was vengeful enough to kill him as she lashed out at him with her left fist and attempted to stab him with the knife in her other hand.

Refusing to hit a woman, he took the worst of the beating with her left. He held her right wrist with all his might. She was very stocky and strong from years of tending to a nomadic tribe. She would not let go of the knife. Finally, Robbie was able to outstretch her knife arm and free his right to grab her punching left fist.

Robbie's lower lip was split and he was spitting blood. He was breathing very heavily. He wanted to bend over and rest his hands to his knees. He could hardly get a breath. Each intake of air was not enough and it was a painful effort to inhale more. She stopped her aggression. Robbie let her wrists go.

Hahaya began to repeat something in her native tongue. She held her head high. She would tell of his betrayal. Her friends would help her exact revenge. She needed rest and food after the long journey to the Fort. There was time. He would get a beating that would render him with just enough presence to see her laugh at him. Her new friends would appreciate it. She covered her bosom not because of her modesty but because of the cold.

He waited till she was long gone and walked off to relieve himself. A chill went through Robbie and he knew he still was paying for a mistake. *One must be careful with whom one engages. Not all are well adjusted proper thinking rationalists. Some are fatalistic and myopic in their thoughts*, he reasoned.

"It does not take much for one who feels confident in life to get stuck on an assumption. Either for the laziness of thought or just a mistaken sense of feeling you make an irrational judgment on the facts being presented," Lieutenant Noonan was talking over everyone's head and had everyone befuddled. He was trying to explain the reasons for bad battle decisions.

"From people's experiences they garner emotional responses to be used when they are confronted with similar problems. It is here judgments are at question. Not all people have the same emotional responses and understanding we do." The young Lieutenant just would not stop his babbling.

"Robbie, let me explain," Ivor was now philosophizing. "If I take two batches of brew and without a taste test I might like one because it appears good based on look and color, or what people tell me, while in truth the fact is the other brew was the better choice. I assumed wrong based on an opinion, a bad judgment call, or misinterpreting information and the Lieutenant gets the best mug of suds."

"I get it. Believe me I do." Robbie held Ivor's opinion high. They both had too much to drink and the philosophical ideas were getting too dense. They started poking Noonan, making him stop his over the head philosophizing.

"I've buried the family. Now Matonabbee is taking me out to where my wife was left. I have leave. No extra duties now the Hearne mission has finished." Robbie was calculating what was next.

"The firewood chore for the year is done. I will go with you." Ivor offered. Robbie smiled at that and a few toasts were made to adventure and beautiful women. And then another to beautiful women. The beer was screened just perfectly with only a few shavings of sawdust floating on the top, sort of like a cream.

"Can you really drink that mug in one gulp?" was the challenge. And everyone who dared drank a dare. Everyone felt part of the regiment. Robbie lost his beer for the second time. There were pats on the back and hugs and people crying over missing loved ones and wanting to go back home.

LOVE AND MONEY

H e will melt in my arms when I return," Maggie had overheard Lillian's announcement.

The maid turned from her cleaning and stared at Lillian. She thought, *What now? Is the Major her Prince Charming now?*

"Best be explaining yourself Lillian. I must know when and for whom your engagement party needs preparing for." Maggie was beside herself.

Lillian walked to the cabin's porthole and spread her arms wide. "I have had a few months to consider. I will go and get my money. When everything is said and done I will have my cake and eat it too. I will return Maggie. Yes and seek Robbie out and he will sweep me off my feet when he sees me. He will lust after me and my money. I doubt as little as much. I will be rich and have love – money and Robbie. Oh, the Major is all right, I suppose. He is just not exciting or able to make my heart flutter. When I think of Robbie …" she sighed.

Maggie smiled at the plan. *My lady has an unusual theme for a rich widow*, Maggie thought. *Get away from the city, buy a parcel of land and learn to live off this land with Robbie, me and a few servants of course.*

"I will leave him no choice. He has taken my innocence away. He will be on edge and thirsty for me. What was my Aunt's new perfume? The French one?

The women started to repack for Acadia. Maggie was laughing. They had not arrived in England yet and they were already planning a return trip.

"Next time we pay the Captain twice as much so that we will be properly looked after," Maggie planned aloud.

BECOMING AMERICAN

Lil Wolf, Robbie's son, was entering a new world as he grew up. Gone were the deerskin coverings and fur lined hats and gloves he touted from the past and replaced with only the best of American traditional garb. Wool shirt and weaved waistcoat with watch pocket and tightly weaved trousers, black polished leather boots, and of course a smoothbore musket with seventeen inch bayonet.

Now, a boy of ten, he would grow quickly, become brave, carry on to brave adventures, becoming a soldier in the American Continental Army and eye witnessing America's fight for Independence. Will he find his father and at the same time become a respected man? He has learned that action begets courage, courage comes from habit, and action gets results. Lil Wolf can look forward to his journey onward to fortune, fame and brave deeds as one of the first to call himself an American.

LILLIAN PLANS HER RETURN

I wear red well don't you think? Lillian held up a new wine colored shawl and pear shaped earrings which contrasted with her blonde hair and white skin. "Simply fantastic."

Maggie rolled her eyes up and to her right. "What am I to do with you, girl? I am sure you will find the latest in French fashion to represent your feminine side?" She raised her voice as if in a question.

At the harbor on the Thames, word went out immediately that Lillian Whiltshire the Heiress had returned safe and well. Soon she would know if there were any disputes to her claim and subsequent delays. As there were none, she was informed that night that transfers were being made and that if she wish she could schedule a shopping trip and at the same time hook up with a ship captain going to South Acadia who could bring her closer to the man she pined for.

The fog was bad and gave way to a light mist that caused her to shiver and blocked visibility. There was much to do. Gather some herbs, seeds and cuttings. Pack warm woolen socks and shirts, a compass, bedding, a piece of furniture or two and a medicine chest. Wine and a jug of porter would round out their list.

Lillian did not buy any fancy gowns the next day, instead preferring a plain linen pullover that showed her curvaceous curves yet hung low enough and was plain enough to humble herself to the North American crowd she was getting used to.

She bought some rouge and some oil for her hair and laughed after seeing the name Bear Grease on the bottle. She paid the tidy profits and the merchant's tithe and laughed at how she could buy these body care products in bulk for a piece of bent iron or a dented bronze kettle. She did not buy the beavertail hat that hung so sadly on its hook.

"We will have servants and soldiers to guard us, Maggie. We will be safe." The constant fear of native unrest or deft financiers could still spoil her plans.

"Five should be enough. Plough hands that have soldiering experience and can be savvy in case there is a native uprising or something. I want a house surrounded by a white picket fence with flowers along the whole fence line. And a big warm fireplace for Robbie to come home to." Lillian hummed to herself as she packed away her new belongings.

A fire indeed. For brewing in the winds was to be a scorching confrontation with vicious results. The play would be for keeps. The object would be for Robbie to keep them all apart and save his marriage, soul and reputation.

FEAR DISAPPEARS

Soon Matonabbee and Robbie would be heading out to find his wife's body where it was left, one hundred miles west of the Prince of Wales Fort.

Robbie felt pretty good considering the turn of events. He had proved himself capable of sustaining himself when in hostile conditions. He had garnered some fame as a scout and hunter and some respect from his regiment as he fought with well-controlled fear. He realized that as soon as he engaged in combat the fear went away and was replaced by an attitude of strength. In other words, action or movement calmed his fears.

By taking action he lost his fear not just in warfare but also in pursuing a new love. Robbie concluded that one can find love again; there is hope after all. He faced his fears head on. He realized that being a successful soldier and getting over loss and finding love again were both possible with proper planning and action.

BABY BORN

Like a sheet of white linen, a wall of heavy snow blocked their path. The strong wind drove sleet and pushed her back. Key stood with one leg bent in front of her, head down and eyes blinking to see a few feet ahead. She had already lost sight of everyone else. Maybe she moved too far ahead. The bad weather had everyone holed up at the foot of a big hill.

Stopping the sledge and dropping the gear off her back she spun it in front and propped it against a small shrub and fell onto her belly, knocking the wind from her. Key knew she could be covered in minutes and not be found if she fell asleep. But, the rest felt good. The baby was sleeping and quiet. No kicking to agitate her. A pleasant dream of spring by a meadow had her moan softly in comfort as an arm pulled her to a sitting position.

Together they would spend the night bundled together and resting. As the weak morning light rose on the horizon they would soon be recovering at the Fort. Many months had passed with no blood and her loins ached. Armed with only two things – hope and freedom – she would persevere.

At the break of dawn they were all washing themselves and re-bundling things for the last march. Key being slightly built was uncomfortable feeling overweight. She reached up to her neck to rub her father's little handmade doll for luck.

What should she tell? Where would she start? Would he still accept her? Questions turned over in her mind. If Robbie was not there she would bear the child on her own, then leave a message and proceed with her tribe members to their homeland. They were a patient lot and were not rushed by a time schedule. The Prince of Wales Fort was possibly in view or very close when her water broke and another camp was set for the laborious time of childbirth. Key screamed in pain as one of the older native women held her upright by the arm pits and had her squatting by a frozen river with fresh towels and a knife to cut the umbilical cord. There was a pail of water that they melted from the snow.

Afternoon would come and a beautiful princess would be born, a daughter to replace her murdered two-month-old baby. Though still torn Key would smile over her new arrival. The young warrior who liked her and beat her would be proud. His seed would inherit the line of chieftains of the Dog-Ribbed tribe and strengthen them. She would rest just another day before making her way to the Fort.

Dried deer sticks were her staple that day, delicious dried venison. With the wildness of the meat smoked out, the dried morsels were full of flavor and nutrients.

That evening she fell asleep nursing her little girl and as she drifted off she worried, *Maybe the wolves will get us after all.* Key's heavy eyelids drooped and she cuddled into the warmth of her rabbit fur covering and slept a peaceful rest for the first time in a very long time.

ROBBIE'S SEARCH IS DELAYED
DUE TO WEATHER

The winter was at its dirtiest moment. Full of wind, sleet, snow and frost causing an uncomfortable situation bordering on dehydration and freezing if left to the elements. No one could travel in such environmental fury. Visibility was zero. Some of the gusts gave no warning to their destructive power. A swirl of wind that carried with it deadly rock debris, from the other side a gale or snow-filled squall that may or may not lift you off your feet. "Best wait till the storm dies down," Matonabbee cautioned. Robbie was downcast after being so excited about starting another trek. Matonabbee responded by nodding slightly as he always did.

"Wait a few days for the weather to clear and then we head out just before sunrise." Matonabbee was confident of his prediction that fine weather would return. If you could consider freezing temperatures, snow and frozen rough terrain constituted as fine weather and conditions that is.

The weather would comply eventually so in the meantime they went to the barracks to chow down on one of their last suppers at the Fort. Their commitment to the cause of finding and burying Robbie's wife was still confirmed.

The forest trees that grow on this inhospitable spot were few indeed – a few pines, junipers and poplar.[ix] The larger birch trees were to the west. New settlers would be coming. So would spring. Indians would come with their furs to trade.

Looking to the setting red sun, Robbie heard the wind start to bellow. He saw a mist of snow coming from amongst the flow of pine and juniper. A small group of natives had been defending themselves amidst the backdrop of a blizzard. They were fighting a storm and were moving slowly and having a tough go of it. A snowdrift eight to nine feet high blocked their path to the Fort and it seemed to take forever for them to traverse the drift and get closer to the Prince of Wales Fort. Robbie and Ivor looked over the ramparts to see the incoming travelers. Soon, Robbie thought, he would put an end to his responsibilities by going to bury his wife's bones out in the barren lands.

TURN NORTH

The ground full of drifts and rising terrain gave the small group of Dog-Ribbed natives immense frustration. Their need to travel to the Fort was no longer necessary with the newborn healthy and content on mother's milk. The decision was made to turn north and go eighty more miles to home. The distance shortened by fifteen miles if they turned at this difficult junction spot.

As they walked, Key recounted her story of her daughter's murder to her native friends so that she could get the story straight to tell Robbie.

"Twelve or more jealous women came out of the bushes and surrounded us before we could react. These women had followed me back to the original attack area and immediately without hesitation, bombast or show of emotion took Layna my midwife, who was very frail at the time, and stabbed her in the heart many times. She was a delicate woman who still nursed because she lost her baby a short time ago and had not eaten more than berries and one raw fish in the last two weeks. My daughter did not fare any better.

"One of the taller squaws took my baby and stabbed at her heart which took so little pressure to puncture. I was stabbed twice in the upper back. Beaten half to death and half my hair yanked out I was forced to march back to camp. The warriors were just waking up. The smell of catfish cooking for them was in the air. A man sat on a log and gnawed away at some leftover bone of some kind. Juices flowed from his fingers and he was content on just watching.

"I was dragged to one of the elders and put on mock display. Tears blinded me. I gasped for breath, not knowing what to expect and expected the worst. The women stood by, cheering like a pack of coyotes, anxious for the kill. It was quite common for the women to kill other tribes' families. The men had no time or taste to do women's work."

Key recounted how she went from hysterical to numb when the little thin straps of leather she wore from her shoulders were cut, making her tattered deerskins drop to the ground exposing her nakedness to the small but gathering group of onlookers. She realized even this elder had been influenced by her loveliness and the fresh intensity that had evolved during her stay. He stood admiring her breasts and was wondering if he would make a fool of himself if he tried something with her.

Key told them how she bit her lip when the sharp blade of the elder's knife had swept across her shoulder to cut the coat. She gathered a large amount of blood from her lip and spat it out on her contemptuous admirer. The red spittle sprayed over the eyes and face of the old man. She spat again at his feet.

Speaking in Dog-Ribbed and broken English she cursed her aggressors. Told them she was broken. "Kill me! Why did you kill my baby?"

The old man replied, "It is tradition. So no seed can seek revenge against something from the past. There is no time for revenge here, only survival."

Key realized the Athabascan understood everything she had said. She stood before him in defiance waiting for decisions to be made. It was then it was decided she had undergone too much sorrow and as compensation she would be given to a man as his third wife. He would generously take her into his fold to look after. As part of his family she would be expected to help in doing all the cooking, preparing for the hunt, carry everything and provide comfort for him at his want.

Key told her kinsman how her soul was broken and she had lowered her head in frustration and disbelief. "I bent down and pulled up my deerskin tunic and was taken off to an imprisonment hut to be given to someone I did not even know.

"After four days of no sleep I sat staring at a wall of the interior of the tent unable to understand why I had no more feelings of revenge or suffering, only a peaceful calm. The sun was making the room fill up and if the sun shone upon her from the vent above she believed she would die.

"I scurried to the corner of the room and did not let the sun beat down upon me. I would not allow anybody to expose me to the sun's rays. They would kill me."

"I thought, 'I will find a way to escape. I cannot stay with a group of people who so viciously killed my daughter and family. I will escape.' I vowed this as I moved over from the bright sun's rays."

The vivid reenactment of the horrid scene made for long periods of thoughtful recollections over her losses.

EPILOGUE

M ost of the outlying tribes and the Athapascow south Cree natives were pushed further west, having sustained too much pressure to stay close to the Fort. The further away from the Prince of Wales Fort and the west coast of Hudson Bay they migrated, the situation became worse because there were fewer opportunities to procure weapons, powder, shot, iron, clay pots and knives. This made them less strong as a nation. Like the few Esquimaux who came to trade at the Fort they were few in number so that as soon as they left the Fort for home they would be attacked and at the minimum robbed of the goods they had traded their furs for.

Matonabbee did position himself as the leader of the Chipewyan Nation and had made peace with many Athapascow tribes by being a marching peace activist. One could refer to him as a diplomat, chief, martyr, a missionary, learning under the tutelage of Moses Norton, a half Cree and half French Governor of the Fort. He was able to build the bridge between the English gentlemen and his Indian Brigand.

The fort settled in for a long winter. Not much excitement till spring. Next year they must journey further from the fort for fuel to preserve the emergency forests around the compound. Firewood cut by axe, trimmed by axe and split with wedge and hammer. Rolled, lifted, shifted, carried, stacked, moved, re-stacked, and picked up again. Working and handling each log many times.

Mr. Samuel Hearne would journey to England and return to be Governor of the Fort by June 1776. He went on to retire as a published author. His exploits were more entertaining than beneficial. He received a considerable amount of funds for his manuscript – twice what the best authors received at the time.

Even though his geographical contributions were limited to the science of the day he was discredited by a colleague in England so that he never received those honors. Fortunately it was later confirmed by a famous explorer, a Mr. Franklin, that Hearne's measurement was correct to locate the famous Bloody Falls where the massacre of the Inuit happened. The tragedy included a young girl wrapped about Hearne's leg begging for mercy till she finally died; an eerie situation that would haunt Hearne till his dying day. Samuel Hearne passed away with dropsy at the age of forty-seven in 1792.

The dawn was coming; the future looked bright and promising. With the majority of the French threat curtailed, the British continued taxing the colonists and the American colonists were waking up to the need for independence.

Robbie and young Lil Wolf had before them an exciting period of North American history to witness and become immersed in. Tennessee was started in 1773 and the first democracy was created. Robbie would need to find and make up with his wife, calm the native girl and stop the efforts of Lillian if he was to make good. His career as a soldier would have to be put to the fore and he believed his wife and son's bones would need to be found and buried to rest his soul. Lil Wolf would become a soldier in the Continental Army and serve the cause against taxation without representation. They laughed when he signed his name as Lil Wolf Wolfe.

There were still enemies on Robbie and Lillian's tail. The awful Sergeant Percival Devil and his compatriots Corporal Maxwell Freeman and Private Jim Murphy still needed corralling. They all got off the conspiracy and extortion charges; they were too valuable to the fort's garrison. The charges against Robbie went missing and no one was really hurt. And there was the mysterious grouping of Private Murphy teaming up with Hahaya the native girl and the lame Cree Macounce.

The hero must still travel for hope and love and find his life with his wife, son and new daughter. Watch for Book Two of Robbie's Adventures!

SNEAK PEAK

BOSTON TEA PARTY

On December 16, 1773 at midnight the modern equivalent of one million dollars worth of tea was dumped – 90,000 pounds or forty-five tons – in Boston Harbor. It took over three hours to board the British ships and take command and break open all the containers and then throw it all overboard. The next morning, rowboats were put out to flatten the tea leaves with oars so that none would escape the destruction. The message was intent on being clear.

A group called the Sons of Liberty[16], dressed up as Mohawks with black coal on their faces and a hatchet that was deemed by all to be a tomahawk, stormed the ships.

After the Boston Tea Party in 1773, the so-termed British Intolerable Acts of 1774 stripped Massachusetts of its self-government and historical rights, abolishing everything. A mass of troops in redcoats marched around Boston pushing their weight around. This triggered an outrage and resistance within the Thirteen Colonies. These events were the key developments in the outbreak of the American Revolution in 1775. The major hostilities of the new American nation ended with the War of 1812 and possibly featured in a future Robbie's Adventures novel. What side will the author take on these controversial events? Wait and find

---

16 The Sons of Liberty were a group of men who were first or second generation colonists. They held no false beliefs in the rights of American Englishmen.

out. But first Robbie must face his old loves and foes in a new adventure. Will Robbie find out what happened to his family? Why does Robbie become a southern colonist?

Find out in the next exciting book in the series, *Robbie's Incarceration,* **another novel of the Robbie's Adventures Book series.**

FURTHER NOTES

To note on the harsh and blunt attitudes I wrote about concerning the old native tribes and their barbaric customs. Throughout history moments can be looked upon as being unjust or unfair. It was said the tribes never banded together as one large powerful group. Well how could they? Any group larger than what they could hunt for and feed would die. It was necessary to go as small nomadic tribes in search of food. Certain formalities and savageness must be forgiven as the times were difficult and everyone was in need and in so much want. Living on the edge of survival creates extremes in attitudes and customs. Let it be and grow from it.

Religious Belief:

The Dog Flanked or Dog-Ribbed First Nation, (Canadian term), or natives (American term) held a similar belief as the Inuit, (Esquimaux) and they stated often:

"We don't believe. We fear."

The people were petrified of being scalped by the roaming tribes. Living in an irregular world they did not worship but feared much. Rituals and taboos were tied into the fearful and precautionary culture caused by the harsh environment.

To note of the white man's ambitions:

The Mississaugas were clean, sober, happy and at peace, brought about by the Methodist Church missionaries. To sophisticate, educate and provide a better lifestyle for these impoverished native people. It was their duty.

It was not long ago just a mass of dirty wigwams, surrounded by heaps of fish bones, offal of deer and putrid filth, drunken savage brawls and beastly orgies. Unfortunately it cost the natives in land and many people from smallpox epidemics, compounded with their loss of a simple native way of life. Fortunately, the Mississauga's became successful around Rice Lake and the Simcoe Settlements in what is now Ontario, Canada.

Unfortunately greed and providence controlled their fate. And man is still creating and tolerating inhumanities on the planet.

Life was sometimes horrible in our recent past and luckily we have put an end to the atrocities written about in this novel. Every woman has her own journey. It should be the goal of the intelligent people of the world *to ensure every woman's safety and respect* through active participation in world politics and position, not to just lead the way by example.

AUTHOR NOTES

(Please also see the web page for more info and Author updates)

I had to change the timing of when the quadrant was taken to the first expedition. It was actually taken on the second expedition. I needed Lil Wolf to be in Boston during the actual date so I made necessary literary changes.

Many quotes and facts are true historical events.

The Wife of the Hero and many of her horrible experiences were true:

I would like to set the story straight regarding our heroine, Robbie's wife Key. Most of what happened to the hero's wife were true; her family's ambush, her rape, torture, isolation and experiences with Matonabbee and Indian experiences. I substituted her husband with Robbie so that I could fit her in as best and did add some embellishments to enhance the story.

In reality, her husband died as well as her father, brother and other relatives in a night attack. After the Dog-Ribbed massacre, three other women were kidnapped and turned into wives or repeatedly beaten and raped and treated as slaves.

After a year as the story goes she escaped the Athapuscow First Nations tribe by canoe and spent the next seven months in isolation. With rabbit, the odd porcupine, squirrel and a few herbs for sustenance she lived quite well considering. She was found by the Northern Indians because of leaving a sloppy footprint.

About the only things I changed were her actual dates of offending machinations. To assist me with the story timeline and not throw off any other historical dates, I changed her timed events. The real date she was first kidnapped and the massacre of her family took place was July 13th, 1770 and she spent a year kidnapped and then seven months of isolation followed by an indefinite time period with the Northern Indians. No precise details of her existence past this point are available.

I felt so wounded when I read her story especially how she lost her family in such a way and then having to undergo two different kidnappings and fending for herself in barren and frozen isolation. The pain and anguish from the murders, the beatings and abuse would be unbearable.

Her treatment was just some of the horrible fate that besieged these encumbered uncivilized historical people. Having nothing one can understand the extremes one must go through to survive. Where a piece of iron strapping off a barrel could make two or three knives, a cast iron pot was priceless as was a piece of iron sharpened to a point which made an awl or used as an ice pick. Any one or two of these items might mean three or four lives that do not die of starvation that coming winter. Still it is hard to understand the inhumane treatment they gave to each other. The men always ate. Two or three women a year would die from starvation because they would have to wait for the men to finish eating in all their gluttony before they were allowed to eat. Often the women would find nothing left and starve. But it did not stop there.

If one or two had food they ate and then their families. If they had accommodations and you didn't – too bad, go freeze. Any advantage was kept for themselves and themselves alone. The man or woman next to them might starve while the other would eat well. One might stay warm and dry in a tent while others froze and died while clutching to life amongst the elements. To each his own. A little co-operation would have gone a long way.

I was also inspired to write this story because of reading the Samuel Hearne Historical papers, *A Journey to the Northern Ocean*. Never in my life have I heard of the severe weather extremes and the terrible conditions that he went through. Throw in the distress of this poor captured native girl and I can only weep. My heart was shattered reading her story. I felt it necessary to include her in my story as it took on so little historical significance yet it touched me so. I hope you will accept my decision.

Matonabbee was a true to life hero, Indian legend, diplomat and chief. A strong and large man who was a leader and diplomat and who really did save a companion from a tent on a diplomatic mission.

In 1782 a smallpox epidemic broke out and many Chipewyans died. The French took back Prince of Wales Fort. Matonabbee was a major middleman between the Cree and the Hudson's Bay Company. Matonabbee was a hero himself and held the distinction of having the earliest recorded/documented suicide of a Native North American.

Matonabbee became depressed after the destruction of Churchill Factory, which provided him with his primary source of fortune and fame. So in the same year, 1782, he hung himself.

Longitude: One of the greatest scientific problems of the day was finding a way of discovering the exact position of a ship at sea. For a detailed explanation of the problems see my web page article on Longitude under "Notes To The Inheritance Letter."

ACKNOWLEDGEMENTS

A special thank you goes out to all the service people who fought for survival, independence and democracy and who protect us today in North America, allowing most of us to remain insulated from the first-hand tragedies of war. Bless all the threatened women and little children in countries where conflict and persecution reign and insulate them as well.

A special thank you to the First Nations who will forever regret the loss of their homeland and way of life. Hopefully, the end of tragedies like what happened to Kiwidinok[17] can compensate for some of the loss of your innocence and inheritance.

A special thank you to Matt Begg and Brelan Boyce and the crew at FreisenPress who worked so hard on my book and did such a great job on the developmental edit. Top notch horse traders in the publishing business.

Special thanks to Glen, Lillian, Dennis and Nick. I used my friends' pictures to develop my fictional characters.

Thanks to Chang Wan Hong for the sketches and Mike Coombes for Nick's sketch, and his constant assistance. And to my family, friends and followers -thank you and enjoy.

An especially warm heartfelt thanks to Dorothy Richards who performed major grammatical fixes with a last minute proofread and a vote of confidence. Thanks my Love.

---

17 Kiwidinock, 'Of the Wind' in the Chippewa language, had real-life tragic experiences. See Author Notes.

BIBLIOGRAPHY

David Bercuson, *The Fighting Canadians* (Toronto: Harper Collins Publishers Ltd., 2008)

Stephen Crane, *The Red Badge of Courage* (New York: W. W. Norton & Co., 1898 reissue)

Raymond Gantter, *Roll Me Over: An Infantryman's World War II* (New York: Random House/Presidio Press, 1997 reissue)

Dava Sobel, *Longitude: The True Story of a Lone Genius Who Solved the Greatest Scientific Problem of His Time* (Penguin Books, 1995)

Samuel Hearne, *A Journey to the Northern Ocean*, (Toronto: Macmillan Company of Canada Ltd., 1958)

Farley Mowat, *Coppermine Journey*. (Toronto: McClelland & Stewart Inc., 1990)

Thomas Radcliff, *Authentic letters from Upper Canada* (Toronto: Macmillan Company of Canada Ltd, 1833). Out of print; available used online.

HISTORICAL ENDNOTES AND FACTS FOR THE INHERITANCE LETTER

(see webpage for additional information at www.robbiesadventures.com)

Endnotes

i.   The 49th regiment was a real force. These soldiers who braved the Niagara Fort are in no way to be connected to the fictional conniving devil Percival Devil or the reprehensible Captain Knobbs.

ii.   The Canadian Rangers were the best paid because they made the best scouts and skirmishers.

iii.   The *Stamp Act* and the *Revenue Act* all contributed to the American Revolution by taxing the colonists without representation. The *Stamp Act* of March 22, 1765 was the first direct British tax on the colonists.

iv.   Patrick Henry who had to answer to a call of treason when he gave a speech against the *Stamp Act* was an American. There is no connection. I just liked his name. It is possible that he was in the vicinity of Niagara at some point.

v.   Lieutenent General Drummond was the first Canadian-born General in the British Army.

vi.   Samuel S. Hearne was a British explorer. His memoirs are famous. Samuel Hearne, probably one of the most celebrated explorers whose major claim to fame was his notoriety of documenting the human condition during suffering beyond anything ever heard of – famine, cold, barbaric natives and wild animals. His geographic contributions were disputed, his maps inaccurate, the Copper Mine he sought had no Copper, and he miscalculated the distance north where he thought he had gotten to. This put the southern limits of finding the northwest passage a lot further north than he actually surveyed. His journal was a remarkable and telling tale of an incredible journey to the Northern Ocean. A very good read on human endurance under tremendous suffering and horrible life-threatening conditions. See Bibliography.

vii.	Bee. A necessary requirement would be the construction of a barn, say 60' x 36' x 18' in height. A framer cut out the mortises and prepared the frame from the plans. A BEE, a group of about seventy neighbors was called together and with use of a raising pole, gradually elevated the mighty bents till they dropped into the mortises of the sill. Bents are the perpendicular parts of the framing, which are then secured by pins or wooden pegs. The use of raising poles either buried in the ground or staged and levered assisted in raising the eighteen inch beams. The roof required 18,000 shingles to be cut. The floor could be twenty-three beams of eighteen inch thick slabs in diameter to support three inch thick floor plates doubled up. One hundred pounds of wood for the floor above. The whole construct more realized when one notices the trimming marks made by the broad axes, which were used to trim square trees into trusses and supports – a very laborious achievement, the whole process taking four to five weeks.

viii.	See vi.

ix.	A typical Hearne's quote showing his poor editing style and poor spelling, which I felt compelled to duplicate for example.

Fact

"The guy with the longest leg usually wins as long as he doesn't get quickly hooked by an ankle at the start," roared Corporal Freeman.

Observation

Well now I know why the Native Indians practice leg wrestling so much. That is how they obtained their women. The winner gets all.

WEBSITE

Characters

I was compelled to have pictures of actual characters posted along with their different bios and storylines to assist in my creative writing. Visuals help. Hopefully you enjoy my book and the amusing characters portrayed in the sketches/pictures. A full color picture of Lillian in that splendid dress along with more of her info will be available on my web page.

For complete dossiers on all the characters in the pictures and sketch artists also see my website.

More web

For those interested or need help in following the events, I have posted on my web page more notes, pictures, videos, a timeline chart, and author information at:

www.robbiesadventures.com

(Koni Doll)

Koni dolls are available at the website

A Koni doll was a good luck charm to ward off evil and to protect against the dreaded act of scalping. Fashioned by the need for a diversion from the tedium of survival; the doll was created. Legend has it that the original Keezheekoni dolls were made out of twigs of cedar and strands of human hair.

Keep your Koni doll in a convenient place near you where the spirits may do their good.

For pricing and ordering see the www.robbiesadventures.com website.

One Dollar from every sale of a Koni Doll goes to a Women's Abuse Center.

Hope you enjoyed Robbie's first adventure and it inspires you to look at your historical backgrounds. Reading history can be a reward in itself. Thank you and enjoy the read. I will continue with the other Robbie's Adventures novels and details will soon be posted.

Watch for Book Two of the series: ROBBIE'S INCARCERATION –another Robbie's Adventures novel. Robbie finds himself in prison and in a lot of trouble in this next novel. He has a lot of foes to deal with. What evil are they going to be up to? Will Robbie find out what has now happened to his family? Will love escape Robbie or will Lillian return and still want him?

Printed in Canada